ALSO BY

HANNAH LYNN

Standalone Feel-Good Novels

The Afterlife of Walter Augustus

Treading Water

A Novel Marriage

The Complete Peas and Carrots Series

Peas, Carrots and an Aston Martin

Peas, Carrots and a Red Feather Boa

Peas, Carrots and Six More Feet

Peas, Carrots and Lessons in Life

Peas, Carrots and Panic at the Plot

Peas, Carrots and Happily Ever After

The Holly Berry Sweet Shop Series

The Sweet Shop of Second Chances

Romance at the Sweet Shop of Second Chances

Turmoil at the Sweet Shop of Second Chances

The Grecian Women Series

Athena's Child

A Spartan's Sorrow

Queens of Themiscyra

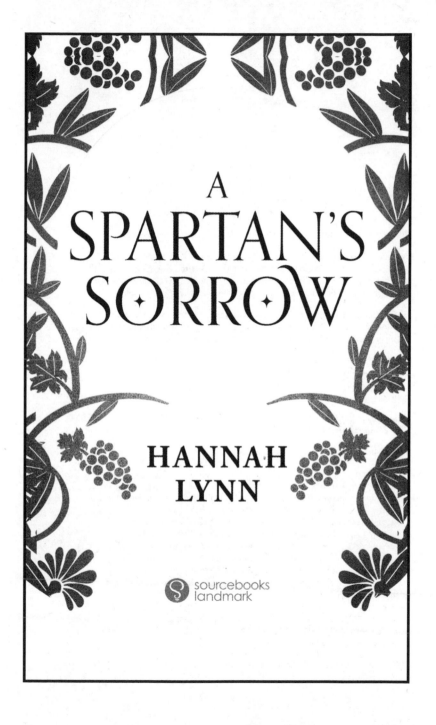

A
SPARTAN'S
SORROW

HANNAH LYNN

sourcebooks
landmark

Published by Sourcebooks Landmark, an imprint of Sourcebooks
P.O. Box 4410, Naperville, Illinois 60567-4410
(630) 961-3900
sourcebooks.com

Originally published as *A Spartan's Sorrow* in 2021 in the United Kingdom by Hannah Lynn.
This edition issued based on the paperback edition published in 2021 by Hannah Lynn.

Library of Congress Cataloging-in-Publication Data

Names: Lynn, Hannah, author.
Title: A Spartan's sorrow / Hannah Lynn.
Description: Naperville, Illinois : Sourcebooks Landmark, [2024] | Summary:
   "All murders must be avenged. While the rest of Greece mourns for the
   war that has taken their husbands away, Clytemnestra fears the day it
   will bring Agamemnon back. When the husband willingly sacrifices their
   eldest daughter to appease the gods, Clytemnestra vows to do whatever it
   takes to protect her remaining children. But history turns strong women
   into monsters, and in saving her family she risks losing them altogether
   and becoming the most hated woman in Greece."-- Provided by publisher.
Identifiers: LCCN 2023024284 | (trade paperback)
Subjects: LCSH: Clytemnestra, Queen of Mycenae--Fiction. |
   Revenge--Fiction. | LCGFT: Mythological fiction. | Novels.
Classification: LCC PR6112.Y57 S63 2024 | DDC 823/.92--dc23/eng/20230503
LC record available at https://lccn.loc.gov/2023024284

Printed and bound in the United States of America.
VP 10 9 8 7 6 5 4 3 2 1

FOR GREAT WOMEN EVERYWHERE.

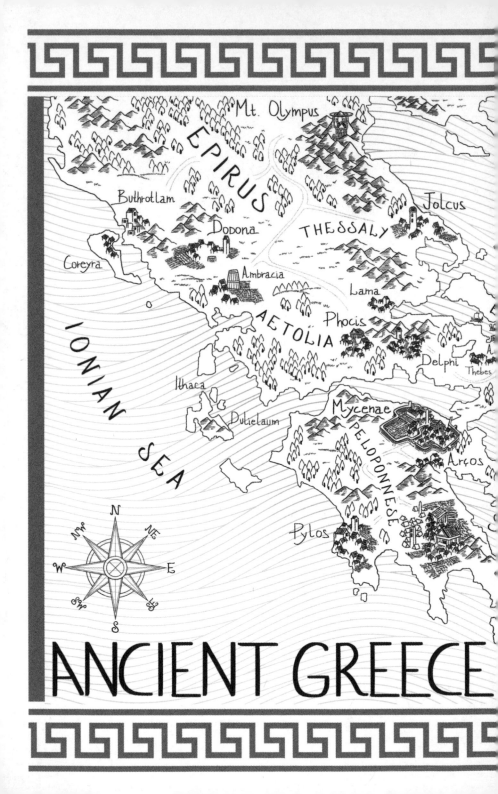

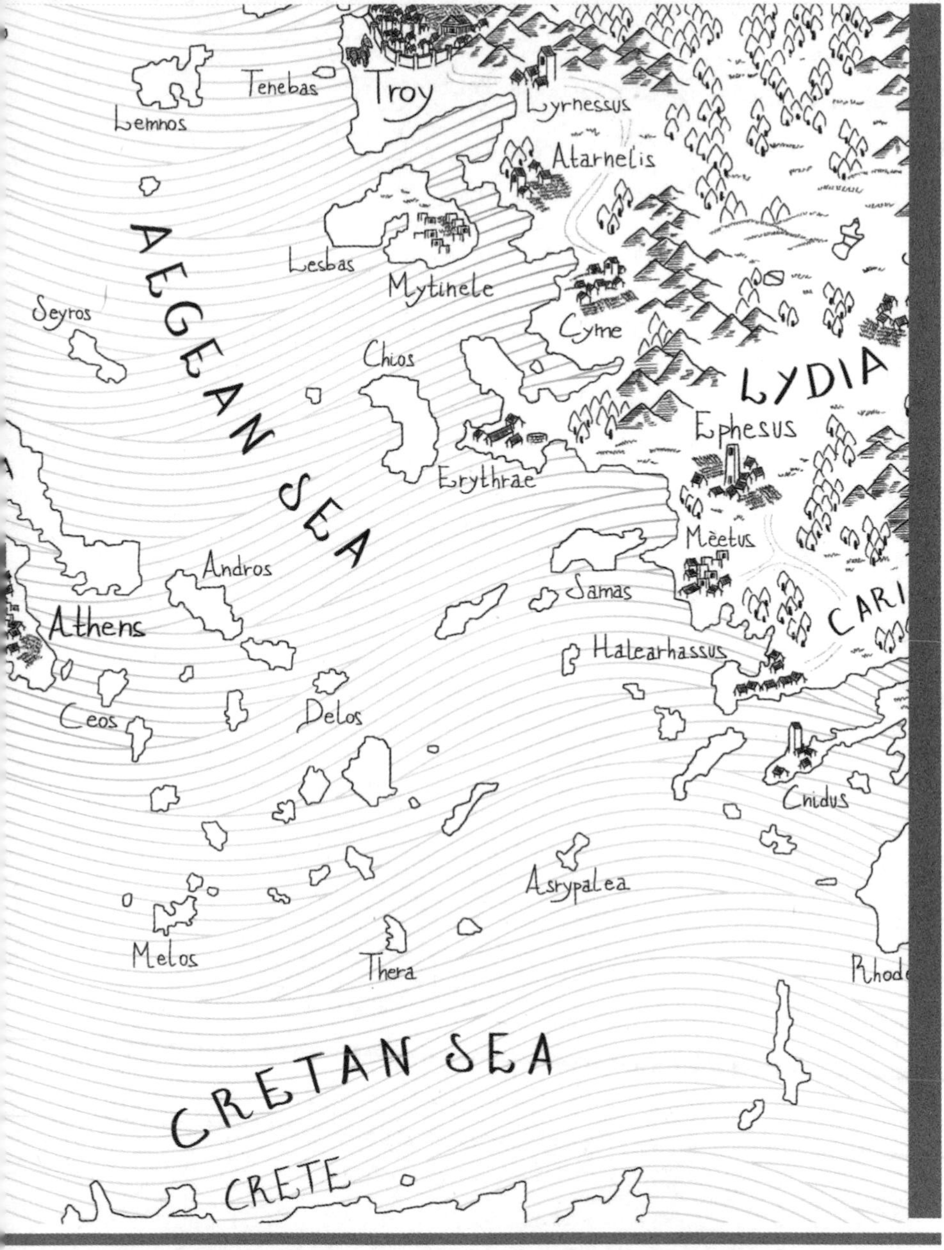
Tenebas
Troy
Lemnos
Lyrnessus
Atarnelis
AEGEAN SEA
Lesbas
Mytinele
Seyros
Cyme
Chios
LYDIA
Ephesus
Erythrae
Mèetus
Andros
Samas
CARI
Athens
Halearhassus
Ceos
Delos
Cnidus
Asrypalea
Melos
Thera
Rhode
CRETAN SEA
CRETE

House of Pelops

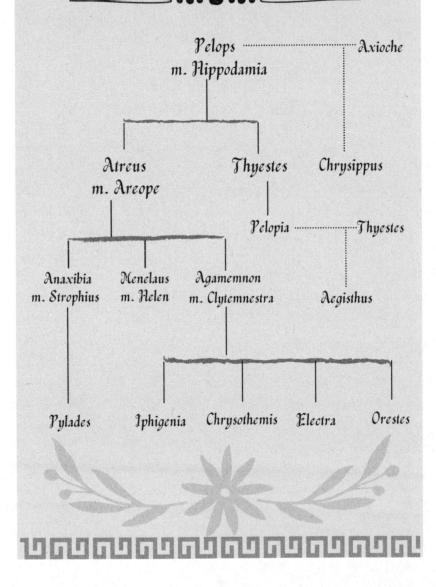

Pelops ⸱⸱⸱⸱⸱⸱⸱⸱⸱⸱ Axioche
m. Hippodamia

Atreus   Thyestes   Chrysippus
m. Areope

Pelopia ⸱⸱⸱⸱⸱⸱⸱⸱ Thyestes

Anaxibia   Menelaus   Agamemnon   Aegisthus
m. Strophius   m. Helen   m. Clytemnestra

Pylades   Iphigenia   Chrysothemis   Electra   Orestes

FOREWORD

T HE STORIES OF ANCIENT GREECE ARE, AT TIMES, AS COMPLI-
cated as the intricate patterns of Arachne's webs. So many
threads, so many paths. From a distance, the weaving seems
strong and secure, and yet, when you look closer, you see that the
fibers are so twisted and damaged that it is hard to tell where one
ends and the next glistening strand begins. Tugging at it doesn't help,
either. This simply causes more fractures. More confusion. The only
real choice left to you is to choose one thread and cling to it. Clutch
at that fiber, hold it close, and have faith that the path you are taking
is one that will lead you all the way through the heart of the web and
out the other side.

PART I

ONE

S WEAT WOVE DOWN AGAMEMNON'S SPINE AS HE STUMBLED UP the rocky path. The journey had taken him longer than he had expected. There were no clouds to lessen the heat or diminish the glare of the sun, and the dry earth was crumbling beneath his feet, forcing him to keep making detours. More than once, he had struggled to maintain his footing and had been forced to crawl on hands and knees in the dust among the scuttling insects, until the terrain had become safer. Even the King of Kings was no match for ground like this.

Before leaving Aulis to make the journey, he had told his men that he would return in the early afternoon. Now he wondered if he would even make it back to them by nightfall. Not that it mattered. Without the guidance of the seer, their ships would be going nowhere, and the mighty armada he had amassed would remain in Aulis harbor, far from the shores of Troy.

For weeks, his fleet had remained as still as paper boats on a glass pond, with not a hint of the wind they needed to take them across the Aegean Sea to fight for Helen's return to his brother, Menelaus. Sacrifices had been offered in the names of each of the gods: goats, sheep, and enough fish to feed an entire village. But nothing seemed to satisfy them. And so, he and his fleet waited—hundreds of ships—like stagnant algae.

Stumbling again, Agamemnon cursed himself and the situation he was in. Not only was he brother to Menelaus, but their wives, Clytemnestra and Helen, were sisters. His men should have been the first to land on the sands of Troy to wrest Helen from the clutches of the brazen upstart Paris. And yet, unless he could get back in the gods' good favor, they would be going nowhere. As such, this infuriating trek through parched lands was unavoidable. It was the only route to get to the seer Calchas.

The old man was the greatest prophet in Greece, if not the world, and so it was no wonder that he kept to himself. Gone were the days when he would mingle with the common folk, or even take a position at a temple, nearer the towns. A man with his gifts deserved a certain level of privacy, although that didn't make the arduous journey any more agreeable. Every few steps, the king slipped on the brittle earth, the hardened skin on his feet already cracked and bleeding. Ideally, he would have brought slaves along, to carry food and water, and possibly even him. But he had been a king for long enough to know that there were some people you could impress with such displays of wealth and power, and others whom you could not, and Calchas was most definitely one of the latter.

At last a small house came into view on the edge of a hill. A patch of grass shone slightly greener there, and the white walls looked clean and bright, as if they had been freshly painted that summer. As he took a moment's respite, he could have sworn he smelled the aroma of freshly baked bread drifting across to him on a warm breeze. Whether it was real or not didn't matter as, with a newfound energy, he hastened to the abode.

Filthy, tired, and with his eyes stinging from the dust, he found the seer cross-legged beneath a fig tree, gazing upward toward a small flock of birds that wove in the sky above him. The garden was simple, with fruit overburdening many of the trees, and Agamemnon was tempted to help himself to a peach or a plum to slake his thirst, but he resisted the urge and moved toward the seer. Calchas's robe was draped over his arm and trailed in the dirt by his feet. Agamemnon was gratified that he had not brought his slaves with him in the end. There would be no standing on ceremony here. No formal vestments or altars bearing offerings. Not even any incense burning. Just a simple man, gifted by the gods to read the signs they gave him.

"Greetings, great Calchas." He stepped forward, casting the old man in his shadow. Moving a little to the side, he cleared his throat. "Forgive the disturbance."

"It is not a disturbance." His eyes remained skyward as he spoke. "I know why you have come. You wish to learn why the winds will not take you to Troy—which god you have affronted and how you can repent."

It was a skill that was both impressive and irritating to the king. Given that the seer already knew of his need, couldn't he have sent word of what they must do straight to Aulis? The old man had to leave this hovel of his at some point, to replenish his stores of oil and grain, if nothing else. He could easily have relayed the information then. Perhaps the gods wished that he should suffer a little first. That would be likely. Given how the insects had beset him every step of the way, he considered that sacrifice already sufficiently well met. Now all he needed to know was what type of beast he should slay and on whose altar he should lay it.

"You are a hunter, are you not?" For the first time, Calchas's eyes left the sky and turned to Agamemnon. "You hunt all kinds of creatures."

"I am a king," he answered. "All monarchs should be able to subdue the rest of the animal kingdom. But yes, I am better than the average man with a bow and arrow."

"Is that so?"

"Well, at least that is what those who wish to get in my good graces tell me." He smiled wryly to himself. He was playing the part well. Showing a level of humility. The fact was, he would challenge any man on his ship to beat him in a hunt, Achilles included. Yes, the warrior was strong and fearless, but still no match for him. There was not an animal on land that Agamemnon could not track and kill, if he wanted. Before they had attempted to set sail, he had enjoyed one last hunt, through the forest of Aulis. There he had taken down a deer that had been so quick, so swift, he doubted even Artemis herself could have felled it. A fact he'd told his hunting party with pride.

"Do you recall the stag you killed?" The seer's words broke into his thoughts as if he were reading them. "That beast was sacred to the Goddess Artemis."

The words struck like ice, and the heat of the day was replaced by a bitter chill that spread the length of Agamemnon's spine.

"Surely not?" he whispered. But the old man's eyes said it all. For the first time in decades, fear bloomed in the king's chest. "It was a mistake. I did not know."

"I do not doubt it."

"Then what should I do?" he asked, trying to hide the quiver in his voice as he broke out into a cold sweat. If he did not appease the Goddess, the likelihood was that his ships would never sail at all. But the punishment for killing a sacred beast would not be insubstantial.

"A feast? A sacrifice?" he offered. "I can do both. I will kill a

4

hundred beasts, five hundred, in her name. Tell me, what must I do? How do I seek her forgiveness?"

Without a word, the old man's gaze returned to the sky. The smallest of breezes sent a ripple through his beard as dozens of birds took to the air once more, circling up and around toward the sun. A bitter taste burned in Agamemnon's throat as he waited to hear how much of his wealth he would have to forfeit. Calchas's gaze came back to him.

"You are a man of the gods, Agamemnon. The King of Kings, no less."

"Tell me, what is required?"

"You have faced difficult situations before, such as reclaiming your father's crown from your treacherous uncle."

"I know this. I know what I have done." His throat had grown so dry he could barely swallow. Seers should talk about the future, he thought, not drag up the past. "What is it I must do?"

The old man's eyes went back to the sky, where a single bird was hovering just a little way off in the distance. Around it, larger birds began to swoop and circle.

"She seeks only a single sacrifice," he said. "One single death on her altar in the Temple of Aulis."

Agamemnon nodded rapidly. "Yes, whatever the Goddess wishes. I will return now. I will do it this very evening."

A single death. That was straightforward enough. He just needed to know the beast. He bowed his head in respect to the seer. But when he lifted it again, the old man caught his hand.

"It is no animal she requires," he said, with a voice that could have been a thousand years old. "It is a child. Your fairest daughter, Iphigenia."

TWO

THE EVENING LIGHT LINGERED ON THE COURTYARD IN SOFT hues of tangerine and blushing pink. It was the largest in a palace full of open spaces and had always been a favorite of Clytemnestra's. Her eldest and youngest, Iphigenia and Orestes, were sitting on a mound of cushions they had placed beneath a lime tree, feeding rabbits that hopped around their feet. Yesterday, it had been frogs from the pond; tomorrow it could be goats or chicks or whatever else they could get their hands on. Two dogs lay nearby, chewing on scraps of food that the children had given them. Sometimes she thought they would rather live on a farm, surrounded by animals, than in the palace of the great citadel of Mycenae, but that would never be. She would keep them here, by her side, for as long as was humanly possible.

The children's laughter floated on the breeze as dulcet as any tune she had ever heard. Breathing in the warm air, she leaned back in her seat and watched them play. Queen of Mycenae, a grand title but one that came with more shackles than anyone could have imagined. It was a far cry from her life in Sparta as a warrior princess—placid, mundane even. Or as mundane as was possible, when a constant veil of fear overshadowed your every move. Since her marriage to Agamemnon, her life had been divided. The public face and the private.

In private she cowered from her husband, flinching at the sight of him, knowing she had to obey his every command. She would stifle her cries, cover her bruises, and try to act as if the Clytemnestra her subjects saw was the real one. Her public face was the Queen Consort who smiled at every occasion and dressed exquisitely in elaborate costumes that would have been an anathema in her old life in Sparta.

Even after all these years, she would find her thoughts drifting back to her homeland, to the clang of metal on metal that would accompany the evening cicada chorus, the smell of sweat ripe in the air. She remembered the fights she had won as a young girl growing up when, when she was only fourteen, her swordsmanship had been good enough to defeat half the boys her age, if not more. They had been so proud of her. Her father, her family—and Tantalus. With a heavy sadness, she recalled two sets of brown eyes she could lose herself in. She had been so happy. And then *he* had come.

"Orestes, you are stroking him too hard. You need to be more careful. Watch. Like this. That's better." Iphigenia took her little brother's hand and guided it gently across the rabbit's back. At two years old, Orestes was already showing himself to be far more like his elder sisters Iphigenia and Chrysothemis, than Electra. His patience, his sensitivity, and his thoughtfulness were a far cry from the attributes of Clytemnestra's youngest daughter, who approached every task as a potential battle and had done so practically since birth. The queen had already found herself embroiled in more disputes with eight-year-old Electra than she had ever done with Iphigenia, who was seven years her senior. Electra's attitude was attack first, possibly apologize later, but only if there was no alternative. Iphigenia and Chrysothemis were the opposite. Still, Clytemnestra worried about them all in their own way, and they were what made her life in Mycenae worth living. They were the one thing that stopped her falling down the dark abyss that Agamemnon had created with his spear, all those years ago. She treasured each one of them, no matter what squabbles occurred.

Across the courtyard, Electra had joined her siblings and was attempting to feed the rabbits the long stem of a dandelion, only each step she took toward them sent them scurrying under the bushes.

"You need patience, Electra," she said, rising from her seat and approaching her children. "Sit down. They will not come to you if you charge at them."

"I am not charging at them. I am trying to feed them. What kind of animals run away when you give them food? It will be their fault if they starve."

Clytemnestra smiled to herself. If any of her children belonged in Sparta, it was Electra.

"Here, sit with me." Iphigenia patted the cushion on the ground next to her. "This one is the tamest. He will let you feed him."

Electra huffed grudgingly as she dropped to the ground, her frown lifting slightly as the rabbit on her sister's lap craned out its neck to nibble the weed from her hand. When the creature finally moved across to her to finish it, Iphigenia picked up her lyre and began to play a tune. As the notes sang out, Clytemnestra closed her eyes and let her thoughts drift away. In moments like this, with her children gathered around her, she felt as though the joy of what she had might just outweigh all the terror she had suffered, and she would try to focus on what he had given her, not what he had taken away. Although she could never forget that. Nor forgive.

Time passed. She remained there, lost in the sounds of the strings and the young ones' chatter until, when the music finally stopped, she opened her eyes to find Orestes's arms bundled with three small balls of fur.

"Rabbits tired. Rabbits sleep in my bed?"

"Oh, Orestes."

"Please?"

This time she let her laughter break free. As the future king, he was the one she worried most about. His gentle nature would be remarkable enough in a girl, but to think of her son ruling the entire kingdom with such a soft heart was enough to make her sick with worry. His kindness could be taken advantage of. He could end up succumbing to threats or being manipulated by false friendships. Or, worse still, his heart would become hardened, until that compassion had been bled from him altogether. Hopefully, with her guidance together with Agamemnon's conduct as an example of how not to behave, he would find a path somewhere between the two extremes.

"Mother?" He spoke again, having still not received an answer to his question. "Rabbits sleep in my bed?"

"What do you think your father would say to that?" she replied with a broad smile.

"He is not here," Iphigenia replied matter-of-factly. "You are the one who will have to say no to him on this matter. But I do not mind. We can have the rabbits in our chamber for the night."

"I mind," Electra responded.

"Well, I do not object at all," said Chrysothemis as she lifted her head from her needlework and weighed in on the subject. "That means it is three against one."

"I suppose that means you get your way, Orestes," Clytemnestra said, grinning.

Despite the majority verdict, it proved far more challenging than any of them had anticipated to ferry the young rabbits from their home in the courtyard to the children's chamber. The palace extended the length of the citadel, and while the creatures had been mostly content to be picked up and carried short distances, they managed to squirm their way free from their hands and make a bid for freedom several times, bounding along the marble corridors. After many screams of delight—and several more of disappointment—Clytemnestra, with the help of Iphigenia and Chrysothemis, managed to move a half dozen of the small creatures to their chamber. While Electra had relented and attempted to help, it quickly became apparent that her stomping feet and yells of frustration were more of a hindrance to their cause, so she instead went to the kitchen to fetch them more food.

By the time they were all in bed, nightfall was well and truly upon them. The sound of dogs barking drifted through the open windows. Clytemnestra moved from one child to the next, brushing aside their hair and kissing them gently on the forehead as she bade them good night. When she reached Iphigenia, her daughter sat up.

"Have you any news of father?" she asked. "I heard Orrin talking to one of the guards earlier. He said that there are still no winds. That the ships still cannot move."

"You do not need to worry about such things," Clytemnestra responded. Stroking her daughter's hair and tucking the loose strands behind her ears, she made a note to herself to talk to her Chief of Guards about discretion. Such conversations should not be held within hearing distance of her children. "The gods will bring your aunt and your father home."

"But ten years. That is what the guard said—that there is a prophecy that the war will last for ten years. Do you think it is true?

Orestes would be twelve by the time he sees Father again if that is to be believed."

Still stroking her hair, she fixed her gaze on her eldest daughter. To an outsider, Electra was the most beautiful of her children, stunning in fact. Striking and bold. But her looks were growing more severe with age, whereas Iphigenia, still only fifteen, had a fairness Clytemnestra had never encountered before. She would never dare utter the words out loud, but she wondered if, one day, her daughter would rival even Helen for beauty. The thought tore into her like a knife. Beauty—the most tainted gift there was. Being beautiful didn't stop a man's hands from striking you. Nor did it stop his eyes—and the rest of him—wandering when he grew tired of the same person in his bed at night. The thought of her daughters experiencing even a fraction of what she had endured made her dizzy with fear. Before Agamemnon returned from the war, she would find Iphigenia a place in one of the Temples of Artemis. That way, she would be safe. Or as safe as any woman ever could be in this unfair world.

"A thousand rumors wash onto these shores every day," she replied to her daughter's question. "If we were to believe each of them, we would never leave the palace."

"But these are not rumors, Mother. They are prophecies. Prophecies from the gods. Prophecies from a seer are as true as the word of Zeus."

"Did *you* hear the words from the seer? Or, better still, from Zeus himself?"

Her daughter pressed her lips together in thought.

"Let us talk no more of this." She smoothed down the blanket of a girl already old enough to have children of her own. "Your father will do everything right by the gods. You know this. No doubt I will have a messenger with me by morning, telling me they are already halfway to Troy. Now sleep. Tomorrow, you are going to have to help your brother clean up the mess these rabbits are making."

A motherly pride glimmered in her eyes as Iphigenia laid her head down on her pillow.

"Good night, Mother," she said.

"Good night, my love."

With the children in bed, Clytemnestra wove her way back through the corridors and out onto the veranda, where a large carafe of wine had been placed on a table beside her seat. Next to it was a platter of dates and figs. During the day, she favored the courtyards, where a cool breeze would drift across the marble flooring, but at times like this on her own, she preferred to sit on the veranda, on the edge of the fortress. Here she would gaze out over the rolling hills and remember.

Sometimes, if she could rouse them before sunrise, she would bring the children here too. When they were babies, she would hold them to her breast and feed them as she drank in the view. With no servants or nursemaid in attendance, she could mother them as she wished. Unfortunately, although perhaps predictably, the older they grew, the less inclined they were to wake with her, particularly during the shorter days of the colder months. Apart from which, even as a small child, Electra had had a penchant for danger, delighting in perching herself on the edge of the limestone wall. On more than one occasion, Clytemnestra had feared for her daughter's life. So now, they spent most of their family time in the courtyard together, where there was more than enough room for them to run around, without her needing to worry about the perils that could befall them.

Ignoring the food, she poured herself a small cup of wine, which she cut with water, and sat back in the seat with a sigh. Ten years. She had heard the rumors of the prophecy too, and from a far more reliable source than gossiping guards. Could it really be possible? Was she really to govern Mycenae single-handedly for that long?

The thought was appealing. Raised as the daughter of a king, she had been accustomed to the duties of a ruler from a small child. There was even a time when she had been a queen herself. Not just an ornamental one, but a true monarch, with the promise of real power. But those days had been short-lived, and she knew better than to dwell on what could have been. Still, now she was to have a second chance. Who was to say Mycenae could not thrive without Agamemnon's hot temper? Of course, that and his ruthlessness were what had gained him respect. Without them, he could never have overthrown his uncle and cousin to take back the throne. He was powerful and brutal. And if, by chance or the hand of the gods, he did not return from the war in Troy, any tears she shed would be purely for show.

She was busy thinking about new ways to while away her evening hours with her husband gone—her weaving and domestic skills remained feeble, despite all the time she had spent on them— when her attention was drawn to a man waiting by the balustrade.

"Orrin," she said, beckoning him closer. "Is something wrong?"

According to the history of the citadel, he had once been one of its fiercest warriors, but now his muscles had weakened with age, and the wounds he received took longer and longer to heal. Agamemnon had placed him in charge of guarding his family in his absence, rather than taking him to Troy. She knew, as such, his first loyalty lay with Orestes, and yet, unlike many of the men of the citadel, he had always shown her a level of respect, which she in turn reciprocated. Ultimately, his true loyalty was to Mycenae. To its citizens and its citadel. While she would never say so out loud, she always got the impression that he did not really care who sat on the throne, as long as the people were cared for.

"There is a messenger, my queen. He has word from the king. He will speak only to you."

She gulped down the remainder of her wine.

"Send him in. Send him to me now."

Without the need of further instruction, he disappeared back into the corridor. In just a few minutes he returned, accompanied by a man who looked as though he had traveled nonstop for several days. His coat was covered in dust, and the skin on his lips was dry and flaking, while his eyes were bloodshot, as if he had gone the longest while without any rest.

"Come in, come in." She motioned him forward, while filling a cup with water. "Drink, please. And take a seat. Then tell me what news you have of my husband. Have the winds picked up at last and sent him on his way?" *Or have the seas toppled his ship once and for all?* she silently hoped.

She extended the cup. He hesitated before accepting and swiftly emptying the contents. The cold water brought some color back to his cheeks, and when he placed the empty vessel down, she filled it halfway with wine.

"There are no winds to sail out of Aulis," he said, "which is why I had to come to you overland."

"But did he meet with Calchas?" she questioned. "Did he find the seer?"

"He did, my queen. He learned that it is the Goddess Artemis who has been wronged."

A cool breeze chilled her. "How?"

"I am afraid that is not of my knowledge. The king told me, however, that the Goddess has decreed a blessed union will appease her and return the winds to the sea."

"A union?" Confusion twisted her brow. Angered gods wanted

sacrifices and repentance, not blessed unions. Then again, her gripe was likely with one of the crew members and not Agamemnon himself. Perhaps she wished to repay him for the inconvenience he had suffered.

"It is your daughter Iphigenia," he said. "You are to send her to Aulis."

"Send her to Aulis?"

The messenger's eyes finally lit up, and a look of awe crossed his face. "At Aulis your daughter is to be married," he said, "to the great warrior Achilles."

THREE

OVER FOOD AND MORE WINE, THE MESSENGER TOLD HER all he knew. They were to leave as soon as possible.

Iphigenia was to be dressed in the saffron robes of Artemis, and a great feast would be held in her name when they reached Aulis, after which the wedding to Achilles would take place in the temple. Then, assuming the Goddess had been appeased enough to return the winds, Iphigenia would travel to Troy with Achilles as his wife. There she would stay, in the safety of the camps, until the war was over. Where she would live afterward was not a matter that had been discussed.

"Thank you. And thank you for your journey," Clytemnestra said, standing up. "I shall pack our things now. And I will wake the children when I am done. We will leave at first light."

A shadow crossed his face. "I mean no disrespect, my queen, but the king said that I was to bring Iphigenia to Aulis on her own. He specifically said that."

"Surely not? A wedding is a celebration for the whole family. He cannot think I would allow my eldest daughter to be given to a man without my presence? I am her mother."

"I am merely relaying what I was told," he said. "That your daughter Iphigenia is to travel alone."

Lowering herself back down to her seat, she thought through the quandary. A marriage to Achilles would be no small event. For her not to be there would only add fuel to the rumors that Agamemnon was tired of his wife and was looking for someone new. Someone younger. Perhaps he had already chosen that person to accompany him to the feast. Yes, that would be it. The thought caused her face to flush with anger. This was her eldest daughter's wedding. She was to be handed over to a man she had never even met. Agamemnon couldn't possibly think that this would happen without her. Damn him and his whoremongering.

"The children," she said to the messenger eventually. "That is what he must have meant. Iphigenia is not to travel to Aulis with her siblings. Orestes is far too young, and the voyage will not be easy. No doubt he wants to save them the discomfort of such a journey." One she knew her other two daughters would gladly endure. While only twelve, Chrysothemis more than once had mentioned the desire to marry a war hero. And Electra just hated missing out on anything. But it made sense, leaving them behind. Taking Orestes, the future king, out on the open sea when Greece was already at war with Troy would be an unnecessary risk. But she would be going, whether he liked it or not.

"It will just be I who accompanies Iphigenia then," she continued. "I will go with her. The rest of the children will stay here, in the safety of the citadel."

The messenger nodded but looked somewhat uneasy at her response. "Of course, my queen. I will ensure the captain knows that you will be joining us. We will leave for Aulis at daybreak."

———

They had, as she had promised, been ready to leave first thing. The small party left by horse from the citadel in the gray dawn, the animals picking their way over the rocky terrain that led toward the coast.

She delayed telling Iphigenia where they were going and why until they had boarded the ship. The young woman responded with nothing more than a nod. Not until the port had faded into the distance did she finally begin to question her mother.

"What do you know of him?" she asked. "Will Achilles make a good husband?"

"I know little more than you, I suspect, my love," Clytemnestra answered as truthfully as she could. "Little more than the heroes' tales that are told across all of Greece. But these do seem to be favorable. As does this union. You are a child of Artemis; of that I am certain. You seem to see the world through her eyes. I do not believe she would have requested these nuptials had she not believed it would be a good match."

Silence fell on them then as they both gazed out to sea, where white-crested waves broke on the hull of their ship. Anticipation rippled through Clytemnestra, but it was Iphigenia who spoke once again.

"The stories say that he is handsome, do they not?"

"They do."

"But being handsome or strong does not mean he will make a good husband, does it?"

"It does not, no." She wrapped her arms around her daughter and squeezed as tightly as she could. How she had borne such a wise child was beyond her. And to be so astute at such a tender age. Her heart ached with the thought of their separation, and she let the embrace linger on a little longer still.

"I hear tell that he is kind too," she continued positively. "That he is generous to those around him and that he does not seek conflict, although his reputation means that it may well come and find him. Remember, it is not just the Goddess who believes this marriage is well matched; your father knows him too. He would not agree to this if he thought it would put you in harm's way."

"Even if it helps with the war?"

Stepping back, she placed her hands on her daughter's shoulders. There was so much she would like to tell her. So many things she wanted her to know before she was gone. Her chest swelled with love for this perfect young woman.

"Your father is a king, and it is his job to protect Mycenae at all costs. But he is your father first, which means it is his job to safeguard you too. That is his duty to all of you children. He will be there with you, in Troy, and will never let anything happen to you. You have my word."

Clytemnestra avoided talking of Agamemnon whenever possible, for the pain that rose in her chest at the mere mention of him. But Iphigenia required comfort, and it was her duty as her mother to reassure her.

"Do you think I will have children?" Iphigenia asked after a pause.

"I very much hope so," she replied. "Because that is the only way you will understand how much I love you."

"I think I already know that."

"Trust me, my child, you do not."

As the day wore on, they whiled away the hours reminiscing, not knowing when they would next be able to do so.

"I still think about that robe you made for Father," Iphigenia said, recalling an amusing incident. "I still do not know how on earth you managed that."

Clytemnestra did not need reminding of the garment. Swordsmanship had come as naturally to her as to any child of Sparta. Needlework had not.

"That was deliberate. I just wished to make you all laugh," she said, shrugging off the comment with a grin.

"No, you did not. You sewed the neck shut! How could anyone do that? Do you remember how Electra ran around the house, wearing the thing over her head?"

"Of course. Do you know how many vases she broke that day? I am only amazed she did not break her neck too!" Her daughter's fond smile as she recollected the incident brought tears to her eyes.

"I made sure she was safe. Do you not recall? I followed her everywhere, catching her every time she stumbled."

"That is right. I remember now," she said with tears brimming. She had forgotten how they had all laughed until their sides hurt that day. Orestes had been just a baby, crawling around them, but even he had been swept up in the euphoria of it all. Such a wonderful memory. Children at their purest, finding joy in simply being with one another. That and their mother's disastrous sewing.

"Do you still have it?" Iphigenia asked.

"I think so. Maybe I should dig it out. See if Electra would wear it for us again."

Iphigenia laughed. "I would like to be there when you ask her," she said.

As the hot sun gave way to a cooler dusk, they went below deck to try to get some sleep before the ship made port in Aulis. After all, the next day promised to be full of excitement.

FOUR

T HE PAIR WERE SLEEPING WHEN THE MESSENGER CAME TO
tell them that Aulis was in sight. They dressed hurriedly and
headed up on deck.

"Is that Father's fleet?" Iphigenia asked as she stepped outside.
The view had changed from distant, craggy mountains to a
horizon of ships. Hundreds upon hundreds of them, sails furled,
floated motionless beneath the morning sky like a tableau. No
wonder Agamemnon was worried. Even with others at his side,
Menelaus would have no hope of bringing back Helen with this
many men prevented from joining him.

"Yes. We will arrive in Aulis soon," Clytemnestra replied.
"Your father will be waiting to take us to the celebrations. Go
quickly and change."

The sails on their own ship were also now obsolete, and the crew
rowed them the rest of the way to shore. The change was palpable. It
was not only a lack of wind but an uncanny stillness. It was almost as
if the Goddess was controlling everything around them. There was
not so much as a ripple on the sea.

When her daughter next appeared, she was dressed in a robe of glittering saffron. The material flowed in perfect pleats as the silken gown glimmered and glinted in the early light, a bold contrast to her freshly oiled hair. The only thing that outshone the beauty of the outfit was Iphigenia herself.

"Do you think this will be all right? Do you think he will like me? Do I look like I would make a good wife?"

Stunned to silence, Clytemnestra stifled the tears that threatened to fall.

"If he does not see that you are the most beautiful woman in the world, then he is a fool. And do not forget, this is your day too, my love. He may be the hero, but you are his reward. The one the Goddess picked for him. Never believe yourself to be worth less than him, or any man for that matter, because thinking it is the start of it becoming true."

Iphigenia's eyes sparkled, and Clytemnestra felt fit to burst. There was something about her that was so pure, it was as if the very sunlight converged on her.

"You know you have always been perfect," she said, a stray tear finally escaping.

"Mother."

"It is true. You never whined. Never cried at night. You are the kindest child I have ever encountered."

"You have to say that; I am your daughter."

"I do not. I say it because it is true. You are the prize here, Iphigenia. You."

The two held each other in yet another fond embrace, and while Clytemnestra wished it could have lasted longer, the young woman broke away in excitement.

"Look, Mother; there is Father. He is waiting, as you said he would be."

It did not take her more than a moment to pick out Agamemnon, standing on the dockside with a crowd of soldiers and servants gathered around him. Her eyes went first to his attire, a plainer ensemble than she would have predicted. But the off-white silk, with golden amulets and bracelets, made him look every bit the king, yet a father not wishing to outshine his daughter before the Goddess. But beyond the smart clothes, there were signs of stress. His shoulders hunched a little and he had lost weight too. Although she could not be sure from a distance, she suspected his tight curls had grayed from the worry of the lack of wind. As he spotted them standing on the ship, his mouth rose in a yellow-toothed grin, only to immediately fall again. She was not the only one who noticed.

"Is Father all right?" Iphigenia asked. "He looks worried."

Clytemnestra felt her stomach knot. "He will be fine. It is just the look of a man realizing he is going to be handing over his little girl to another, that is all." Then, hoping she was right, she turned to her daughter and squeezed her arms before smoothing down the dress. "Remember, *you* are the prize," she said again.

In as stately a manner as possible, they made their way down the gangplank.

Agamemnon's attention went straight to his wife.

"My king," she said.

"What are you doing here?" he growled. "I told the messenger he was to bring the girl by herself."

The girl! She gritted her teeth and forced her face into a smile. Even now, with the honor of a goddess bestowed upon their daughter, he still failed to see her for what she was worth. He always failed to acknowledge any of them, except Orestes. She swallowed, controlling her anger.

"I left the other children at home. Electra and Chrysothemis are under orders to keep Orestes out of trouble, no matter what. Believe me, they were disappointed. Surely you could not imagine that I would miss the wedding too? Of my eldest daughter? To Achilles, no less?"

His eyes flitted between them. "You dressed her in Artemis's colors. That is good. We will go there now." Without another word, he turned on his heel.

Clytemnestra grabbed Iphigenia's hand, holding her to the spot. "The messenger said there would be a feast first and then the ceremony."

Jaw locked, he spun back around to face them. "Then the messenger got it wrong. I am to take her straight to the Temple of Artemis."

"Why?"

"To pray."

Still she refused to loosen her grip on her daughter.

"It is all right, Mother." Iphigenia turned to face her. "I can go to pray at the temple. I believe it is the right thing to do, given all the blessings she is to bestow on me."

"See. The girl understands."

That word again. *Girl.* Like she was not of his blood. As if he could not even be bothered to recall his own daughter's name. Her grip tightened.

"I spoke to the messenger at length," she said. "He recalled everything you told him with great clarity."

"Clearly, that is not the case."

"Do not lie to me, Agamemnon!"

Her voice resonated around them. Several of the servants and soldiers who had been waiting shifted uneasily. She might have played the role of obedient wife well enough all these years, but she was still the daughter of the King of Sparta and had recognized her husband's lies from the very start. He was not taking this child from her until he told her the truth.

A look of sheer venom flashed in his eyes, but she countered it with one of her own.

"You have not greeted your wife. You have barely said two words to me, and now you wish to whisk Iphigenia off to a temple, without so much as a word about the wedding arrangements. You can barely look me in the eye, Agamemnon. What is it? What are you not telling me?"

The rancor was still there, but it was now clouded by something she recognized all too well. Guilt.

"As the gods are my witness, I will put her straight back on that ship if you do not tell me!"

A muscle was now twitching in his face as the King ground his teeth together. The straggling hairs of his beard no longer hid his pitted, yellowing skin. She despised that beard, just as she hated everything else about him. With a wave of his hand, his minions moved a short distance away. He stepped to her side and lowered his mouth to her ear.

"It was me," he hissed. "I am the one who angered the Goddess. I am the one who is responsible for my ships bobbing here uselessly, like legless ducks on a pond. I have brought this upon my men and upon Menelaus. So I am sorry if I seem brusque to you, Clytemnestra. I am sorry if my way of greeting you was not how you had envisioned so fancifully in that florid imagination of yours, but I have many things playing on my mind. And, right now, my priority is to appease the Goddess. Given how much she clearly thinks of our eldest, I felt it would be prudent to pray at her temple, before the feasting or the ceremony begins."

A small pang of guilt stirred within her. Whatever she thought of Agamemnon, she prided herself in her wisdom. In knowing how to behave appropriately in any situation. Growing up in Sparta had taught her that. Tantalus had given her that.

"I will come with you," she said, releasing her daughter's hand. "We will pray together." She took a step forward, only to find her path blocked.

"No," he said. "Iphigenia and I will do this alone."

FIVE

A THOUSAND EMOTIONS SWEPT THROUGH CLYTEMNESTRA AS she meandered through the bustling port market. In a few hours, another of her children would be gone from her life. But this one was different. Iphigenia was simply getting married. She would not be truly gone. Not like Alesandro.

The thought of him stung sharply, and she hurried to quash the feeling before any other memories surfaced to join it. She had been doing so well these past few years. Besides, Iphigenia would know in an instant if something was wrong with her mother, and she refused to let her grief overshadow her daughter's wedding day.

The market was a hive of activity and a feast for the eyes. A myriad of trinkets and treasures, many of which she had not seen at home in Mycenae, glinted on the stalls. Her eyes wandered from jewelry to fabulous materials, to crockery and even birds, colorful and flightless, tethered with string to wooden posts. She would have to take back presents for the children, she thought, as she continued to amble over the cobblestones. Not that they needed anything, but it was never about what they needed.

Still thinking of gifts, she made her way to a stall selling daggers and picked out a small knife. The handle was inlaid with mother-of-pearl and the shaft engraved with a simple filigree pattern. Boys just a few years older than Orestes would use such a tool to skin rabbits, although she suspected that even in another five years he would still rather use it to cut plants to feed them. Perhaps it would be a more suitable present when he was older. Leaving the knife where it was, she continued her stroll. The breeze was warmer than at home, and the air had a salty tang to it. A mix of different accents buzzed around her, with men and women in all forms of dress. It would be an exciting place to live, she thought, if only for a short while.

For Chrysothemis, she bought a necklace of garnets set in silver. Her middle daughter's tastes were far from her own, but the general rule was that if something sparkled, then she would like it. Still looking at the gems and bracelets, she considered what to buy Electra. Such raw beauty would be set off wonderfully with a bright stone—an emerald or citrine perhaps—but any time she had bought her youngest daughter jewels, they had lain abandoned at the bottom of a drawer, or else been pilfered by Chrysothemis, to go with some outfit or another. And so, she returned to the stall with the knives and picked one out for Electra.

Aromas of salt fish and dried meats wafted around her as she slowed her pace trying to absorb it all. There was a freedom that came with ambling around a foreign market, where no one knew who she was. A freedom that came with no guards hovering nearby. In Mycenae, traders would drop their prices ridiculously low, or else simply give her their wares if she so much as expressed the slightest interest in something in their stall. But here, while Agamemnon was a well-known figure, she was not. As such, they treated her like any other rich foreigner, hiking their prices up to at least double what something was worth, which made her smile rather than offending her.

As she wandered, her focus shifted back to the wedding, now just hours away. Given that it was to happen in Aulis, it would seem fitting that she wear something to pay her respects to the town. And then there was Achilles. Agamemnon should have already arranged a suitable wedding gift for the pair, but given how preoccupied he was, the thought might have slipped his mind. What did you buy the world's greatest warrior who was about to wed one of the world's greatest beauties in a union arranged by a goddess? Somehow a vase or amulet didn't feel appropriate.

She was rifling through a selection of silks, feeling the fineness of a particularly pretty one as it ran over her fingers, when a voice in a nearby stall caught her attention.

"You cannot be serious, Patroclus. I cannot wear something like that."

"I think it would suit you."

"Do you know me at all?"

Patroclus. The name stirred somewhere in her memory. Abandoning the fabrics, Clytemnestra walked toward the pair, the hubbub of the market lost to her the closer she came. The two men were sharing a wistful smile. At a glance, they appeared similar in age; a little younger than her, most probably. Both were dressed in fine clothes, both deeply tanned from hours spent in the sun, but while one of the men was, by common standards at least, attractive enough, the other could have been a god. With his chest swathed in folds of deep maroon, he stood a half foot taller than his friend and would have made most of the men in Sparta look like runts by comparison. She could not help but admire his physique, from his neck to his arms and all the way down to his calves, which rippled with muscle. At his waist was sheathed a small blade, although she could not conceive of a situation in which he would need to draw it. She couldn't imagine that even the bravest man would dare to challenge him.

"Achilles?" she said, interrupting their conversation. The gaze between the two men broke, and as the taller of the men—Achilles, she was certain—lifted his hand as if to dismiss her, his eyes caught sight of the gemstones on her fingers and a crease formed between his brows.

"Do I know you?" he asked, placing the sandals in his hand back on the table in front of him.

"I am Clytemnestra," she said.

The crease remained, deepening as he tried to place her name, but his companion had no such problem.

"Your Highness," Patroclus said, bowing. "We were not expecting to see you."

"Of course." Achilles followed suit. "Clytemnestra. Agamemnon's queen. You do us a great honor being here."

Now embarrassed by his delayed response, he held his bow low until she reached her hand out and beckoned for him to rise, smiling demurely when his eyes finally met hers. She hoped that his manners were not an act. It was difficult to tell, but as far as first impressions went, she considered this one to be fair. At least he was not spending the hours before his nuptials drinking. Realizing a somewhat awkward silence had developed, she smiled again.

"Agamemnon's queen, yes, I am she. But soon I am to be more than that to you, of course."

"You are?" The furrow between Achilles's brows reformed. "I am sorry. I do not understand. Are you to come with us to Troy? I heard that you were a fearsome swordswoman when you were younger."

"No, no. I wish." She laughed at his geniality. "But it is today, is it not, that you are marrying my daughter?"

A rumble of laughter caught in Patroclus's throat, although it was so quickly stifled that she did not hear it. Achilles shot him a look.

"I am sorry, my queen. I think there has been some misunderstanding. You believe I am to marry one of your daughters?"

She blinked and shook her head. Either his confusion was in earnest, or he was one of the most gifted actors that she had ever come across.

"Agamemnon sent a messenger. I was to bring Iphigenia, my eldest, here. The union has been blessed by the Goddess Artemis. She has commanded it. You are to marry my daughter today, and then the winds will return."

The frown was still there but had now changed to one of concern rather than confusion.

"I am sorry, but if such a bargain had been struck, I am sure that I would know of it. Today? You say I am to marry her today? No, there has to have been some mistake. Even Agamemnon would not make such an assumption as to commit me to my own betrothal without consulting me first."

Though he sounded certain, his red-tinged cheeks suggested he was not completely convinced. Agamemnon could easily pull such a stunt, and they both knew it. It was Patroclus who spoke next.

"Let us go and find him. I am sure we can clear this up in no time. Where is he now? Is your daughter with him? Iphigenia, is it? I have heard the most favorable reports of her. Of all your children."

"He has taken her to the temple."

The words had barely left her lips when her world began to tilt. The noise of the market disappeared. The warmth of the day evaporated. Nothing remained but an icy cold that was filling her veins. She had been right all along. Gods did not delight in human happiness. They would not see a wedding as atonement for an offense. Gods sought retribution. And if it was Agamemnon who had wronged the Goddess, as he had said it had been, then it was he who would have to pay the price.

"The Temple of Artemis," she gasped. "Where is it? *Where is it?*"

"The Temple of Artemis? It is just at the top of the hill. We will take you there."

He looked toward Achilles for confirmation, but Clytemnestra was already racing away.

"Move! Move!" she screamed at the crowd.

The sight of Achilles in the market had caused quite a gathering around the three of them. With all her might, she pushed past one person and then another.

"Move! Move!" she yelled again. "Get out of my way!" Her heart raced. Tears blurred her vision. Finally, she escaped the throng and was out into the open, but there was still so far to go. The temple was at the top of the hill, as Patroclus had said. She could see it gleaming white, above the trees.

"I am coming! I am coming!" she called out. "I am coming for you, Iphigenia!"

Her feet moved faster and faster as she strode out. No, she told herself. He wouldn't. It couldn't be possible. She must have got it wrong. But, in her heart of hearts, she knew the truth. As she fought her way up the steep hillside, her muscles began to burn. Damn her legs. Damn her pathetic body. Why had she allowed herself to become so unfit? Her muscles had grown weak and her mind weaker still as she'd wasted her days just sitting around talking, or on her useless weaving. How had she not seen this coming? How had she not read the signs?

"I am coming, Iphigenia!" she called again as she ran. She had promised her children a thousand times that she would keep them safe. She had promised, too, that Agamemnon would protect them. And now she had delivered her daughter to be slaughtered at his hands.

"Please, gods!" she screamed up to the sky as she ran. "She is only a child! Please! Take me! Take me instead!"

She stumbled again. Her hands bled as she clawed at the rocks and gravel. Behind her, she could hear the voices of Achilles and Patroclus calling her, asking her to wait. But she would not. She could still get there in time. She had to. She would not let it happen. Not again.

As she neared the temple door, a man stepped out from the shadows. Agamemnon. And in his hands, a knife, the blade gleaming red.

A pain tore through her heart as the thousand scars that had never truly healed reopened in a blinding agony.

"No! No!" She pummeled his chest.

"I said you were to wait in the town."

"You murdered her! You have murdered our daughter! My child! You have done it to me again!" She didn't know what she was doing. She was only aware of the agony that seared through every part of her being as she clawed at her husband. She reached up on her toes and spat squarely into his face.

He grabbed her arms, pinching her skin cruelly.

"You had no life before me, my queen!" he snarled. "Remember that! I did what had to be done!"

"No life? You stole my life! And you have stolen it from me again!"

"You ungrateful bitch!"

His words fell on deaf ears, as she writhed back and forth. Her arms were already bruising from his fierce grip as his fingers inflicted the same injuries as they had a hundred times before. Still she did not give in. With almost superhuman strength, she shook him off and pushed past him.

There, on the altar, was the crumpled figure of her daughter.

"Iphigenia!" Tears streamed down her cheeks as she climbed up onto the slab and pulled the limp body into her arms. Her skin was still warm to the touch and her lips still glowed pink, but the saffron robes, which had shone so brilliantly in the sun only an hour earlier, were now stained deep red as her blood seeped away.

"My darling. My darling, darling girl. I am so sorry. I am so, so sorry. He will pay for this, I promise you. He will pay."

The moment seemed as if trapped behind glass, a tarnished mirror that offered only the darkest of reflections. How could she live with this? How could she survive this again? She squeezed her daughter tighter, as if by doing so she might somehow imbue her with her own life force. Then, as she clung to her, she recalled with sudden clarity the knife she had bought in the market. Lowering Iphigenia gently back down, she pulled the blade from her bag. The metal glinted in the candlelight. New, unused. Sharp enough to skin an animal. Her eyes turned back to the doorway, where Agamemnon stood staring out with his back to her. Her pulse soared. This was it. It would be the only chance she would ever get.

Fixing the knife in her grasp, she dropped quietly from the altar. Her heart hammered in her chest as she darted toward her husband. Despite the years of idleness, her muscles now responded quickly, but the attack was ill-timed. She was still an arm's length away when he turned, with a look oh so familiar. There was not the smallest flicker of humanity in his eyes, nor any finesse in his movement as he backhanded her viciously, connecting directly with her jaw. Even in her youth, she would have struggled to maintain her balance against such a blow. Now, with her heart and will totally broken, she collapsed to the floor, eyes watering with the physical and mental pain. Sneering, he glared down at her, just as he had all those years ago.

"Bury the girl," he ordered. "The winds have returned. It is time I left."

SIX

CLYTEMNESTRA REMAINED AT THE TEMPLE UNTIL THE BLOOD on her hands and the floor had congealed to a deep red. Iphigenia's eyes were closed and her lips tilted up, as if in a slight smile, although all the color had drained from them now. Shadows formed and lengthened as the time passed. Birdsong rose and fell, but for her, time had ended.

She wouldn't have known what was about to happen, Clytemnestra told herself. Agamemnon would have granted her that mercy, surely. He was a huntsman. He knew how to kill cleanly and swiftly. Her daughter would not have realized what was coming.

The image played over and over in her mind. Her daughter kneeling to pray, full of thoughts about her upcoming nuptials, her wedding night. She would have been at peace, joyous even, when he struck. That smile, which lifted her eyes and made them shine brighter than Helios, was all her mother could see. That beautiful smile and then…

As birdsong was replaced with the nighttime chorus of the cicadas, a chill breeze blew through the temple pillars, fanning the fabric of Clytemnestra's robe and cooling the air around her, but she did not feel it. She did not feel anything.

Taking a damp cloth, she was wiping the blood from her daughter's face when a small cough caught her attention. Stumbling to her feet, she turned to see a young woman dressed almost identically to Iphigenia. A priestess.

"I wished to let you know that we can bury her here, on the grounds." She kept her head lowered as she spoke. "She will be at home with the Goddess that way."

The words took a moment to register.

"With the Goddess?" Clytemnestra lifted her head. "The Goddess is the one who did this to her. The Goddess and her father."

The priestess nodded slowly. "The Goddess is wise. Her decisions are those of divine knowledge. We, as mortals, cannot know their meaning."

The queen, who had been as cold as ice for hours, now felt a raging heat rising within her.

"Their meaning?" She took a step toward the priestess. "This is an act of barbarism! It has no meaning!"

"You must have faith."

"Faith?"

"It is not for us to question the Goddess."

"The Goddess is a selfish whore!"

The priestess flinched at the outburst, but Clytemnestra was not done. She marched toward the woman, her body now burning with fury.

"The Goddess took my daughter, who had done nothing wrong! Nothing! She was innocent!"

"And that is why it is the greatest gift. Of all the children, the Goddess wanted yours."

"Well, I want her too. I want her back!"

"The Goddess—"

"Damn your Goddess."

The priestess turned pale and looked up, muttering under her breath. Clytemnestra cared not a jot. Whatever wrath Artemis would feel for her, what did it matter anymore? What was the worst she could do to her now? With a sickening jolt, she realized: of course there was more horror the Goddess could inflict. She had taken one child, but there remained three more. They must be protected!

"I must get home now," she said, turning back to the altar. She bent to scoop Iphigenia's body into her arms.

"What are you doing?" The priestess hurried to her side, pushing her away from her dead child. "You must leave the girl here. She was a sacrifice to the Goddess."

"And the Goddess has her now. What remains is coming with me."

The priestess shook her head, looking around for someone who might come to her aid, but they could both see that there was no one. Most likely they were all at the blessing of the fleet that Agamemnon had murdered his daughter for.

"We are leaving now," Clytemnestra said.

The priestess grabbed an edge of Iphigenia's robe, pinning it to the altar. "This is not what we do. She must stay here."

Stepping back, she surveyed the girl with all the patience she could muster. *How old is she*, the queen wondered, *and how far is she prepared to go to please her Goddess?* She might be about to find out. With her eyes locked on the priestess, Clytemnestra reached into her satchel and withdrew the knife once more.

"Just try to stop me."

A look of fear flashed across the priestess's face. Clytemnestra took a step forward. "I have no quarrel with you. I just want my child."

The priestess opened her mouth but made no discernible sound. A chorus of voices floated in from outside. Distant voices, but of people close enough to hear her scream now if she chose to. Fear switched from one woman to the other.

"Please. Please." Clytemnestra grabbed her arm. "She is my daughter. She is my child. The Goddess has her blood and her soul. Please let me take her body home. This is all I have left of her. This is all I have."

The voices grew louder, and the panic within her surged.

"I do not want to hurt you, I really do not, but I will not leave without her."

Still clinging to Iphigenia's robe, the priestess's hands trembled. One scream and there would be more bloodshed in the temple that night. Clytemnestra readied the knife, her knuckles shining white. The priestess, now so afraid that her whole body was shaking, finally dipped her chin in a nod.

As Clytemnestra stepped past her and lifted Iphigenia into her arms, the young girl fell to her knees and wept.

Outside, the Goddess had made good on her promise. A wind had sprung up with such force that it was shaking the leaves from the trees, sending them dancing in spirals above her head. A jarring cold swept in from the sea, and the evening sun was disappearing over the horizon. The fading light caused her to stumble, as she tried to locate the path. She had nothing to light her way and couldn't even use her hands to support herself, as she clung to her daughter's body. It would be in the lap of the gods if she made it down the hill in one piece.

Peering into the shadows, she finally located the pathway. The adrenaline that had kept her going earlier had evaporated, and exhaustion had taken its place. Only then did she realize the extent of the task ahead of her. The route was so narrow, so winding, it was no wonder she had struggled to maintain her footing on the way up. And now she had to return in near darkness, her arms bearing the weight of her dead child. As Clytemnestra considered her situation, one of Iphigenia's hands fell limp at her side, brushing her arm as it did so. The cold of her skin caused her muscles to seize. She would not abandon her daughter. She would take her home and bury her in the grave circle, among the trees and the birds of the citadel that she had loved so much. It could take her a week to get down the hillside for all she cared; she was not giving up now.

Holding on to Iphigenia for all her worth, she picked her way gradually down the hillside. When the wind gusted stronger, she lowered herself to the ground and waited for it to pass, before heaving herself back up and continuing. Time and time again, her muscles trembled and her legs shook, but she waited for the moment to pass, then carried on. One slow step at a time. One step and then another. It was all she could do.

The moon was shining brightly when she finally reached the town. The daytime trinket stalls had been replaced with hawkers selling all manner of food. Thick smoke, full of the aromas of salted meats and grilled fish, filled the air. Her stomach growled but she felt no hunger. Eyes turned toward her. Conversations stopped. Whispers rose and people parted, shuffling backward, creating a path for her. Only now did she consider how she must look, with blood covering her clothes and hands and the body limp in her arms. The whispering grew louder, the looks more pointed, yet no one approached her. Nor did anyone she passed ask if she needed aid. Instead, they retreated from her, as if she were something to be frightened of or, worse still, pitied. Pitied for her failure as a mother who could not save her child. *Well, curse them all,* she thought as she met every stare. They knew nothing of her or her daughter. Nothing of what she had been or could have become. As she walked the cobbled stones, past the hawkers of Aulis, she promised herself one thing: she would never again seek anyone's help to keep her children safe.

The days shortened. Migrating birds passed overhead on their way to warmer climes. The sun rose and then set and then rose again.

No matter how many times they asked, she found it impossible to answer her children's questions with anything that came even close to making sense to them. Of course they knew that their sister was dead. They had been present at her burial, when they had taken her body to the grave circle of their ancestors, placed coins on her eyes, and bade her a safe passage to the underworld.

There would be no one there Iphigenia would recognize, Clytemnestra realized as she attempted to drown the images of her dead daughter in wine. Her grandparents had passed over the river Styx, but she had never met them. And a brother she had not even known existed. It should be a parent's job to go first, to welcome their children to the next stage of existence. But as much as she thought about joining her daughter, she knew she still had three children left in the world to protect.

As the first week had bled into the next, the whole of Mycenae was rife with rumors of what had happened to Iphigenia in Aulis.

"They must not leave the palace grounds," she ordered Orrin as she paced up and down the steps of the throne room. "You are to place guards on every entrance. They are not allowed out. Not with anyone. You understand?"

"I do, my queen."

"And they are to meet with no one, unless I am with them. You understand that too? No one!"

"I understand."

Not all of her servants were to prove quite so biddable.

"You need to tell them, my queen," Laodamia said one evening as she prepared a cup of wine for her mistress.

Two weeks had passed, and the children had not so much as stepped out on the veranda without her present, for fear of what words could drift in on a breeze. Chrysothemis and Electra were arguing about something on the other side of the courtyard, while Orestes bounced on his mother's knee.

"They will hear one way or another. It is best it comes from you."

"They are too young to know the truth."

"I believe that they are too old to be lied to," Laodamia replied. "It is for you that I fear, my queen. If they hear by some other route…" She left the sentence hanging in the air. Clytemnestra swallowed a mouthful of wine. She knew it was true. Rumors had a way of squeezing themselves through the smallest of gaps into the most unwelcome of places. But she needed more time.

"Not tonight. I have a headache. Besides, I am with them. There is no chance they will hear anything."

"Then tomorrow? Would you like me to prepare a room for you?"

"We shall see."

Placing Orestes down next to her, she sipped again at the wine and waited for her servant to leave. Laodamia had been there the very first day she'd set foot in the palace, and the queen confided in her more than any other person in Mycenae. But it was not a friendship, and should she need to be reminded of that, Clytemnestra was ready.

"Chrysothemis, Electra, what are you arguing about now? Come here, the pair of you."

Across the courtyard, the girls ceased their bickering and ran to join their mother.

"It is her fault…" Electra began, and a small smile played on the queen's lips. At least some things never changed.

Despite her desire to keep the truth of Iphigenia's death hidden, the subject came up at their meal. Unexpected rain had forced them into one of the dining rooms, where silver platters and glazed ceramic bowls were spread out along a marble-topped table. The stonework had stunned her when she had first arrived. Marble slabs and obsidian pillars. Marble thrones and colonnades. So much space and the endless reflections—not surprising for one as vain as Agamemnon. Oh, how she had hated it! These days, she barely even noticed. Tall beeswax candles were lit the length of the table. She had requested these years ago. She had found candles made of tallow emitted a scent so pungent that it affected her appetite. Yes, there was something pleasing about a good candle and its delicately dancing flame. So much more captivating than the oil lamps that burned nightly throughout the rest of the citadel.

Lost in the amber flames, she watched as the molten wax rolled down each slender pillar, fraction by fraction, until it puddled on the holder beneath it. One drop, then another, then another. Soon it would all be gone. The remaining wax could be used again, of course, melted down and reformed. But the original candle would be gone forever.

"She was a sacrifice," she said suddenly, breaking into the children's conversation without warning, surprising even herself. "She was a sacrifice to the Goddess Artemis, so that the wind would return and the fleet could leave for Troy."

Her two daughters turned to look at her. Chrysothemis spoke first.

"Iphigenia?"

"At the temple. She was sacrificed at the temple."

Disbelief stunned them into silence for a moment.

"I thought… You said there was an accident."

"No, there was no accident."

"But…but it makes no sense. A sacrifice? Why?"

Orestes continued to play with his food, oblivious to what was going on around him.

Dropping the bread from her hand, Chrysothemis shook her head. "There must have been some other way. We have animals. We should have used them. They could have had all the animals."

"The gods did not want animals," Electra snapped, speaking for the first time. "If they had wanted goats and sheep, they would have asked for them. They must have wanted Iphigenia."

Tears now streamed down her face as Chrysothemis looked to her mother, pleading for an answer. "But, surely, they could have tried another way?"

"That is not how it works. If the gods ask for something, you do it. You have no choice."

"But surely—"

"They wanted Iphigenia," repeated Electra.

"Be quiet, Electra!" Chrysothemis covered her mouth, trying to stifle her shuddering sobs. "Mother, please, why? Why did they need her?"

The queen shrank back into her seat, her throat tightening as she willed the question away. Why? Had she not asked herself the same thing every moment since that day in the temple? What answer could she give them that they deserved? There was none. She picked up her cup and quickly drained the contents before they could see how fiercely her hand shook.

"You should finish up now," she said, standing. "There is a storm on the way."

Indeed, a storm did come that night. Winds, loud enough to drown out even Clytemnestra's weeping, battered the walls of the palace. Men and women raced around the building, sealing what doors and gateways they could. She did not help them. It was not a queen's place to do so. Instead, she stood at her open window, challenging the gale. Sheets of rain sliced down, soaking her robe and hair.

"What do I do?" she called out. "How do I face this again?"

A gust of air blew in so brutally that it knocked her backward onto the stone floor, snuffing out the lamps and plunging the room into total darkness. Panting against the pain, she forced herself back to her feet.

"Please, please tell me what to do!"

The bolt of lightning was so pure, so vivid, it was as if Zeus himself was speaking directly to her. And when the storm had passed and she woke the next morning, her head was as clear as it had ever been. She knew exactly what she must do.

SEVEN

FOUR YEARS HAD PASSED SINCE SHE HAD SCOOPED UP HER daughter's body from the altar in the Temple of Artemis, and the war continued to rage on. Four of the ten years foretold to them. While most of the women in Mycenae were longing for their husbands' return, Clytemnestra accepted the absence of hers with gratitude as she ruled alone.

Mycenae was thriving. *She* was thriving in her role as queen and guardian, commanding the polis and politicians with a grace and wit that many had doubted possible. Each year, their faith in her grew. Throughout the trials of long, hot summers and bitter winters, she had shown frugality but not miserliness. Compassion but not weakness. One by one, she had earned the respect of even Agamemnon's most loyal devotees. But however well she played her part and kept the wheels of Mycenae turning, her focus remained not on the kingdom but on her children. Their health. Their happiness. Their safety.

"You need to stand with your feet apart." She moved to her daughter and adjusted her shoulders. "I have told you before, you must hold your balance better."

"I do not need to balance when I am weaving," Chrysothemis whined, shifting her feet a fraction, in a vain attempt at making herself more stable. "Why are we still doing this? As soon as the war ends, I will be married. Besides, we have been practicing this for years, and no one has ever tried to hurt us."

"That is because we are never allowed to leave the palace," Electra observed.

Clytemnestra ignored the remark. The evening sun had been a little above the horizon as the family had gathered together for their evening sparring session. As was normally the case, she had brought them out onto her veranda. The orange-hued light glinted off the wheat that grew in the pastures below and reflected off the marble that surrounded them. This was their regular routine, as set in stone as the rising of Helios.

"Come, raise your elbows a fraction." The queen continued to guide Chrysothemis. "Hold the blade higher. That is it. Now strike at me."

Wielding the weapon with distaste, Chrysothemis dragged her feet along the ground from side to side, then tentatively thrust the dagger forward, only for Clytemnestra to knock it to the ground in one swift motion.

"You need a stronger grip," she said.

"It is the tightest I can manage."

"That is not true. You just need to keep working at it. It is already better than it was."

"How is it possible that you are still so bad at this?" Electra asked, looking up from where she sat, polishing the blade of a sword. "We have been doing this for four years now."

"How are you still so bad at weaving?" Chrysothemis sneered back, picking up her knife. "You have been doing that for even longer."

"Yes, but I am bad at weaving because I do not bother with it. Weaving is dull. Why anyone would wish to waste time on it is beyond me. You have actually practiced this, and you are still terrible."

"Well, I am sure your husband will appreciate your swordsman-ship when you are stuck in his palace looking after his babies all day every day. I do not understand why we keep doing this."

Clytemnestra opened her mouth to respond. She had dozens of reasons listed in her mind, all day-to-day dangers facing a woman in this world and all of which she had shared with her daughters many times. But something caught her eye again. For the last two rounds of their training, she had noticed a figure sitting on a rock in the distance. He seemed to be looking their way, yet had made no movement to leave the field and take the path toward the citadel. He'd no sheep or goats to tend, nor did he wear the normal garb of someone who roamed the hills.

"You are still practicing so that I get the chance to laugh at you every day," Electra said as she continued to goad her sister.

"Girls, please!" Clytemnestra drew her eyes away from the man, bringing the bickering to a halt. "That is enough. Now, Electra, it is your turn. And put that thing down. What have I told you? You need to be able to defend yourself at a moment's notice. You will not always have a sword in hand. Where is that dagger I gave you?"

Grudgingly, Electra dropped the sword, rose to her feet, and pulled out the blade that was sheathed at her waist. The very same one her mother had bought her all those years ago. For a while, Clytemnestra had regretted the gift. The sight of it only brought back memories and caused her heart to yearn once more for Iphigenia. But the manner in which Electra, not easily pleased, cherished the weapon was to her mind the way her daughter expressed her love, without using words.

"Good—now your aim is to strike me. Do not worry about hurting me. No need to hold back."

The orange light scattered around her as, instinctively, Electra began to move her feet in small sidesteps, keeping her body low. From the very first session it had been like that. The ease with which she held a weapon, the focus that she displayed. Their Spartan heritage showed itself far more in her than in any of her siblings.

"How about we make this a wager?" Electra offered, her eyes still trained on her mother.

"A wager, you say?"

. For a twelve-year-old, she was far worldlier than either of her older sisters had been at that age, but Clytemnestra enjoyed the challenge.

"What wager might you have in mind?"

Electra continued to move her feet, her eye contact with her mother unbroken.

"Orrin said he is heading to the shore tomorrow, to the port at Argos. He is guarding the meat and wine we are sending to Troy." She hopped forward briefly before retiring again. "The journey will take half a day. Less, perhaps, if the men are quick loading."

"You still have not said what the wager is," the queen replied.

Running her tongue across her bottom lip, Electra narrowed her gaze. "Let me go with him. Let me ride with him."

"You went riding yesterday."

"In the paddock. Always in the paddock. And always with you and the guards. I cannot gallop there. I cannot jump or be free."

"The paddock is where I can keep you safe," Clytemnestra replied, switching her own blade from one hand to the other and back again.

"But I would be with Orrin. There is no man in the whole of

Mycenae that I would be safer with. You cannot keep us locked up like this forever."

"Locked up?" She lowered her blade. "Is that what it is called when you protect your children?" She studied her daughter. Yes, Spartan blood ran through her veins all right, but there was so much of Agamemnon there too. The stubbornness. The refusal to see another's point of view. It was no wonder she idolized her father. Fire burned in her eyes now. If her mother didn't appear to contemplate her request, it would result in a sulk that Clytemnestra knew from experience could go on for weeks. What risk was there really in accepting her challenge?

"Fine. If you disarm me, or strike me, you may ride with Orrin."

A grin spread across Electra's face, and she quickened her step. "I will let him know the moment I am done here."

Her posture changed as she transformed from princess to hunter. Now fierce and unrelenting, she lunged once, then again. Chrysothemis and Orestes stopped what they were doing to watch the scene unfolding. With gritted teeth, Electra skipped to the side, readying herself to make a third strike, but her mother swiveled on the ball of her foot, and before she had time to figure out what was happening, the queen had her around the neck.

"You are moving too early," she said.

"You told us to anticipate your moves."

"I am not saying *do not* anticipate. I am saying be more subtle. You are giving yourself away."

Her hand was still around Electra's neck, pinning her daughter to her chest. She loosened her grip by a fraction, which was all the girl needed. Twisting under her mother's elbow, she spun around and sliced the knife at her belly. The tip of the blade snagged on the fabric of her robe before Clytemnestra pushed her away with a kick square to the stomach. Unable to keep her balance, her daughter tumbled backward and landed with a thump on her behind.

"A good attempt," Clytemnestra said, reaching out a hand to help her back up. "Maybe next time."

"I had you!"

"No, you had my robe."

Red faced and covered in dust, Electra glared at her. "That is not fair!"

Realizing she would not accept her help, Clytemnestra pulled her hand back and turned around.

"I said disarm me or strike me. Your knife caught in my clothing for a moment. That is not the same thing."

"That is not fair! It was the wager!"

"It was. One that you lost."

"You were never going to let me go, were you? You are going to keep us like this, as prisoners, forever." Standing up, she threw her knife to the ground.

"I guess next time you will have to beat me."

"Or I could just go with Orrin anyway!"

The threat rang clear, causing the queen to stop in her tracks. Jaw locked and eyes now blazing, she spun back to face her daughter. "You are a princess, Electra. I am the queen. Orrin does not answer to you. Nobody does. If you want to see what happens when you go against my authority, then by all means try it. You will experience what a real prison feels like!"

Tension sizzled between them, Electra's eyes still flaming and her teeth grinding so fiercely it was audible. Finally, she turned and stormed up the steps to the palace.

"I cannot wait until Father returns," she yelled as a parting shot when she reached the top.

"Electra!" Chrysothemis chased after her sister. "You cannot speak to Mother like that! Wait! Come back!"

And with that they were both gone.

Her words had stung, but Clytemnestra allowed for the fact that her daughter didn't know the truth. The father she idolized, the one she practically worshipped, was a figment of her imagination. If they understood, they would never leave their mother's side. She had somehow managed to conceal the truth of Agamemnon's role in their sister's death over the years. She had told them that they had both been tricked by the priestesses of Artemis into bringing Iphigenia to them. That they had been praying together when the act had been committed. He had tried to stop it. That was what she had said. Not for his sake—never for him—but for theirs.

Knowing that it would be pointless following her angry daughter, she turned to her youngest child, who, for the whole of the sparring session, had been seated on the ground, playing with a collection of insects he had gathered.

"What about you, my darling? Do you wish to fight with your mother this evening?"

"Could you read to me instead?" he asked.

Warmth bloomed inside her. Dear sweet Orestes. He was even less enamored with the idea of fighting than Chrysothemis. Fortunately for him, he had been born with the advantage of being male. But his gentleness was what Clytemnestra loved most about him, and she would do anything to preserve it as long as possible. She didn't want to push him too much.

"Come then—let us go inside. Perhaps we should get your sister something to eat while we are there."

As he clambered to his feet, she gazed back down the hillside to where the man was still sitting motionless. It would be dark soon.

Wolves and wild dogs would prowl the fields, yet he seemed perfectly at ease where he was. A fool perhaps?

"Mother, are you coming?"

Her eyes remained on the figure a moment longer.

"Yes. Yes, I am," she replied and followed her son up the steps.

But before moving inside, she turned again and cast one last glance toward the man on the hillside.

"Who are you?" she asked.

EIGHT

N O MATTER HOW MUCH SHE WISHED OTHERWISE, Clytemnestra felt the loss of Iphigenia's presence everywhere she went. Every corridor, every nook and cranny brought her to mind. The wide-open hallways, where she had pretended to be some wild beast and let her younger siblings chase her. The kitchen, where she had on more than one occasion become covered in flour while helping the cooks prepare bread. And then the drawing room, where she had first picked up a lyre and plucked a simple tune, then practiced every day until her songs were more beautiful than those of any musician Agamemnon had ever hired to entertain them. Every room seemed to hold her memory in the fabric of its walls, refusing to release her from its grasp. Some days, Clytemnestra thought she caught her scent on a breeze, or she would run out of her chamber, sure she had heard her voice. It was grief. Clytemnestra had experienced this enough in her life to recognize it for what it was, but it didn't make it any easier to bear.

And there was no place she longed for her daughter so much as in the gardens. Large pillars tapering up to ornate stone moldings marked out the edges, while the area inside was sectioned off, with gazebos and enough seating for fifty people to enjoy their surroundings. But the children loved it most of all for the fruit there. Grapevines hung on trellises over the daybeds, offering shade and refreshment in the heat of the summer, while the herbs and flowers exuded scents as varied as rosemary and passionflower. Electra would only ever pick fruit for herself or, occasionally, for Orestes too. But Iphigenia had always attacked the vines, armed with a basket that she would fill to the brim, before offering the contents to anyone who was relaxing nearby.

The space felt barren now without her daughter singing to the birds or plucking flowers from around the fountains. Every rosebush, every patch of grass or cushion reminded Clytemnestra of her, and she would feel her eyes burning, just approaching the area. Yet it was the heart of the palace. A place she knew she could not avoid, if only for her children's sakes. And so, she found a way to distract herself there.

While the departure of the men for Troy should have seen the place grow quieter, the opposite was true. It had been easy enough to find women willing to spend a few hours each evening sitting in the luxury of the palace, drinking wine and eating food at Clytemnestra's invitation. Most wives now found themselves freer than they had ever known, and they always had plenty to talk about. Some she knew from her previous social circle—parties Agamemnon had held, to honor himself mainly, or feasts organized for one god or another. Once the children were asleep, Laodamia would often appear too, to take a seat and converse, although Clytemnestra secretly suspected that her servant's presence there was mostly to ensure that nothing too raucous occurred that might wake the children again. And so, the gossip and laughter went a small way toward filling the silence that would otherwise have left her heart and mind to wander. Or, at least, she told herself it did.

That night, after distancing herself from the women, she gestured to her servant, who rose and approached her.

"Laodamia, there is a man whom I have seen loitering today from my veranda. He was outside the citadel's walls. I believe he was watching me and the children."

"A local herder, my queen?" she asked in a hushed voice, turning away from the rest of the women as she spoke.

"I do not think so. I did not recognize him. Almost all the husbands have gone off to fight, and it is mostly the women who tend the sheep now. Besides, there were no animals with him that I could see."

"Then why else would he be there?"

"I am not sure. That is why I have asked you."

Laodamia nodded. She could not have been more than five years older than her mistress, yet in moments like this she seemed infinitely wiser.

"Have you alerted Orrin, my queen?"

"Not specifically."

"It may be wise to. But I shall keep my ear to the ground and let you know if I hear of anything."

"Thank you. And could you ask the guards to place an extra man on duty outside the children's chamber tonight, please? I am sure it is nothing, but you never know."

"Of course. I will do it now."

"Thank you. You can bring the women more wine when you return, if it is needed."

The servant looked back with a smile that creased the corners of her eyes and yet never quite shone within them. Something had probably happened many years before to make that sparkle leave, Clytemnestra suspected. The loss of a child, perhaps. Was that not the curse of the nursemaid? Maybe they had more in common than she had realized. No matter. She would never pry.

On the other side of the gazebo, singing had begun, Iphigenia's lyre now in yet another young woman's hands. Tension gripped Clytemnestra.

"Actually, I think I will go," she said, jumping up. "You stay here. The day has tired me more than I thought. It is probably best if I head to bed now. I will see to the children first."

"Are you sure? If it is too noisy here, I can ask them to leave. You can have the place to yourself if that is what you would prefer."

"No, no. Stay. Please stay. Enjoy your evening. There is plenty of wine. Help yourself. Be merry here."

"Thank you, my queen. Sleep well."

"I can but pray."

Sleep well? Wishful thinking, as Laodamia well knew. Since arriving at Mycenae, Clytemnestra's slumbers had been fraught with nightmares. And now, nearly two decades later, those same bad dreams still tormented her. It did not matter how tired her body was when she closed her eyes; scenes of her past would unravel in her mind to haunt her.

She had already learned that it was not possible to exhaust herself into restful sleep, but still she tried, sparring daily and not just with the children but also with one or two of the palace guards. Sometimes Orrin himself would take a short break from his duties to allow her to practice against him, but there was little satisfaction to be gained from this. Even skilled Orrin was fearful of a slip that might cause her pain or injury, and therefore he treated her with even more restraint than she did the children. Never did they really test her, truly push her to her limit.

One of her newer nightmares found her racing up the hill to the Temple of Artemis, sick to the stomach, a feeling of helplessness growing as every step weakened her muscles. The sense of desperation, realizing her body could not do what she needed it to and was not strong enough to get to her daughter's side in time, was all-consuming. Through the lethargy she had allowed herself as queen, she had failed Iphigenia. She would not let it happen again. So, in the mornings, she had taken to running. She would head to the veranda to watch the sunrise, and the moment the sky lit up the earth enough she would race out of the Lion Gate, past the grave circle, and around the citadel. Sometimes she would go up and down the mountainside until her muscles burned and her body dripped with sweat, and then she would push herself harder still. Never again would her legs or lungs let her down. Never would she fail to reach a child in need. Each night, her aching body yearned for a rest that her mind could not grant it.

In the children's chamber, she took a spare pillow and blanket from the pile and lay down in front of the doorway. It was far less comfortable than her bed, yet this stone floor was the one place in the whole palace where she slept easiest. Anyone who wished to reach her children would have to go through her first.

Clytemnestra lurched awake, her pulse immediately racing. As she could have predicted, sleep had been fitful, and she had woken at least a dozen times in the night. Dawn had almost broken when she finally fell properly asleep, managing just an hour or two, before another nightmare had forced her out of her slumber yet again.

Across the room, the children were all snoring softly and would be, she suspected, for several hours to come. Folding up the blanket, she returned it and the pillow to the pile. There was no point trying to go back to sleep now. Better that she should go for her morning run, before facing whatever business awaited her in the citadel.

Gradually, yet far slower than she would have liked, she had regained a modicum of her Spartan strength. It had not come easily. The fitness of her youth had dwindled away, thanks to overindulgence at the table and sedentary pursuits. When she had first attempted it, she had not managed one lap around the citadel's walls before collapsing onto her knees, panting. But those days were behind her now. When she wanted to stop, she would make herself carry on a little further. When she wanted to slow down, she forced herself to run faster. And when she wanted to turn back, she just changed direction.

That morning, she took a trail that wove slowly down the mountainside. When she reached the bottom of the valley, she switched onto a different path, where the incline back up was steep and unforgiving. It was a favorite route of hers and caused her thighs to burn and sweat to stream down her back. The lack of trees also meant that the guards, who watched her on Orrin's orders, could do so discreetly from a distance. There was no need for them to chase after her, breaking her concentration and invading what little privacy she had. Sometimes, on longer runs, they would jog beside her, occasionally offering a small amount of conversation. But running alone was far better.

When her legs were finally shaking with anoxia, an unpleasant sensation yet one that caused her no end of satisfaction, she felt content that she had tested her body enough that morning and should return to tackle the many tasks that awaited her.

Hot springs dotted the surrounding countryside. At the end of the winter, they would overflow, creating gushing rivers that raced through the valleys and pools in lower-lying areas. In the height of summer, people would gather in droves around these ponds to relax and gossip, but their distance from the palace made a quick visit impossible. So, instead, she decided to head beneath the citadel to the large reservoirs, where she could cool off beneath the rock and quench her thirst at the same time. These cisterns were a feat of engineering, fed by water pumped from nearby Lake Kopais and yet another reason Mycenae was such a force to be reckoned with.

When she finally reached the city walls, she bypassed the Lion Gate and took the winding staircase that led down beneath the buildings. Later in the day, this would be busy with men and women coming and going, filling their urns with as much water as they could carry. But, at this hour, she rarely saw a soul. She raised a hand to one of the distant guards, and he nodded back in acknowledgment, leaving his post in a leisurely stroll to join her. Gone were the days when they would be glued to her side, especially within the citadel. She would often manage to reach the reservoirs, quench her thirst, and be halfway back up again before they had joined her.

Knowing how long it normally took the guards to appear by her side, Clytemnestra was surprised when about a quarter of the way down she heard footsteps echoing behind her. Turning, she saw a man's silhouette above her. From just his outline, she could tell he was not one of her men.

"I suppose I should not be surprised that a Spartan princess, even as a queen, would rather spend her mornings running up mountains than being served bread and honey in bed. I have to say, I find it most refreshing."

She squinted in the semidarkness, angling herself to better see his features. Despite the shadow that fell across his face, a churning rolled through her gut as she recognized the stranger.

"You have been watching me. Me and my children. Who are you?"

Her hand felt in the belt of her robe. She had brought nothing with her in the way of a weapon. Not even a simple dagger. How often had she told her children that they must always be prepared? Yet here she was, cornered, with nothing more than an exhausted body to defend herself with. She straightened her back, trying to hide her growing fear.

"I asked you a question. Who are you, and why have you been watching my family?"

He nodded, a small glimmer in his eyes. "I apologize, Your Highness. Forgive my impertinence. I am merely a little taken aback. I have never seen Helen, but I find it impossible to believe that the gods could let anyone more beautiful than you wander the earth."

She moved her left leg forward, into a more stable stance from which to strike at him. She would go for the neck, using the side of her hand. And she would do it quickly, if he did not answer to her satisfaction.

"I have asked you a question twice now. I can assure you there will be no third time."

With a hurried bow, he lowered his head. "Forgive me, please. I have not been following you, Your Highness. I was thirsty, that is all, which is why I am here."

"And yesterday? You were watching me then."

"Yes, but not deliberately. The view from that veranda on which you stood was the one I most treasured in all Mycenae."

"The veranda is in the palace. It is not part of the common area of the citadel."

"I am fully aware of that." His eyes locked on hers. There was a familiarity to them, although she would swear on her life that she had not met him before. He tucked a strand of hair behind his ear before he spoke again. "My name is Aegisthus."

"Aegisthus." It took less than a heartbeat for the name to register. "Agamemnon's cousin?"

"Yes."

A cloud floated in front of the sun, plunging the staircase into even greater shadow.

"Then you are the man who killed my husband's father."

NINE

YEARS EARLIER, AEGISTHUS HAD KILLED HIS UNCLE, KING Atreus, the very man who had raised him as a son, and stole his crown for his own father, Thyestes. Agamemnon and his brother, Menelaus, fled to Sparta for refuge. When they eventually returned, fully grown and formidable warriors, they had taken back the throne from their traitorous uncle and cousin and sent them both fleeing from Mycenae. This had been just a few months before the wedding of Agamemnon and Clytemnestra.

That was where the story had ended. Agamemnon and Menelaus had their respective thrones, Agamemnon in Mycenae and Menelaus in Sparta. Whatever had happened to Thyestes and Aegisthus was rarely discussed. There had been a time when the brothers were hungry for vengeance—one as slow and painful as possible. After all, the law of the gods dictated that a son must always avenge the murder of his father, and they had fully intended doing so, but the business of ruling had gradually dulled the bloodlust, and the desire for revenge had waned. Thyestes had eventually died of old age while exiled in the city of Cytheria, and Aegisthus had seemingly disappeared.

As the years passed, people ceased to mention the cousin's name anymore. But Clytemnestra knew her husband well. It was possible he was merely biding his time, waiting for a moment when he would have the approval and backing of the greatest number of people before carrying out the task.

"How do I know you are telling the truth?" she asked, stepping further away from him, back down the staircase.

"I decided that no other name I could give you would enamor Your Highness less to me than my true one. Surely, only a fool would make up something like that?"

"There are many fools in this world."

"There are, and at times I have been one myself. But believe me, this is the truth."

"Then why are you here? To steal the crown again, while my husband is at war? I assume that is your plan."

Wordlessly, he cast his gaze beyond her, to the long staircase leading to the reservoirs below. One push was all it would take, she realized. One shove and she would tumble all the way down. It would look like an accident. And then he would be free to ransack the palace with whatever forces he had standing by. Where were the guards? Why were they being so slow today? Perhaps they had thought to wait, to afford her more privacy. What a day to offer such consideration. Or perhaps they were already dead.

"I come seeking nothing but your husband's forgiveness," Aegisthus said, bowing again.

"Then you have timed things very badly indeed, for it has obviously escaped your notice that he and the other men are gone and have been for some time now."

Color rose to his cheeks. "I am aware of that, my queen. I will be honest. I hoped that while he was away I could make myself of use here. Earn your good favor, so that he would see I am no threat to him anymore."

Anymore. The use of that single word added a new dimension to their conversation. The already claustrophobic stairway seemed to be closing in on her. If she didn't take her chance to leave now, she might never get another. Steeling herself against the tremor in her legs, she moved toward the king killer.

"I am done here," she said.

Her body shook as she pushed past him. He wobbled slightly, not unbalanced, but caught by surprise enough for her to make her escape. Her breathing faltered as she raced upward, the freedom of the open air only a short distance away now. She would send Orrin back immediately. She would see him off her land before noon. Sunlight dazzled her as, only one step from the top, he grabbed her wrist. She turned to face her attacker, eyes wide.

"Please, my queen, I am sorry if I have offended you. I have been lost for a very long time and had hoped that, perhaps, I would manage to find something of myself back here."

She glared at the hand on her wrist, pinching her skin. With a flick of her arm, she snapped it out of his grip.

"Stay away from me and my family," she hissed. "Stay away from our palace. This is not your home now. It is mine. And if you do not, I shall not hesitate to finish the task that Agamemnon and Menelaus failed to complete. And trust me, I would do a much more thorough job than any man."

A nod of the head turned into a half bow.

"I thank you for your generosity, my queen."

"There is no generosity here," she said. "Now leave!"

With her feet now securely above ground, she waited for him

to move, but for the longest while he simply looked at her, his dark eyes pleading. Then, without further apology or farewell, he walked past her and along the walled pathway. Only when he was out of sight did her knees buckle and she fall to the ground, gasping for breath.

"My queen!" A guard was at her side, his leisurely stroll down from the lookout point having changed to a sprint when he saw her fall. "What has happened?"

Kneeling, she attempted to slow her ragged breathing. He could have hurt her, killed her even, and yet she'd suffered nothing more than a sore arm. Why?

"I...I must have pushed myself too hard."

The lie left her mouth before she knew she was going to say it. Why she had chosen to, she didn't know.

"I am fine now," she said, standing up and brushing the sand from her robe. "I am fine. Please, let me be."

When she reached the palace, she headed straight to the south tower. With the citadel perched on a mountaintop, the view from the highest point was incomparable, stretching as far as the sea on a clear day. If Aegisthus had any troops hidden in the valleys, she might be able to see them from there. What she would do then, she wasn't sure.

A flurry of nerves continued to run through her. Aegisthus, a murderer, had roamed the citadel unchallenged and yet had walked away from her when she told him to. Why, when to kill her would have made taking Mycenae that much easier? He'd had the upper hand there on the staircase and again when he caught her arm, and yet he had withdrawn and left. Why would any man do that? Could it possibly be true that he had come only to seek forgiveness?

She shook the thought away. The number of guards would need to be increased and she would order foot patrols too. She would not tell Orrin the name of the intruder, just that she had been approached. That in itself was enough. Whatever Aegisthus was planning, he would not succeed.

From her vantage point, the mountainous lands of Mycenae rolled out in front of her, a bare, arid region. Summer had always been her least-favorite time of the year. The hillsides that during the rest of the year could be so vibrant and green seemed brittle and charred, a sea of browns and ochers. The air worsened too as heat ripened the stench of the animals, flies buzzed in droves around them and their food, and the plants that had not been harvested withered away. Spring, autumn, and even winter were so much more pleasing to the eye, for all the senses to enjoy. But for now, she did not care about the peonies or sideritis; there was only one thing she was searching for, and there he was, walking away, alone.

"My queen?"

Startled by another presence in the tower, she turned to find Laodamia in the doorway. "I am sorry, my queen, I have been looking for you."

Her stomach lurched, her mind leaping immediately to the worst thought imaginable.

"The children? What is wrong? Where are they?"

"The children are fine. I thought you would want to get ready for court."

"It is court? Today?"

"It is. The Assembly will be gathering for food shortly."

A heavy sigh drifted from her lips.

"Then yes, please help me prepare."

"You must pay for the animals that were killed," Clytemnestra said, having listened to yet another dispute. "Or they can be replaced with beasts of the same value as those lost. Is that understood?"

"Yes, my queen. Thank you, my queen."

"But what of the yarn? All his sheep are already shorn. Mine were not. I have lost that too."

She sucked in a lungful of air.

"Then they will give you fleeces as well," she said. "The same number. Now, is there anything more to be discussed?"

Eyes darted around the throne room. It had taken over six hours to deal with the month's squabbles, though she considered the time quite reasonable, compared to the many days she had lost there, silent at Agamemnon's side. At least now her voice was heard and she was making a difference.

"My queen, there are rumors that the armies have breached the walls of Troy. Is this true? Has the war ended?"

It was a woman who spoke. They were supposed to have no voice in the chamber, and several of the old men shuddered, as if disgusted by her audacity. There was no denying it was not the wisest of questions to ask, but without the efforts of the women, the younger men would have nothing to come home to. Clytemnestra looked her in the eyes as she spoke.

"Do not listen to stories," she replied. "They are quicker to change than the weather, and I can assure you, I have heard of no such thing. Until we see the beacon glowing on Mount Arachneus, we can assume that our roles here in this room and out in the kingdom remain the same and will continue as such for as long as is needed. Do you understand?"

The woman nodded. "Thank you, my queen."

When all was dealt with, the Council retreated to the dining hall to enjoy the buffet, which she always provided, and to continue their conversation, only to fall silent any time she approached. *Curse them*, she thought. If the war lasted just a few years more, most of them would be dead by the time Agamemnon returned. Maybe she should help this along—get the kitchen to provide only the fattiest and richest foods every time they visited the palace. Still, it was a better situation than some queens faced with their husbands absent.

She was still turning this over in her mind when Electra suddenly appeared and came rushing toward her.

"Mother!" she shouted, pushing past tutting old men to reach her. "Mother! Mother!"

"What is it?" Clytemnestra bent at the knee to hiss at her daughter. "What are you doing in here? You know this is no place for you."

"It is Orestes. We cannot find him. He is gone!"

TEN

S HE DID NOT WASTE TIME ON APOLOGIES AS SHE RACED OUT OF
the dining hall and into the wide corridors of the palace. Her
heart was pounding, and panic was muddling her thoughts.

"When did you last see him? When were you with him last?"

"We were playing hide-and-seek. He was to hide from us. But
we cannot find him. We have searched everywhere."

"Where have you looked?"

"Everywhere. The courtyards. The throne room."

"Your chamber? Did you check the chamber?"

"I…I think so. I think Chrysothemis went there."

Instinct had taken over. Clytemnestra pushed aside the curtain
into the children's room. This was always his favorite place. After
all, since he was only six, where else would he have the imagination
to hide?

"Orestes? Orestes? Where are you?" The beds were pristine. The
room was empty. She pulled aside the drapes, in case he was hiding
there, but when all she found was the whitewashed walls, her fear
spiked again.

"My queen, is everything all right?"

She spun around. Standing there, with furrowed brow, was Laodamia.

"Orestes has gone. He is missing. We must alert the guards. Call them immediately."

"Orestes?"

"Aegisthus!" Her eyes suddenly widened in fear. That had been his plan all along. To distract her with a sob story, then sneak in and kidnap her child. "He has taken him. But where would they go?"

She paced back and forth, trying to decide what her next move should be. But this was just wasting time. She needed to find them before it was too late. She would not let this happen again.

"When?" Laodamia had turned pale. "When did this happen?"

"I do not know. But he is gone."

Guards had gathered around them now. Orrin's men.

"Fetch my horse! I will find them!"

"My queen, have you checked the kitchen?" Laodamia asked.

"The kitchen?"

"I saw him head that way. Not so long ago."

She hesitated, her eyes going from Electra to the guards to the children's nursemaid, finally returning to Electra.

"Was the kitchen checked?"

"I...I do not know. I think so."

Her attention moved back to the guards.

"My horse and a dozen men. Send half of them straight off now. The others will wait for me. I will follow. You are to look for a man. Aegisthus."

She turned and sped back down the corridor, toward the kitchen, where staff were milling about, filling and refilling platters for the men in the dining hall.

"Have you seen the prince?" she demanded.

"Orestes?" one of the women asked. "Not since he came for food after breakfast."

She swept around the room, crouching to peer beneath the tables. "Orestes! Orestes!"

The place was full of baskets of bread and fruit, but no sign of her child. Angry that she had wasted yet more time, she rushed back to the door, colliding with a young man.

"My queen, I apologize."

"Get out of my way!" she yelled, pushing past him. "I need to find my son!"

"You are looking for the prince?" he asked.

She stopped. Misreading the tiny twist of his lips, the slight widening of his eyes, she felt her hands fly to his neck, and she slammed him against the wall, the thud reverberating around them.

"What did you do with him?" she screamed. Whatever she might lack in strength, she was making up for in pure rage. "Where is he?"

His face was turning red from the pressure on his throat.

"I... I... He...." he spluttered.

"My queen, please." Laodamia was at her side. "He cannot speak. He cannot tell you."

Clytemnestra dug her nails into his skin before releasing him. The young man's knees buckled, although he was wise enough to keep his eyes on her. He managed to choke out the words:

"He said he needed a good place, that was all."

"A good place?"

"To hide. To hide from his sisters."

"What do you mean?"

"I did not think it would be a problem. He just wanted to win. They were all playing."

"Where is he? Who took him? Where did they go?"

"Go? No, he is still there. I just checked. He is still hiding."

The flood of relief was short-lived and now mingled with a new sense of fury. "Where? Where is he? Where is my son?"

Tears filled the young man's eyes, as he whimpered, "He is hiding in the food store. In the pantry. Behind the sacks of flour."

She should have told the guards to march him outside the citadel, never to be allowed to return, she thought, as she bolted for the stairs that led off the kitchen, but she needed to check first. If her son was not where he said, it would be more than just banishment awaiting the cook.

It was a part of the palace that she had never visited. As queen, she had no need to go there, but she knew exactly where to head. The air cooled as she ran down the staircase and into the dark storeroom, where the smell of salted meats caught in her throat.

"Orestes? Orestes, are you down here?"

Her eyes adjusted slowly to the darkness. This could still be part of a trap. A ploy to give her enemies more time. She was ready to turn around, to find a knife and slit the cook's throat, when a small squeak came from the back of the room from behind the flour store.

"Orestes!"

Tears blurred her vision as she pushed the sacks aside. There, dusty and disheveled, was her son, his bottom lip protruding in a pout.

"Did I win?" he asked. "It surely does not count that you found me. Vander said this was the best place to hide. Did I win?"

Her heart was fit to burst as she pulled him to her chest and breathed in the aroma of his floury hair.

"Yes, my darling, you won. You won."

A smile split his face. "I did!" he yelled with glee.

She did not dispose of the young cook as she had originally planned. As she carried Orestes back up the stairs, her son's face lit up at the sight of him.

"Vander, I won!" he announced, beaming from ear to ear. "You were right. I won!"

"I am very pleased, my prince," he replied.

Clytemnestra clenched her jaws as she considered a fitting reprimand. But punish a man who had done nothing more than help her child play a game? Relief finally won out, and she realized that this would not be appropriate.

"We will eat in the children's chamber," she said instead. "Be quick with the food."

Later, her body quaked with the delayed reaction of almost losing another child. Anything could have occurred down in that cellar. What if something had happened to the cook, and no one had known where Orestes was hiding? What if something had fallen on him? So many what-ifs whirred around her brain, she could barely sit still. So, instead, she headed out into the warm summer evening, to sit in the grave circle and talk to the stones that housed her daughter's bones.

Situated to the south of the Lion Gate, it was one of the few places within the citadel where she could rely on being on her own. This burial site was only for monarchy and thus no one but the queen, her family, or the gardeners had need to be there. And yet, as she approached, she realized she would not be alone.

He knelt in the grass, by the stelae of Atreus, Agamemnon's father—the man whom he had murdered.

"I told you to leave."

Stumbling to his feet, Aegisthus kept his head bowed.

"My queen, I am—"

"Enough. You have come here to gloat. To taunt those you have already taken."

"No, no, that is not it."

"Then give me one good reason why I should not kill you now."

As he lifted his chin, his eyes met hers, and only then did she see how they glistened with tears. He had been crying, she realized. He had been kneeling at the grave of the man he had murdered, sobbing. His voice cracked as he spoke again. "I do not have one," he said, in answer to her question.

"You should just do it. Please, kill me now."

ELEVEN

T HIS HAD NOT BEEN AT ALL WHAT SHE HAD EXPECTED. Clytemnestra found herself standing in the grave circle staring at the weeping man. Getting to his feet, Aegisthus wiped his cheeks with the edge of his robe.

"Forgive me, my queen. I will leave you now. I will leave Mycenae this very night, as you requested."

He went to move away, but this time it was she who caught his arm.

"No," she said. "You will tell me what it is you are doing here in my kingdom. Here at this grave."

"I told you. I seek forgiveness."

She tightened her grip. "I do not take being lied to lightly."

"Nor should you," he said. "But it is the truth."

In the fading light of the summer evening, she searched his eyes for a hint of deceit yet could find nothing but sorrow. Her grip loosened. With a small dip of his chin, he conveyed his thanks.

"If you have time to walk with me, I would like to tell you a story," he said.

The evening chorus of the cicadas accompanied them as they strolled slowly around the east side of the walls toward the stables. Neither had spoken since leaving the grave of Atreus. She somehow found herself drawn to his pain and was keen to know the reason behind this usurper's reappearance. This time, she had the reassurance of a dagger sheathed at her side. They arrived at a stone bench, and he gestured for her to sit. Even then, he did not speak.

"Why would you come back here?" she asked. "When he dethroned your father, Agamemnon swore he would kill you if you ever returned, remember?"

"He never saw me when he took back the throne."

This caught her by surprise. She had heard the story many times, how Agamemnon and Menelaus had sent Aegisthus fleeing into the night, barefoot and sniveling.

"What do you mean, he did not see you?"

"By the time Agamemnon came for my father, I had already left Mycenae. Atreus and Thyestes were petty and spiteful men who used Agamemnon, Menelaus, and me in their bloody feud. I wanted no part of that. If you still think I am here to avenge my father, then you are very much mistaken."

If he was lying, then he was even more dangerous than she had first feared, for she couldn't read so much as a hint of trickery in him.

"I thought it was the will of the gods that every son must avenge his father," she said.

"My father was not murdered. Not directly. He was exiled and died a slow and, hopefully, extremely painful death."

"Surely you were there with him?"

His bitter laugh came as a harsh contrast to the tranquility of their surroundings.

"Then what happened?" she asked. "What is the truth of the

matter? And why have you come back to a land where you are despised?"

"It makes no difference where I go. I am despised everywhere. I have been since the moment I was born." As he drew in a deep breath, his shoulders lowered into the posture of an old man.

This was why he had come, she realized. This was what he needed to explain.

"Tell me," she said.

A long moment passed before he lifted his gaze to meet hers.

"You will know of what happened to my siblings, I assume. How Agamemnon's noble father, Atreus, chopped them up—his own nephews—and served them as a meal to his brother, my father, Thyestes."

She'd heard the story. Few hadn't. It was one of the most despicable acts in all history. When she had first met Agamemnon, she'd thought it impossible that anyone could be as brutal as his father. Now she knew he was just as bad, if not worse.

"I was raised by Atreus. An abandoned baby, gifted a second chance by the generous King of Mycenae. I am sure you know that much too. And it was only in my attempt to please him, by killing Thyestes, that I discovered who my true father was. You cannot imagine the torment that I faced when I found that out. Atreus, despite his faults, had raised me. But I had always felt out of place in his palace. Always felt as though a part of me were missing. I think that happens when you are abandoned as a child; you will always wonder what was wrong with you."

A feeling of sympathy arose in Clytemnestra, although not directly for Aegisthus. It was for a woman she had never met. She could not imagine what would force a mother to abandon her child like that. From the moment she had birthed each one of her own, all she had ever felt was unadulterated love and the desire to protect them, even if it cost her her own life. To feel anything less was unfathomable.

"Thyestes was my father. The man Atreus had raised me to hate was of my own blood. And, for all the compassion he had shown me, Atreus had served up my siblings and made my father eat them. So, when I discovered the truth and Thyestes, in his turn, asked me to kill Atreus, I did not know what I should do."

He shook his head.

"My father was sly; I will give him that. The way he worded it, I truly believed that Atreus was the one to blame, not only for the murders but for how my life had turned out—for the way I had been abandoned, left in a field, still bloody from my birth. Thyestes laid it all on the old king and, somehow, I believed that killing him would give me vengeance for all I had been through. But he was not to blame. I killed the wrong man."

Even in the warmth of the summer evening, Clytemnestra's arms prickled with goose bumps.

"What do you mean?"

Aegisthus brushed beads of sweat from his forehead, his mouth working soundlessly before he spoke again.

"I killed Atreus, with the sword that Thyestes, my father, had given me. On my return, I was hailed a hero and a great feast was thrown for me. That was when I learned the whole truth. As I triumphantly brandished that weapon and while all around were cheering me, my sister Pelopia's eyes were fixed on the blade, now wiped clean of my uncle's blood. She recognized the markings on the metal, knew it from another place, another time. It was the sword that had been held to her neck, to stop her from screaming while she was being raped, impregnated with an heir who would do the bidding of the man who was violating her. Our own father. And my sister, my sweet, loving sister, was also the heartless mother who had abandoned me to die in that field all those years before.

"When she discovered the truth, when she learned who I was... who our father had been..."

He paused, battling his emotions to finish the story. Clytemnestra's own pulse raced, as she feared she already knew the ending. It took but a moment for it to be confirmed.

"She seized the sword from me and fell upon the blade."

Aegisthus's eyes, once more overflowing with tears, rose to meet hers.

"I did not come to Mycenae for vengeance, Clytemnestra. You must believe me. I came here for forgiveness from your family, for what I did to them. I did not understand what I was doing. I was not my own man. Please, please, I beg your pardon."

She saw it all there, etched on his face. The young boy, yearning for a family. The headstrong son, only wishing to do his father proud. And then the blow. The discovery of who he was and how he had been conceived.

How could anyone get over that? she wondered. And then find the courage to reveal it and not just to a stranger, but to a member of the house that he had betrayed.

Never, in all her life, had a man asked for her forgiveness. And never had she felt it less warranted. But she knew now why he had come and what she should do.

"You have it," she said. "You have my forgiveness."

"And your husband, Agamemnon. Do you believe he will show me the same kindness?"

The last image she had of him came to mind, walking away from her, his hands stained with Iphigenia's blood. She could not bring herself to even utter his name.

"My husband has enough forgiveness of his own to seek," she said.

TWELVE

FOUR DAYS PASSED, AND CLYTEMNESTRA FOUND HERSELF FULLY occupied with the business of running the citadel. Arguments had gone back and forth on how to allocate the food they had harvested, so that neither the women and children of Mycenae nor the armies would suffer. It was not just a case of dividing the grain and meat and rationing the salt, but of sacks and baskets that needed to be woven. Everything took time, and the women, in addition to spinning the yarn and weaving it, were now also having to tend the herds and shear the sheep. Their workload had not only doubled, but they were doing jobs once deemed capable of being undertaken only by a man, a fact that her politicians seemed unable to grasp. Around and around they would go, bickering worse than infants. Any spare time she could find, she spent with her actual children.

And so, when Laodamia came to her one evening as she lounged in the courtyard, after a full day of battling the polis, Aegisthus was a thousand miles from her thoughts.

"My queen, there is a gentleman wishing to meet with you."

"Where is he?" she replied.

"He will not come into the palace. He says he will wait for you outside. Down at the stables."

She snorted. Another of Agamemnon's cronies, ready to tell her how to do her job, no doubt.

"Do you have his name?"

"I do not, my queen."

"Well, if whoever it is cannot be bothered to drag himself up to the palace to see the queen, then he will just have to wait."

She sighed and closed her eyes. The nursemaid hovered a moment longer, before disappearing, no doubt to relay the message far more diplomatically than it had been given.

Night had truly settled in, when she finally left the courtyard to head to the children's chamber. As she wandered through the colonnades, her thoughts returned to the man waiting by the horses.

There was very little chance he would still be there, she considered, and yet she was intrigued. So many men viewed a palace without a king as an opportunity for the taking. Rumors from Ithaca told how Penelope had been inundated with suitors, despite the fact that her husband was still alive and fighting. That this man wanted to keep his distance from the palace told her something. Only what that was, she wasn't quite sure. Grabbing a shawl and an oil lamp, she headed out into the night.

"You have been waiting here all evening?" she asked as she reached the stables and realized who it was.

He rose as she approached. "I was hoping you might find the time to take a stroll down this way."

"Or perhaps you thought you could summon me and I would come?"

Bending at the knee, Aegisthus bowed awkwardly. "No, that is not the case. I apologize if that is the impression I have given you.

It was not my intention. The palace... I... For me..." He stopped and regathered himself. "The palace is not a place where I would feel comfortable," he said eventually. "I apologize if my request came across as inappropriate."

Stopping a short way off, she observed him. How was it possible that this was the man who had slain Atreus and had been raised as a brother to Agamemnon? In this brief exchange alone, he had offered more apologies than her husband had in their entire marriage. And he had plenty to apologize for.

"I did not want to take up your time, Queen Clytemnestra. I merely wished to thank you for listening to me the other day. I will confess, I had not planned on unburdening myself quite so freely. In fact, I had intended never to reveal to anyone what I told you."

"But you did." She still kept her distance.

"I felt you might understand, on some level. You know what it is to be betrayed by your family." Seeing the pain in her eyes, he bowed his head. "I have already said too much. I am sorry. I heard the rumors of what your husband did."

"So that is why you came. To flaunt the fact that the great Agamemnon is despicable?"

"No, never. I told you. I came here to seek his forgiveness."

"Forgiveness from a man who is himself a monster?"

He locked eyes with her. "I am a monster too, my queen. I did an appalling thing to the man who raised me. But that does not mean that I am incapable of forgiving those who have wronged me. Of forgiving my mother for what she did to me, for example."

There seemed nothing false in what he said, no hidden layers of meaning that she could discern. And yet she was angered by his words.

"Your mother was a child when you were born. She did what she thought was best. To protect you both."

"My mother could not look at me when I was born; that was why she abandoned me. There is no point in pretending otherwise. I heard it from her own lips, when she thought she was only my sister. When she spoke to me, her younger brother, in confidence about that terrible experience, she told me how she had despised the child she had borne, from the instant of its birth. Please, my queen, I do not wish us to part on bad terms. I came only to say goodbye, that is all. I leave in the morning."

"You are going?"

"I have done all I can here. You will pass on my message to Agamemnon, when he returns?"

The abrupt end to their conversation surprised her. Blinking, she considered what he had said. "I will do so, but tell me, where will you go from here?"

"Wherever fate will take me. That is the beauty of belonging nowhere, bound to no one. Of course, it also means that I will never be missed by anyone."

In the quiet of the night, she thought that perhaps he wanted her to remark on this, but having spoken to the man properly only twice before, she felt there was very little more she could say. Whatever situation he found himself in, he was a man of stature and eloquence. He would be able to find his way in any city. Perhaps that was his game, to try to best Agamemnon by bedding his wife.

"I have made you uncomfortable," he said as if reading her thoughts. "That was not my intention. But, as I have you here, I might as well speak the truth. You amaze me."

Clytemnestra scoffed at this remark. As far as compliments went, she had received far more embellished ones in her time.

"Well, I thank you for your kind words."

As she moved to leave, he reached out his hand to her, only to recall her previous threat and quickly withdraw it.

"The way you cherish your children. The way you protect them. You are like a lioness with her cubs."

"It is a mother's job."

"That may be so, but that does not mean all do it as well as you."

She scoffed again. "Trust me, my children would not agree with you. Especially those who no longer live."

He stared into her eyes. "Tell me. Do you blame yourself for what happened to Iphigenia?" he asked.

The warm air turned suddenly icy, and her lips curled in a snarl.

"You have no right to even speak her name."

"No, of course I do not. But I just want you to know, to understand, that you are no more to blame for what happened to your daughter than I am for what happened to my mother."

A horse whinnied in the distance. She held his gaze.

"I do not blame myself," she said. "I blame her father. And I blame the gods."

Tension smoldered between them, and she found herself torn. The palace and her duties beckoned, the same that would be there tomorrow and the day after, and the one after that. Nothing new. Squabbling farm women and lazy politicians. She could see the next six years stretching out in front of her, until Agamemnon's predicted return. More and more of the same thing. But here was something unexpected, unknown. Someone to whom she was unfamiliar. Biting down on her lip, she looked at the son of Thyestes.

"Aegisthus, what are you like with a sword?"

THIRTEEN

O NE MONTH ROLLED INTO TWO AND THEN THREE, AND soon Aegisthus had been a presence in her life for almost a year. They met in private. He was still adamant that he would not set foot inside the palace without permission from Agamemnon. Her husband's name grew more distasteful to Clytemnestra with every day that passed.

News had drifted in from supply ships returning to their shores of the progress of the war in Troy. The siege was still firmly in place, the current idea being to starve out the Trojans. It felt like the type of plan her husband would adopt. One that caused the most death and despair, without him having to lift a sword or get his hands dirty. There was always the chance of sickness, though. Maybe a disease carried by sand flies would strike him down. Or perhaps his death would come at the hands of one of his own men. With every messenger who arrived, there was the possibility of the tidings that he, rather than Troy, had fallen. But until that day came, she had the children and her role as queen…and she had Aegisthus.

He did not hold back as the guards always did, and while he was at first out of practice, skills built up during years of training with Agamemnon and Menelaus did not take long to resurface. Once he knew her limits, he pushed them, tested her, just the way her training would have been carried out in Sparta. The clang of metal, that sonorous ring that accompanied the quiver of the blade in her hand, was like a tonic to her. At Orrin's insistence, she wore armor, and although it was not the Spartan way, the extra protection around her body only served to drive her harder. She started to feel youthful again, as if anything were possible.

When they finished sparring, they would sit and talk, and he would tell her about his travels in his life of exile, although not since that night near the grave circle had he mentioned his father or sister. Yet he was the one person in front of whom she felt free to use the name of Iphigenia. Aegisthus, unlike her children, had been privy to the rumors that had spread around the Aegean and, as such, was well aware of Agamemnon's role in her death.

"I wonder if he feels remorse," she pondered. "If he feels it was worth it now. Nearly five years they have remained on the shores of Troy. How important was that wind, really? He wanted it so urgently, and yet what advantage has it really gained them?"

"That is a question only the gods can answer," he replied. "But, as to whether he feels remorse, I cannot doubt it. No man could kill a child and not feel that, regardless of whether it was kin or not."

Resisting the urge to tell him more, Clytemnestra broke off a piece of the bread she was holding, before changing her mind and throwing it toward a group of sparrows. Orrin stood a short way off, close enough to watch her but not so close as to hear their conversation. This was the unspoken agreement that they had come to. If she had to be accompanied, it would be by him, Orrin, who understood discretion and knew how to hold his tongue; after all, he'd had enough practice with Agamemnon.

"I should go," she said, standing up and gathering her weapons from the ground. "I have a meeting with the polis at midday. But I will see you tomorrow?"

"I shall be here, if that is your wish."

"It is," she said. Then, before her eyes could betray her, she mounted her horse. Noting her movement, Orrin did the same, and together they galloped toward the citadel. With a little bit of luck, she would be back before the children woke.

Some days she and Aegisthus would ride north as far as the gulf, or west into the mountains. On others, they would simply lie in the grass and stare up at the sky while they talked. As a princess, she had been trained to be strong but quiet, curious but never emotional. Her feelings and worries had been subordinate to the egos of the kings in whose palaces she had lived—her opinions trivial, her desires negligible. After all, what more could a queen truly want? Had Helen understood what she had done, fleeing with Paris the way she had? Did she realize that she had exposed the unthinkable: even all the riches of a kingdom could not buy happiness? Not that Helen was the best example. She had been the same as a child, always wanting something she couldn't have. Always drawing attention to herself in any situation. But Aegisthus's attention stayed firmly on Clytemnestra, and her sister's name was never even mentioned, unless by her. He listened to her. He didn't offer advice, never criticized or pried. Just listened.

One morning, during those few pleasant weeks at the start of summer, when the ground was still lush and green, the two met together at one of the hot springs that littered the land. It had been her suggestion. Soon the days would become too hot to ride out far just for the fun of it, and the pair did not meet close to the citadel for fear of being noticed. So, while she sat at the water's edge and dangled her feet in the warm water, Aegisthus lay flat on his back, staring up at the wispy clouds that sped across the sky. Orrin, her chaperone, was on the other side of the water, holding the horses' reins while they grazed.

She had been pondering a question during the journey there. It had been at the back of her mind for quite a while, for weeks in fact, perhaps even months. But she had never asked it, for fear of what the answer might be and the repercussions it could have. But, in the quiet of the spring, as birds flitted between the vines that clung to the sandstone rocks, she found herself asking him anyway.

"What are you here for, Aegisthus?"

She lifted her feet out of the water and twisted onto her side, so that she could face him.

"I thought we came to bathe."

"I do not mean here at the spring. I mean with me. What are you doing here with me?"

Propping himself up onto his elbows, he locked eyes with her, and she could see the pain that was always there, just beneath the surface. Maybe that was why she found herself so at ease in his presence. He had known sorrow beyond his control too.

"Whenever I ask for you, you come," she said. "We talk and I leave, and you disappear and I do not even know where you go."

"Does it matter?"

"It matters to me."

He continued to hold her gaze for what felt like an eternity. When he finally spoke, the words came out as a sigh.

"Why? Are you not happy with things as they are? Is this friendship not enough?"

"This friendship is one of the few things that keep me sane."

"Then why question it?"

Why? She had asked herself the same thing many times. Why was she not content? Why was this not sufficient? Perhaps it was because she had so few friends. No genuine ones, at least not in Mycenae. And those in Sparta would have forgotten her by now. Perhaps it was because he was a man. Weren't all men meant to be constantly lusting after a woman, or women? So what did it say about her, if he was content to spend so much time with her, without a hint of impropriety?

And when they weren't together, she found herself thinking of him more and more, anticipating their next meeting—what he would say, how he would act. He was so close to her now on the rocks that she didn't know if the heat she was feeling was from the spring or from his presence. And, although she hadn't noticed when her pulse had started to hasten, as she lay there only inches from him, she realized it was drumming so hard it could have marched Agamemnon's army into battle.

Slowly, she pushed herself upright. "I could be happier," she said.

Her movements were slow and deliberate, and as she reached up, her eyes stayed fixed on his. Deftly, as if her body knew automatically what her mind desired, her fingers found the knot at her shoulder and her robe slipped down.

"Clytemnestra…"

She saw the apprehension in his eyes and understood the nervousness he must be feeling. Her own pulse was racing now, just as it had been on the night she had wed Tantalus.

"No one need know about us," she said. "Besides, what does it matter if they do? Agamemnon will be filling his tent with whores, as usual."

"He is your husband."

"He is a murderer and a brute who thrust himself upon me."

She reached to her waist, but no sooner had her fingers landed on the metal pin there than Aegisthus's hand was on top of hers.

"It is not that I do not want to," he began.

Everything changed in that instant. Whipping away her hand, she pulled up her robe and stood up.

"Forgive me. I do not know what I was thinking. I must have drunk more than I realized."

"Clytemnestra, do not do this."

He was on his feet now too, reaching for her hand. But she turned quickly and hurried away across the rocks. He followed.

"Please. Let me explain."

"No, no. There is nothing you need to say. Nothing I need to hear."

"Yes, you do."

She had reached her horse, but as she grabbed its reins, he snatched them from her.

"Clytemnestra, will you stop? You are not wrong. It is not just you who feels like this. I want this too—more than anything!"

The old guard led his own steed discreetly away from the pair.

"Please, Clytemnestra."

"So that is why you stopped me? I do not know much, but I am fairly certain that men do not reject the woman they desire."

"I came to Mycenae seeking forgiveness from your husband. Tell me how he would respond to this, if it were to reach his ears."

"I do not care about him or what anyone thinks anymore. You still do not understand, do you? You do not know the monster he is."

"Monster or not, he is still the king and he is still your husband."

"But I do not want him. I never wanted him. He…he…"

The words caught in her throat. She could speak their names to Aegisthus, surely. She could tell him about Tantalus and Alesandro. Maybe then he would understand. Or perhaps he would just pity her even more. That was it, she realized. Their friendship was based on pity. That was why he didn't desire her. All the time he had spent with her had been merely out of compassion. She had been wrong to see it as anything else.

"Do as you wish," she said. "I am done with you."

FOURTEEN

GALLOPING BACK TO THE CITADEL, SHE THRASHED THE horse, swallowing down the urge to scream. How could he? How could Aegisthus still show loyalty to Agamemnon, after all that he had done? Loyalty to the man who had murdered her children. Would Aegisthus still feel the same way if he knew the truth about Sparta? About Alesandro and Tantalus? Well, damn him, Clytemnestra thought, as she dug her heels into the horse's flanks once more and leaned forward against the air whipping past her. Damn Aegisthus and his misguided loyalty. She did not need him anyway.

At the entrance to the citadel, she dismounted and handed the horse to one of the guards, before striding up to the palace. Even Orrin had the sense to give her a wide berth.

Why string her along in such a manner? After all, he must have known how she felt about him. These last few months they had barely gone a day without seeing each other. Last moon had seen the Festival of Thargelia, a grand feast for the Goddess Artemis that had made her sick to the stomach. To have to pay tribute to the one who had taken her darling daughter had been almost more than she could bear. But she knew better than to risk the Goddess's displeasure and had sacrificed sheep and offered the first fruits of the year, as prescribed. Afterward, she had wept and Aegisthus had cradled her in his arms, as though he truly cared for her.

Much as she would have preferred to continue to vent her anger on her horse—or anyone who crossed her path, for that matter—she decided the best course of action was to distract herself with her children. Thus, she found herself enduring her least-favorite occupation—tapestry. How Chrysothemis found any pleasure in it was beyond her, and yet this was how her daughter chose to spend her time.

Grudgingly, she sat at the loom, tugging so hard on the thread that it snapped clean off. It would only be for an hour or two, she reminded herself every few minutes, and then she could unleash her anger with Electra. At least one princess would get the experience with her mother she was hoping for.

"You do not need to do this, Mother," Chrysothemis said as the queen cursed at yet another breakage. "I know you despise any sort of needlework."

"That is not true."

"It *is* true. Besides, you are terrible at it. You know that I am going to have to unpick it all and fix it for you after you leave, just so the others do not see it."

"Is that what you have been doing?" she asked, looking at her work and realizing that, yes, the earlier rows were most definitely more delicate and accurate than the ones she was currently managing.

"Quite possibly," she replied, with a glint in her eyes.

Huffing, the queen tried to reattach the thread.

"Well then, I am being kind, am I not, giving you extra practice?"

While she rated weaving as more torturous than childbirth, time with Chrysothemis was always pleasant, just as it was with Orestes and had been with Iphigenia. Her daughter's relaxed manner and ease of conversation never failed to calm her. The same could most definitely not be said of Electra, whose devotion to Agamemnon blinded her. On more than one occasion, when she had been pushing her mother's patience to its limit, Clytemnestra had literally bitten her tongue rather than scream the truth at her: Agamemnon has all he has ever wished for in Orestes. He has no need of daughters. He has already disposed of one to his advantage and would no doubt do the same to you or Chrysothemis, should the occasion arise. But she could never reveal that. It was, after all, her job to protect them. Even from the truth.

"I was listening to the servants in the kitchen today," Chrysothemis was saying, working with such dexterity that she did not seem to need to look at what she was doing. "They say that the war will be over in a month. That all this time they have been planning and plotting, and now they are ready to make the final attack on Troy and rescue Helen."

"Is that what they say?"

"Yes. That we will see the beacon glowing on Mount Arachneus by the next feast." She paused, her hands momentarily stopping their work. "I wonder what it must be like," she said.

"War? It is something you should be grateful you do not have to experience. Starving in squalid tents or picking maggots out of your food while the flies buzz around. Tending the injured or not being able to sleep for their screams. And, all the while, waiting for the inevitable."

Chrysothemis shook her head. "I did not mean the war," she said. "I am sure that must be terrible for all the men whom Father commands. I meant to love someone so greatly that you would be willing to die for them. The way our uncle does Helen."

"Love?"

A lump wedged in her throat. Love? Ha! It was the puerile behavior of two selfish adults, putting their own desires above the wellbeing of thousands of others. Helen was not capable of genuine love, and neither was Menelaus. They were vindictive and malicious. If only someone close to them had slit one of their throats at the start of all this, it would have all been over years ago. Love? What did love ever achieve, anyway?

"You were right," she said, standing up and letting the shuttle drop to the floor. "I am terrible at this. You carry on. I told Electra I would see how her training with Orrin has been going. She thinks that she can disarm me now. Apparently, she will prove it when we spar today."

"Well, I think I should stop this too then," Chrysothemis responded. "For that is one thing I would not want to miss."

Electra's comments about her skill and strength equaling or even surpassing her mother's had been growing in frequency and confidence with every passing moon. Now that her daughter was thirteen, there was barely an inch in difference in their heights, although she had inherited her father's bone structure and was thicker set and more muscular than Clytemnestra had ever been. After nagging her for countless evenings, and then invading her morning sanctuary in the courtyards, the queen had finally agreed—one sparring session with no holds barred.

Perhaps naively, she had thought it would be an intimate affair, just her and her daughter clashing swords, until Electra made an error or—and she did not actually consider this a possibility—Electra disarmed her. However, when she turned the corner of the corridor, she saw a crowd had gathered outside the throne room.

"Mother. Good." Electra was standing there already, waiting. "You are here. We can begin. I hope you do not mind; I invited a few friends along to watch your defeat."

Electra did not have friends. She had people she ordered around, although they all looked as excited as she was to be there.

"Did you know it would be like this?" Chrysothemis whispered in her mother's ear.

"I did not. Did you?"

"No. Electra must definitely think she will win."

Men and women parted to make a path for them down the central steps. At the far end was a large throne, with a smaller one on either side—one for herself and one for Orestes. Currently, they were littered with an array of weapons. Without another word to her mother, Electra went over and made her choice.

"Two kopis?" Clytemnestra asked, noting the two short swords in her daughter's hands. She personally preferred something with more length and found it easier to maneuver one blade than two.

"I find the combination suits me well," she boldly replied.

"Very well."

Stepping forward, Clytemnestra inspected the selection that remained. One she suspected—judging by the weight of the items—had been especially chosen by Electra. Clytemnestra favored thin, light weapons. These were all heavy and cumbersome. But it did not matter. Sparring with Aegisthus, she had practiced with many different types. Picking the least unwieldy of the bunch, she stepped forward to face her daughter.

A hushed silence descended on the throne room. Kicking off her sandals, Clytemnestra read the texture of the floor through the balls of her feet. Slick and cold, the tiles offered good traction on her bare skin. She could use that to her advantage. Her daughter was light on her toes—she had seen that often enough, but she was used to practicing outside, on the gravel and dust. That kind of surface was quite different. A slight slip and you could easily recover. In here, it would not be the same. Clytemnestra shifted her weight back and forth, sensing what her limits would be. From there her attention moved to the sword, finding its point of balance in one hand and then the other.

By contrast, Electra was focusing solely on her opponent. She knew her weapons, had specifically picked them out. Her stance was strong, her gaze so intense that Clytemnestra could almost feel it burning into her. There would be no surprise disarming this time. She would need to work a little harder. No sooner had that thought crossed her mind than the fight began in earnest.

Electra dodged one way and then another, before she finally appeared to engage, but it was a feint that Clytemnestra went to block, only having to twist away again to counter the real attack. Electra's poise with the two blades was impeccable as she swung time and again at her mother. There was a rhythm to her movement. An ease that the queen quickly matched.

"You are taking a long time to disarm me." Clytemnestra goaded her, in good spirits.

"Am I? Or am I learning all your weaknesses?"

"Maybe you are giving me too long to find yours."

Electra drew one kopis back and brought it down with all her force, but her mother struck up at the same time. The clang of metal resonated as Clytemnestra slipped her blade beneath her daughter's and twisted her wrist, ripping the weapon out of her hand and sending it flying across the chamber, where it landed just a few inches short of a spectator. A disappointed murmur rose from the crowd. Clearly, they had chosen their favorite.

"We should stop now," she said, watching Electra grimace at her bad fortune. "You have put up a good fight."

"I am not completely disarmed yet," she replied. "Or are you too afraid to continue? Maybe all your talk about protecting us is just that. Talk. Perhaps it should be I who is in charge of the family's security while Father is away. Maybe I should be in charge, full stop. Clearly you have never been up to the task."

It was obviously said to bait her. But it worked far better than Electra could have expected. She was right. Clytemnestra had not been up to the task. She had arrived in Mycenae weak and broken and it had taken losing another child to make her see that. But now, now she was ready.

Clytemnestra refocused. Her senses heightened. The feel of the sword in her hand. The flow of the air across her skin. The ripple from the impact down her arm as she struck Electra's remaining kopis again and again. She had not checked her blade for sharpness, assuming it to be a blunt training sword, so she forced her daughter further and further back without a second thought, until she was soon at the edge of the steps, with nowhere left to go. This was what it had felt like in Sparta! Fighting in public, with people watching, judging her talent and skill. So much more exhilarating than just practicing in private, even with the man she had wanted to take as her lover. She did not need Aegisthus. She did not need any man. Why would she waste another breath thinking about someone who had rejected her? This was what she had been born to do, to feed off the energy of the crowd. And the crowd was certainly enthralled. Every breath was held in anticipation.

She could see the whites of Electra's eyes as they widened in panic, looking back and forth around her, searching for any kind of answer to her mother's attack. But there was none. The moment she leaned back, Clytemnestra knew it was all over. With another flick of her wrist and a well-positioned leg behind her daughter, she sent Electra and the second blade spinning to the ground.

A mere heartbeat passed between the disarming of her child and the flood of sounds that rushed to her ears. Cheers filled the air, honoring the queen. Applause and adulation, the likes of which she had not heard for decades. Turning around to face her subjects, she smiled, offering a small bow, as if entertaining them were part of her royal duties. Only when she turned back did she see the tears in her daughter's eyes. Thirteen. Only moments ago, she had seemed so close to being an adult, but now she was lying there, a humbled child.

"You did not need to humiliate me," she cried.

FIFTEEN

T HERE WAS NOTHING SHE COULD SAY OR DO. AS SHE REACHED down her hand to pull her up, Electra shunned the offer, pushing herself up onto her feet unaided. Clytemnestra edged backward.

"Electra?"

The crowd was already dispersing, coins changing hands she noticed, with slaps on the back and laughter, or groans. And then a guard appeared and headed straight toward her. "Excuse me, my queen. There is someone here to see you."

She looked to where Electra was picking up her kopis, only to throw them back down again.

"Tell them I will be there shortly. I am busy."

"He told me to say that his name is Aegisthus."

She stopped. "He is here? Inside the palace?"

"Yes, my queen."

Her eyes went to the corridor, then to her child. Having abandoned her weapons, Electra was now talking to Orrin, and Orestes was by her side too. Both were comforting her. Both doing what should have been her job. She moved toward her, but Electra turned her back. As she prepared herself for yet another battle, a hand appeared on her shoulder.

"I will talk to Electra, Mother," Chrysothemis said. "You go and see to this visitor."

"I should explain. I should…apologize."

"She will not listen to you right now. You know that. Give her a little time."

"I am her mother."

"Yes, but you know that I am right."

With her gaze still on her youngest daughter, she tried to swallow the guilt that she was feeling. How was it that they clashed so frequently when really they both wanted the same thing? A safe home for them all. If she could only make her see that.

When a throat cleared behind her, she remembered the guard and Aegisthus's presence in the palace.

"Tell him I will come now," she said.

In the privacy of the empty corridor, she allowed herself a moment to catch her breath. She pressed her hands onto the cold stone of the pillars, then wiped the sweat from her skin. So much space, yet why did it so often feel like she was suffocating? Chrysothemis was right—Electra needed time. Perhaps this duel had been a good thing. Maybe now she would wish to train with her mother more often, knowing there were still many things she could learn from her.

Her feeling of guilt was superseded by nerves, which multiplied as she made her way through the colonnades and finally caught sight of him, head bowed, futilely attempting to dig his toes into the marble floor.

"I thought you said you would never set foot inside the palace without his permission."

Aegisthus's head sprang up and his eyes darted from side to side. She laughed.

"You think I am hiding him away here? Believe me, you would know."

Still visibly tense, he spoke. "Is there somewhere we can go to talk privately?"

She cast her eyes back toward the throne room. No doubt it would take a few hours, at least, for Electra's temper to cool.

"Not in here," she said. "The palace walls have ears. We can walk outside."

Orrin was still occupied with Electra, and so the pair were entirely alone as they took the path down to the winery. With the men still away, much of the produce of the previous year's harvest was waiting in barrels for a ship that would take it to Troy. This would be higher on Agamemnon's list of necessities than food, but he must have other sources to keep him satiated—probably the villages he plundered where, no doubt, he also found his whores.

They walked in silence, Clytemnestra adjusting her robes, which had loosened during the duel. Aegisthus held his hands clasped in front of him. They moved past the grave circle, keeping a respectful distance. At this rate, it would be nightfall before either of them said anything.

"What is it that you want? Why are you here again?" she asked at last.

"I am not sure."

"Then what a fantastic use of our time this is. If you have nothing to say—"

"Please, I need you to understand." He went to take her hand but quickly stopped himself. "Do you imagine I wanted to say no to you this morning? Of course I did not. I think...I am..." he stammered before stopping and trying again. "I have dreamt that you would feel this way, but you are married, Clytemnestra."

"To a man who thinks nothing of me."

"I do not know if that is true, but it does not change the fact that he is a king. The King of Kings. You belong to him. Please understand that I am trying to protect you."

"Do not flatter yourself. I do not need you or your protection." There was bitter venom in her voice. "You know nothing of me. Of what I have been through. Of what I can survive. You are worried about Agamemnon's wrath? That man has killed me three times over now. He has already taken so much from me. And it seems he is taking you too."

"I have not gone anywhere, Clytemnestra. I am still by your side."

"But we cannot return to what we were now, can we? And that is my fault and I am sorry."

"It need not change things."

"So you will stay? You will stay here in Mycenae? We can still meet?"

Her words sounded so pathetic, so needy, she immediately wished she could take them back. But it was how she felt. Young. Heartbroken. Her questions were met with a silence that threatened to undo her.

"What you want from me—what we both want—cannot happen," he said at last.

"I know. I understand that."

"If we continue to meet privately so often, rumors will start. They may have already begun."

"So what do you suggest?" A flicker of optimism was growing. Could this be the beginning of the one precious thing that would belong entirely to her?

"I will come to the palace," he said. "I will make it known publicly that my intention is to seek forgiveness from Agamemnon. We will show everyone that we are just friends. Our presence together, out in the open, will prove we have nothing to hide, and this will silence the scandalmongers."

"Do you think that will work?"

"Why would it not, Clytemnestra? We have done nothing untoward, and anyone who sees us together will know that."

A warmth started to fill her. He would do that for her? Come to the palace, as he had vowed he never would? And she would have him there, beside her, a steady rock in the tempest of her life.

"You know people here?" she questioned.

"I do."

"That is good. In fact, that is very good. Invite them to come to the palace with you. Everyone will see that our relationship is part of a wider friendship, nothing beyond the ordinary."

Without thinking, she took his hands in hers and squeezed them tightly, but the smile she hoped to see in return did not appear on his face. Instead, his brow was knotted with worry.

"Clytemnestra, you must face facts, though. If Agamemnon gets word that I am here, he *will* send someone to kill me. You do know that."

She shook her head with so much force it sent her braid whipping about her shoulders.

"It will not happen. No one will hurt you while I am on the throne."

The desire to reach up and kiss him surged through her. A kiss of friendship, nothing more, she told herself, although she knew it for the lie that it was. So, instead, she thought better of it and simply squeezed his hands again, then turned and sped away, before the urge overwhelmed her.

When she arrived back at the palace, her cheeks were flushed, not only with the exertions of the past few hours but with a new feeling of hope. She would go straight away and speak to Electra, she thought. Today was a day for building bridges.

SIXTEEN

ALTHOUGH IT TOOK SEVERAL DAYS, ELECTRA EVENTUALLY accepted her mother's apology and became even more determined to beat her, with a sword this time, setting the date for another duel after a three-month interval. Clytemnestra agreed, promising herself that, this time, she would allow her daughter to win, however well or badly she fought.

The following day, Aegisthus visited, as part of their new arrangement, bringing half a dozen friends with him: a musician, an artist, and a few others, whose talent or vocation she did not catch. The pair, who had been used to long, easy, private conversations, did not speak a word to each other after their initial greeting. But a thousand subtle smiles and glances passed between them, the rest of the group oblivious to it all.

The following night, she spoke to him directly.

"Aegisthus, is it not?" she asked. "My husband's cousin. I am surprised to find you here. I cannot say he would think too kindly of your presence in his palace."

His cheeks reddened, just the way she had hoped they would.

"I am here wishing to rectify the mistakes of my youth," he said.

"From what I hear, that will take you some time."

With that, she turned and struck up another conversation, refusing to pay him any further attention, even when he left. She was playing her part well. She knew he would understand what she was doing, and anyway, she would speak to him again on their own the next morning.

Somehow, meeting in public view made their now rare, private ones even more exquisite, although they served only to compound the feelings that had been growing in her for months. As the days turned into weeks, she found herself focusing more and more on the physical aspects of her confidant—the callouses on his hands, the symmetry of his lips, the way his beard was dappled, the first signs of gray around the temples. She could feel him doing the same with her. Watching her. Studying her. And it seemed the most natural thing in the world. They could not touch, but nothing could stop them looking.

The months passed and he continued to attend the parties, now even better camouflaged as he found more suitable men to join them. This would look quite normal, Clytemnestra told herself. Many queens hosted such events since their husbands had gone away.

With official introductions long over, they would sit together, still in public view, debating methods of farming, fighting, or whatever topics took their fancy. In this way, she gradually learned more about him. His travels. His likes and dislikes. Him as a person. With Aegisthus by her side came a feeling of tranquility that she had struggled to find since arriving in Mycenae. But, unfortunately, even this did not stop the nightmares.

Despite Orestes now being close to seven, Electra recently entering womanhood, and Chrysothemis already sixteen, Clytemnestra would still find herself curling up in their chamber at night. She would lie awake for hours until she eventually closed her eyes, only to be greeted by visions that set her heart pumping hard enough to crack a rib.

It was after one such bad dream that she had awoken so slick with sweat that her sheet was clinging to her, almost translucent. She decided to head out early to meet Aegisthus on the mountainside.

"I feel there is still so much about your past that I do not know," she said, sitting cross-legged on the ground, a blanket around her to ease the morning chill.

"That is the same in every good friendship, is it not?" he replied somewhat dismissively.

"Why do you say that?"

He shrugged. "No one should know everything about another person, Clytemnestra. You put two people together for long enough that there are no secrets left; they will start to pick at each other's little foibles until they are all that they can focus on. It is better to be content with what you do know."

"I do not believe that is true."

"No? You think you could live with one man forever and only see good in him?"

"I know I could. I nearly had the chance."

Only when she saw the look of concern flash across his eyes did she realize what he was thinking. That he was that man. The one she had hoped to live out her mortal life with. Her throat became dry with embarrassment. Maybe he could have been, once, but not after everything she had lost. She had kept the story to herself for so long. It had been easier that way. Easier, but never easy. Maybe this was the chance to share her burden at long last. She turned to face out across the water.

"There is a legend, you know," she started. "Some believe it to be a prophecy, surrounding my father."

"I am sure there are many."

"Yes, but this one is the reason I know I will never be allowed lasting happiness. My father denies it, of course, but when you look at Helen and me, it is impossible to believe that it could not be true. You see, he is a godly man, but he favored certain gods, just as some gods favor certain humans. He would make sacrifices and throw feasts in honor of Ares and Apollo, the likes of which you would have never seen before. Hecatombs, and even greater offerings still, were not unusual. Anything to garner their approval. But the gods whose patronage he did not require he ignored."

"Such as?"

"One in particular."

He cocked his head.

"Aphrodite," she answered.

He was still confused, which was completely understandable. She and her sister, Helen, had certainly been blessed with great beauty, but this was not the only gift available to the Goddess, nor even her greatest.

"My father did not care for such trivialities as love or passion, nor even beauty, except in as much as it could help him make powerful alliances through his daughters. He neglected the Goddess, failed to make offerings to her or hold feasts in her name. But it was not he who was to feel her wrath, suffer her curse."

Aegisthus lifted a hand and cupped her cheeks. The warmth from his fingertips spread outward from his touch.

"My darling Clytemnestra, you are not cursed."

"You say that because you do not know."

"Do not know what?"

Above them the trees billowed, scattering leaves that then danced on the breeze. What good would come from telling him? she wondered. None. But then again, nothing good could ever happen.

"What do you know of Tantalus?" she asked.

"Tantalus, the late King of Pisa? Was there not enmity between him and your father? He died very young, did he not? I do not know all the details."

"No," she said. "Few do."

The story had remained locked in her heart for two decades. To use the key to that lock now was to open the floodgates to more pain.

"I know that you think I am most like Electra. Everyone comments on it. The fiery temper. The dogmatic opinions. But it was not always so. When I look for myself in my children, I see Chrysothemis." She paused to see if he would respond. When he did not, she continued. "She wants to be married. I have told you this before. She has an idea in her head that it will be all about love and passion, and I try my best to bring her down to earth. But the truth is, I actually had that once. I had a marriage of love."

"I...I did not know."

She could see from his expression that he was telling the truth.

"My father had a long-standing friendship with Tantalus's father. The marriage between us was expected, and we both welcomed it even though I was young. Only fourteen. But his father had recently passed, and the new King of Pisa needed a queen. A year and a half we lived in wedded bliss, remaining in Sparta because of my youth. The plan was always to return with him to Pisa, but two things happened. Firstly, I fell pregnant. Secondly, you killed Atreus."

"And Agamemnon and Menelaus fled to Sparta?"

"Yes. Our child was but a few days old when they arrived. Naively, I thought nothing of their presence. It was without doubt that one of them, if not both, would fall in love with Helen, and that suited me. I would be left alone in my little world, just Tantalus, Alesandro, and me."

"Your son?"

"My first child. My first boy." Worry suddenly flashed through her. "The children do not know about this. They cannot know. Orestes believes *he* is my only son."

"Clytemnestra, you know I will not tell a soul. Please, carry on. Tell me what happened."

"He happened," she said.

"Agamemnon?"

She nodded. "I do not know when he first noticed me. I cannot think what diverted his attention away from my sister."

"Why do you do that? Why do you always belittle yourself? You are the most beautiful woman I have ever laid eyes on."

She laughed. "That is because you have not met Helen. But I am not seeking compliments, and I am not jealous. It is just a fact of life. I believe I do have something over her though, a greater spark. Maybe that is what Agamemnon saw in me and made him want me for his wife—a challenge. He spoke to my father, who, no doubt, must have seen the advantage to himself in such a union. The years of friendship with Tantalus's father counted for nothing, now that he was dead. Nor did my happiness, nor the fact that I had just borne a child.

"I think my father wanted it to look like an accident, to save my feelings to that extent, at least. But Agamemnon? Oh no, he wanted me to see. He wanted me to know. I was called for dinner, a private meal, with just him and my father present, to discuss Helen's wedding supposedly. But when I arrived, he was standing there, over the bodies of my husband and child. Three days later, I was in Mycenae, brought here, as his wife.

"It is not my imagination, Aegisthus. Nor am I mad. Agamemnon will not be satisfied until he has ripped every last ounce of happiness from my heart. First Tantalus and Alesandro, then Iphigenia. And each night, all I can think about is which child he will take next."

"I will not let that happen."

"You promise?"

"I do."

He wrapped his arms around her. Allowing her head to fall against his shoulder, she felt a warmth she had not experienced for decades.

"I do," he said again.

They sat in silence then, each needing time to deal with what she had told him. And as uncertainty faded, she experienced a feeling of lightness in place of the heavy weight that had burdened her for so long. Finally, someone else knew the truth, knew the extent of the horror she had suffered at the hands of her husband.

When they returned to the citadel, he left her at the Lion Gate, placing a small kiss on her forehead. She continued on her way to the palace. She would fix the children's breakfast, she thought, or maybe have a cook pack one up, so that they could head out on horseback together and enjoy an early picnic.

As she mounted the palace steps, her mind was still lost in what to eat and where to go. A short way from the entrance, she started at the figure in front of her. Electra's cheeks were flushed red. Her clenched fists shook at her side, and her body was as tense as she had ever seen it. A low growl rattled from her throat.

"Electra? Is everything all right? Where is your brother?" She placed a hand on her daughter, who flinched as though the touch had scalded her. "Electra, what is wrong?"

The growling sound continued for a moment before she finally spat out the words.

"I know," she said. "I know who he is, and I know what you are doing. And it will stop now. On Father's life, I swear you will stop."

SEVENTEEN

"Everybody knows, Mother. It is the talk of Mycenae, how you are busy screwing Father's treacherous cousin behind his back, while he defends the family honor fighting in Troy. You are nothing but a common whore. That is what they are saying about you."

"You will watch your mouth, Electra!"

"Why? Is Aegisthus more polite when he fucks you in Father's bed?"

Clytemnestra could feel the anger rising up within her. "You should choose your next words very carefully."

"I am sorry the truth upsets you."

"You do not know the truth. You have *no idea* what you are speaking about. I have done nothing wrong."

"Oh, I know plenty. Tell me, did you always wish to become as big a whore as your sister, Helen? Let us be honest, though; Father would never go to war for you, you pathetic old woman."

Her arm moved before she even realized what she was doing. The flat of her hand struck Electra squarely across the cheek. The sting shot through her palm as a wash of red bloomed across her daughter's face.

"Electra…"

A lesser person, man or woman, would have at least flinched at the blow. But Electra held her head high and turned her cheek, so that her mother could see the true extent of her action. A red handprint. She'd had so many of the same marks on her own skin, thanks to Agamemnon, but to realize she had inflicted the same injury on her own child sent a gasp of shock from her lungs.

"Electra," she said again, reaching out, only to have her hand swiped away.

"Do you even know what he did?" Electra sneered. "He killed my grandfather."

"Of course I know. Electra, I am sorry; I am. But this is not what you think. Many men are responsible for the death of another, for many different reasons."

"He was a usurper."

"He was practically a child. He made a mistake. As you are doing now."

"It is no mistake. I have heard it from the guards. They are saying he has come back for the throne again. Well, he will not succeed this time. I will not let him take Father's crown away from him."

Sighing, Clytemnestra shook her head. So much strength and yet so much arrogance, and an inability to even consider the truth that was right in front of her.

"Electra, you are too young to understand the complexities of this family."

"What complexities? There is nothing complex here. It is your place to serve your husband. To serve my father, the king. But instead, you have betrayed him. You are a traitor to Agamemnon."

The way she said his name with such pride, caused bile to rise in Clytemnestra's throat.

"Look me in the eye, Electra, and tell me you honestly believe your father has never killed anybody undeservedly. That he has never killed anyone just to get what he wanted."

The girl was trembling with resolve. "You are jealous of his power. You and this man would take it from him."

"Electra, you have no idea of what you speak."

"I know what you plan. He is here to overthrow Father, just as he did Grandfather, and you are either too blind or too stupid to see it. Five years Father has been gone, and you open your legs to the first dog that comes sniffing around."

The itch returned. The urge to strike her daughter for a second time. Had it been anyone else, it would have been a knife in their guts. Instead, she stepped backward, putting her daughter out of reach.

The girl smirked. "Do you want to hit me again, or worse? What would you do to keep your little secret? Not that it is even that anymore. But you have shown your true colors here today, Mother. Of that I am certain."

"My true colors?" The rage transferred from daughter to mother. "This is what you think my true colors are?"

"I have the evidence here on my skin."

"And I suppose your great Father would never do anything so unjust?"

Electra pouted. "The decisions he makes are for the good of the kingdom."

"He is a murderer. Time and time again."

"For the good of the kingdom."

"He murdered your sister!"

"No!"

"He took a blade to her throat."

Electra paled. "No, it was one of the priestesses. You said so yourself. They took her as a sacrifice. He did not know what they were going to do."

"Really? Your rumor mills have turned rather quiet on this, have they not? Or is it your memory that fails you? It was your father who sent the message that she was to be married. It was your father who tricked us into going to Aulis, who did not even want me there, who lied to us again and again. And it was your father who came up behind her, while she was at prayer, slit her throat, and stole her life."

"No, that is not true. You told us that he was tricked."

"I told you what I had to, to protect you, you fool."

"No, you are lying to me. You are a liar!"

"So now I am a liar, but then I spoke the truth? The thing is, daughter, I was there. I saw the knife in his grasp, the blood on his hands, and my child, your sister, dead on the altar. There was no one else in that temple, Electra. So do not tell me what I know. Do not tell me about the monster you so admire. And do not tell me what I will and will not do for my children. You stand there and support a father who would slit *your* throat for a better wind."

She could see Electra trembling, her hands quivering at her side. But her eyes remained steady and no tears fell.

"He did what he did for us all," she said eventually. "It was his duty as king."

The air rushed from Clytemnestra's lungs. It could not be possible that, even when faced with the truth, Electra would still side with him.

"You cannot believe that!"

"He did what the Goddess required of him."

"No, he could have waited. He could have found another way to appease her."

"He did what the Goddess required of him," she repeated, the resolve in her voice hardening. "That is what a leader does, Mother. They make tough decisions. Painful ones. And if you cannot see that, it just shows how much of a fool you truly are. I am glad he killed Iphigenia. It shows he really is the man I have thought he was all along. I would have offered myself, had he only asked."

Tears now streamed down Clytemnestra's cheeks, weaving pathways to her chin. Could she not remember her sister? Had she forgotten how tender she had been with her when she was young? Most girls would be hard pressed to find a mother as loving as Iphigenia had been to Electra.

"You have no idea…" she said. But this was not the case. Electra knew. She simply did not care.

EIGHTEEN

S HE STOOD TALL JUST LONG ENOUGH FOR HER DAUGHTER TO
turn her back and leave. Only then did she let her shoulders
slump in defeat.

"My queen," Laodamia said as she appeared at her side.

"Did you hear?" Clytemnestra whispered through her tears.
"Did you hear what she said to me?"

"She is a child, my queen. Just an angry child. She does not
mean it."

"Do not coddle me. She knew exactly what she was saying."

"You should rest. I will fetch you something to eat."

Laodamia guided her gently to her chamber, where she pulled
back the bedclothes, and Clytemnestra lay down and sobbed.

Life had come full circle. So many years had passed since she had
been brought to Mycenae, yet here she was again, weeping, alone.
Broken. Nothing ever changed.

She did not meet with Chrysothemis to weave that day. Nor did
she go outside with Orestes to admire the birds or search for lizards.
Even the Council was left waiting for her presence. Instead she lay

on her bed, eyes open, heartbroken. As evening fell her guests and friends arrived, women and men who had been coming for months now and would expect to see her.

"Let me help you get dressed, my queen," Laodamia said, coming into the room and gently pulling the blankets from her.

"Tell them I am sick. I *am* sick."

"No, my queen. I will not do that."

Clytemnestra turned to face her.

"I beg your pardon?"

"I said, 'No, my queen, I shall not do that.'"

"I am ordering you."

Laodamia nodded slowly. "It does sound that way. Even so, my answer is the same. I will tell them no such thing. You are not sick."

She strode across the room and picked out a clean gown. A heavy fabric, predominantly green, with golden flowers embroidered along the hem.

"Do you remember when you first arrived here? Do you remember what you were like? The frailest thing I had ever seen. I mean it. How you were a princess was beyond me. You looked like you belonged on the streets."

"Whatever game this is you are playing, Laodamia, you are treading on thin ice," she warned, although her maid appeared not to hear.

"Nothing more than skin and bones, my queen. And they said you had not eaten a thing since leaving Sparta. Nothing. They said you barely even left the cabin, and I could tell by the look of you that they spoke the truth. You had made yourself a prisoner. Now some people said it was because you were young, that you did not want to leave your family, but I tended to you then, remember? I cleaned your clothes, helped you bathe."

"What are you saying?" she whispered. "What is the point of this prattle?"

"I am saying that I know, my queen. I know that you have gone through the worst thing a mother can go through, not once but twice. I know that when you lost that first child, it was so young that milk still flowed in you. I do not know what happened, and I would never expect you to speak of it to me. I am just trying to tell you, my queen, whatever the princess said today, however much she wounded you, it cannot be so great compared to what you have suffered already. Nothing could. And yet you picked yourself back up. Even when it happened again. Even when he took Iphigenia from us. Now, would you like me to see to your hair?"

Anger and disbelief seized Clytemnestra. For nearly two decades, she had avoided speaking of Alesandro, and now, twice in one day, conversation had focused on him. Were the gods playing cruel games with her, forcing her to recall the horror all over again? She would accept Prometheus's fate and have her liver pecked out every day, in preference to recalling that loss even one more time.

"How much do you know?" she asked, terror gripping her.

"I know nothing, my queen, except what I saw." Laodamia crossed the chamber to the mirror where she straightened out the brushes and combs. "And I am not here seeking gossip either. I have said my piece." She hesitated before turning back to her. "The gods did not see fit to let me keep any of the children I bore, but I have always been grateful to you, my queen, for letting me treat you and your children as if I were more than just a servant."

"Laodamia…"

"These last few years I have often hoped that, had my own children lived, I would have been as good a mother to them as you are to yours."

Clytemnestra felt a lump in her throat.

"You have to say that—I am the queen."

"I think the fact that you are the queen means I should have kept my mouth shut, do you not agree?"

A half smile lifted the corners of Clytemnestra's mouth, setting loose tears she didn't even know had filled her eyes.

"Right now, people are expecting you. Let us remind them just how beautiful their queen is, shall we?"

The courtyard was awash with life. Aegisthus was plucking clumsily at a lyre, much to the amusement of those around him. When she saw him, she felt her cheeks quickly rise in a smile, although the figure behind him made them drop again just as quickly.

"I did not think we would see you here this evening, Mother," Electra said. She had taken Clytemnestra's seat and was lounging, legs extended. "I was just saying you had a fever."

Her fists clenched until her knuckles shone white and her nails dug into her palms.

"A fever? I think not, my daughter," she said with a smile. "I am perfectly fine. Now move along. This time is for the grown-ups."

Her daughter's eyes flashed.

"We do not mind." One of the ladies spoke. "She is so sweet. She makes us laugh."

She watched as the words stung Electra, and a feeling of smug satisfaction rose within her.

"Yes, she is a sweet child, is she not? Such a sweet little girl."

She stepped forward, her glower demanding Electra relinquish her position on the seat. The pair locked eyes, but it was a brief battle. They both knew that to refuse the queen now would only make Electra look as childish as they believed her to be, and there was no way she would give her mother that satisfaction.

Lounging back on the daybed, Clytemnestra waved her hands.

"Wine," she said to the servant who came to attend her. "You will have a drink with us too, Electra, my darling, will you not?"

She had not planned this. She had not planned anything.

Electra kept accepting the wine so willingly, never noticing how her mother kept indicating that her cup should be refilled each time she emptied it. She never realized that less and less water was being added either, until she was drinking it undiluted. An hour passed, and her cheeks were turning pink as the alcohol circulated in her veins.

"Do you not think you should stop this now?" Aegisthus whispered to Clytemnestra. He seemed to be the only one who saw what she was doing. "You have made your point. Send the girl to her chamber."

"What do you think, Electra?" she asked. "Are you ready to go to bed with the other children?"

The girl's head lolled to the side. "I am more of a queen than you," she slurred, reaching a hand down to pull her dagger from its sheath—the very one that Clytemnestra had brought her from Aulis. "I could rule them all."

"I guess that means she wants to stay," Clytemnestra remarked.

Laughter rang out around them, but Electra could barely turn her head to scowl. Her insults continued, not only directed at her mother but at the gods who had provided her with such a weak parent and at a land that raised only men to be soldiers. The land, of course, not Agamemnon. Soon the pink tinge turned greenish, and only when she tried to stand and fell did Clytemnestra make their farewells to her guests and guide her to bed.

She stayed beside her that night, to make sure she did not vomit in her sleep. Not that her daughter would appreciate the concern, of course.

———

The groaning did not begin until long after noon.

"Here, sit up and drink this," Clytemnestra said, hoisting Electra up and pressing a cup of milk to her lips.

She moaned and struggled before finally swallowing a mouthful.

"What did you do to me?" she asked. "What did you do, you bitch?"

The queen stiffened, although she kept her feelings hidden from her daughter.

"Me? You do not remember what I did *for* you?"

"This was your doing. You got me drunk, like a common peasant."

"Really? I forced wine down you, did I? I think you will find that you did that of your own accord. I did, however, stop you pulling a dagger on Christina for no reason that we could fathom. I am also the one who made offerings to Athena this morning, after you so blackened her name last night."

"You lie!"

"Do I? Then, please, tell me what you do remember."

"I...I..." She cradled her head. Unable to stay upright any longer, she flopped back down onto the bed.

"Tell me, my child, if you do not remember those things, do you recall all the times you left your drink unattended, so that it could have been spiked with something far more sinister than spice? Do you remember accepting the request of a man three times your age, to show him around the palace, with no idea of his true intentions? Do you realize all the danger you would have been in, had I not been there?"

The girl's hands had moved to cover her ears, although she continued to shake her head.

"Stupid. That was one of the things you called me, Electra. Unfit to rule this kingdom, you said. I could have let any number of things befall you last night, had I so wanted." She got to her feet. "But I will protect you from every evil in this world," she said, "including yourself."

"Mother?"

Striding to the door, she stopped at the sound of her name.

"Yes, my child." She turned, waiting for the expected apology. A flutter of hope rose within her. Her children needed her. All of them, even Electra now that the consequences of her actions had sunk in. But when her daughter spoke, all hope was dashed.

"I was right. You are a bitch."

NINETEEN

ELECTRA'S FOUL MOOD AND DISDAIN FOR HER MOTHER WENT on for days, which turned into weeks. When months had passed, Clytemnestra was forced to accept that the relationship she had hoped for, of the kind she'd had with Iphigenia and cherished so much with Chrysothemis, would never be there with her youngest daughter. In company, they tolerated each other's presence; they avoided one another in private. They did not eat or drink together, or even converse. There was now only one thing they shared in common—affection for Orestes.

Despite her love for all her children, the young prince was Clytemnestra's greatest delight. His level of conversation had reached new heights, and he could chatter on for hours about animals, fish, insects, or birds, in fact anything that walked, swam, crawled, or flew. Much to Electra's great disappointment, he showed no interest at all in fighting. He was like a breath of fresh air to the queen. As such, every spare hour she could squeeze out of any day she would spend with her son. Only when evening came would she head to the courtyard and her guests, to sit beside Aegisthus.

Reports from Troy remained intermittent and unclear. With each messenger who arrived, she found herself more conflicted. The end of the war would mean the Mycenaean women would be reunited with their husbands and sons, unless tragedy had befallen them. They had worked tirelessly in the men's absence, harvesting food, fishing, fixing broken roofs, mending goat pens, in fact doing anything and everything that was needed. There was not a job they had not tackled between them, and they deserved some respite now and a return to family life.

However, the one blot on the horizon with the homecoming of the menfolk was that it would also mean the return of Agamemnon. If rumors were to be believed, they had somehow survived Trojan attacks, plagues, and near starvation. Not that he would ever suffer. He'd see his men go without before he sacrificed his normal rations. Fortunately, news came so seldom that she usually managed to suppress thoughts of him and focus on her kingdom, her people, and her palace.

One evening, she was seated next to Aegisthus when conversation turned to Troy and the war. The particular topic that night was Helen or, more precisely, what Menelaus would do to her once she was finally *rescued*.

"It was a betrayal," someone said. "She left with Paris of her own volition. That is what they have always said in Sparta. He will make her suffer for it, for the rest of her life."

"I do not believe so," said another. "You do not wage a war so long for someone you only wish to hurt."

"Then what? You believe he loves her?"

"Of course I do. This is more than just a battle of pride. It is a battle of hearts. Which is why he will win. Eventually, Paris will return to loving his own reflection more than Helen. And when she sees this, she will be glad for Menelaus to welcome her back."

"Yes, because his family has such a long history of sympathy and forgiveness!"

No one looked at Clytemnestra as they discussed this. Unspoken rules had been established long ago, and they all knew just how far they could go. Talk of battles was fine. Talk of rape and pillaging was acceptable, but not preferable. Talk of other kingdoms was encouraged, but nothing derogatory of Mycenae. And nothing at all of Clytemnestra or her children. This was their home, and anyone who disrespected that would be quickly dealt with. With this understanding, the nightly gatherings had continued in peace over the years.

Conversation soon moved on to Penelope and her battles with suitors, and then to Hector and Achilles. Who would triumph in hand-to-hand combat? What would be left of Ithaca when Odysseus returned?

The debate had been going back and forth for some time, when a new group ambled into the courtyard. Some familiar faces, some less so. It was an unknown young man, with a limp, who spoke first.

"I heard this was a place for the old folk of Mycenae to gather," he said. "But I am pleasantly surprised. There are more young women in here than in Agamemnon's tent in Troy."

The chattering stopped. A few fearful glances flickered toward the queen. Mention of Agamemnon at all usually resulted in her prompt exit. But she decided to bide her time, hoping the moment would pass. However, the man did not read the situation and carried on.

"What is wrong with you all?" he asked the silent men and women around him. "It is a great joke. I have been waiting for the chance to use it. Mind you, ladies—I fear that you are all a little more aged than our great king prefers. From what I hear, his latest prize is little older than the daughter he slaughtered. Then again, I guess when you are King of Kings, you can take your pick."

You could have heard a pin drop. Every face in the courtyard drained of blood. No one moved. Not even Clytemnestra. No queen would be naive enough to think that her husband was not spoken of disrespectfully in private, but not in his own palace and not like this. She should kill him here and now, she thought. It was no less than he deserved. Everyone gradually turned to her, awaiting her response, no one wishing to make a move before she did. The man, following their eyes, now realized his error and his own grew wide with fear.

"Your Majesty, I...I—"

"No."

The single word was all she could manage. With her heart pounding, the moment stretched out. She could order him lashed to within an inch of his life, and everyone there would understand. But, instead, she smiled at him.

"Come. Drink," she said to him, just managing to control her voice. She turned to the girl with the lyre in her hand. "Please, a tune. Something cheerful."

The music started again and wine was taken in small considered sips. Minutes passed and the conversation slowly increased in volume, the comments about Agamemnon and Iphigenia avoided although not forgotten. When the carafes needed refilling, Clytemnestra saw her opportunity. Lifting two from a side table, she walked out through the columns, as if to do the job herself.

She had barely stepped into the corridor when a figure appeared beside her.

"That is not a queen's job. Call someone...or I will do it myself."

"Aegisthus, this is my home. I do not need you to tell me how to run it."

Two servants appeared from the direction of the kitchen and looked on nervously.

"Go, fetch more wine from the cellar," she said, holding out the vessels. "We are fine here."

Nodding rapidly, they scurried away as instructed, leaving her and Aegisthus alone in the shadow of a pillar.

"I am sorry," he said, resting a hand on the small of her back. "I am so sorry for what he said. Whoever he is, he did not deserve the tolerance you showed him."

Her gaze remained on the departing servants.

"It is not the women. He has had them since the day he first bedded me. But to talk of her in the same breath as…" The image almost choked her. "He took my daughter's life, and now her memory has become little more than a punchline, while he lives a life of whoring and excess. Meanwhile, I am keeping his kingdom going and protecting our children, even when they cannot see they need it. What would happen, I wonder, if we were the ones who required rescuing? What would he do then, if his own family ever really needed him?"

"My dearest Clytemnestra, I doubt there would ever be a situation in which you could not defend yourself."

"That is not the point, is it?" Her eyes burned with tears, one of which escaped and wove its way down her face. Aegisthus caught it with his thumb. "She is the point. What he did to her is the point."

He bowed his head. "I know that it will be of little consolation for you to hear this, but I promise, if you or any of the children were in danger, I would be there. I may have no army, no fleet, but I would fight to the death for you."

She tried to control her tears, finding words difficult.

"That would be a consolation," she managed at last. "A great one."

Laughter echoed through from the courtyard. She shuddered at the sound.

"Let us not go back in there," he said, taking her hand. "Let us find somewhere else."

She led the way through the vast hallways. Their footsteps echoed on the marble floor, and their shadows, cast by the flickering lamps, skittered along the walls. He would have walked this way before, she reminded herself, all those years ago, when he killed his uncle and the palace was his for the taking. *How many lifetimes ago must that feel to him?* she wondered as she pushed open a door and held it wide for him.

"Your chamber?" he asked.

"It is the one place I know we will not be disturbed."

For so many years, this room had been a prison to her. During those first months, before she had fallen pregnant with Iphigenia, she had counted the colored mosaic floor tiles—the white and the gray, the red and the yellow—day after day after day. Anything to stop herself thinking about what she had lost, and what she would have to face when night fell. As the years passed, she had learned to smile when Agamemnon came to her. Learned to appease him and please him, so that he might think twice before taking his belt to her. Only when she had been pregnant had she been safe from his blows, although after the birth of each daughter, she had been the victim of his disappointment.

As she sat on her bed, her eyes returned to those same mosaics. She could not remember how many tiles there were anymore. Perhaps one day she would count them again.

"Do you know that there are no walls to protect us from invasion in Sparta?" The first comment out of her mouth, and she had no idea where it had come from.

"I did know that, yes."

"Yes, I suppose you would. Most people do. Spartans do not need walls. We protect ourselves. Each other. We are so strong together. Ever since I came here, I wondered: Are the walls meant to keep people out, or keep them in? All these years, and I still cannot decide."

There were no sounds to distract them. No music or laughter. No cicadas or rushing water. It was just the two of them, alone. He stepped toward her.

"I need to ask you something."

"Anything. You know that."

"I fear it will cause you pain."

"What further pain can I suffer now? The gods and my husband have seen to it that it is my constant companion."

Perhaps that sounded like self-pity, vile and loathsome as it was to her, but it was the truth. Not since that day when Agamemnon had taken the two loves of her life had she ever felt whole. The dull ache always remained, like a malady she could never recover from.

"There is another story from that day, Clytemnestra. The day that you lost Iphigenia. One you have never told me."

"I do not speak of that day."

"I know you do not. But they say you carried her down the hillside in your arms. They say you did not let her go, even when darkness came and the winds raged around you. They say that no one helped you, no one came to your aid, as you carried your dead child."

"Aegisthus. Please do not do this. Do not make me relive it."

"I do not wish to cause you pain, my love. You must know I would never want to do that." He knelt on the ground at her feet. "You did not let her go, Clytemnestra. And you must believe, by all the power of the gods, that she knows that. And Alesandro. He should have been safe. As sons can avenge their fathers, mothers should be allowed to avenge their children. What has happened to you is a tragedy, but you never let them go. You must understand that. You are strong and fearless, and nothing Agamemnon could say or do will ever change that."

Once again, she fought to control her emotions as he spoke.

"More than anything, Clytemnestra, I wish I could take away the sorrow. I am so sorry for all that you have suffered, and I wish I could have been there to help you. But I will never let you go now. Just like you, I will never give up."

His eyes were brimming with tears, and she realized her own cheeks were wet. Holding her breath, she reached out and touched his face.

"Thank you," she whispered.

"I want you to know that you need never be alone again."

"I know." She could feel the warmth flowing from him, and it was as if something missing had been replaced, something she had been longing for all her life, not just these past few years.

"Clytemnestra..." he whispered.

TWENTY

S HE WOKE TO THE RAYS OF THE EARLY MORNING SUN GLISTEN-
ing through the window, illuminating his face and giving it a
golden appearance. He seemed ageless in sleep. All the lines,
carved so deeply when awake, seemed to have melted away, offering
her a glimpse of a younger Aegisthus. A man she wished she could
have known. Gradually, his eyes fluttered open.

"I have just realized that this is the first week I have slept soundly
since I arrived in Mycenae," she said as he stretched out beside her.
"Can you believe that? Twenty years, and all I needed was you."

"I think it probably helps that you are not lying on the stone
floor of the children's bedroom." He grinned and she nudged him
with her elbow. He caught her wrist and kissed it, moving his lips all
the way up to her neck.

Winter melted into spring, and Aegisthus remained at her side. The
transition had felt so natural—the move from confidant and friend
to lover. He spent his days and nights at the palace, guiding her,

counseling her, but never imposing on her as a queen or as a person. If she thought his knowledge would be beneficial, then she sought his help. If not, she continued to deal with matters herself.

And all of her children, bar one, having been given the time to adjust, couldn't have been more accepting of him. Chrysothemis had at first seemed concerned by Clytemnestra's disloyalty to Agamemnon, but it had not taken long to sway her. Still enchanted with the ideal of true love, she watched the couple with hope. And at last Clytemnestra could show her what a genuine partnership should be based on: equality, compassion, and trust.

As for Orestes, he finally had the father figure he so deserved. Aegisthus did not try to dominate him, as Agamemnon would, using fear or humiliation, but guided him, listening carefully to what he had to say, no matter how tedious those ramblings may have seemed to others, Clytemnestra included. He would sit and nod, as if spellbound by Aegisthus's every word.

"What is this one?" Orestes asked one day, having sprinted through the palace in search of Aegisthus, his hands cupped around yet another new specimen. "I found it in the garden. Have you seen anything this color before? What do you think it is?"

"That..." Aegisthus replied, taking the creature gently from Orestes's hands into his own, "is a bristle worm."

"It is?"

"It is. But you did not find it in the palace, did you? These live in the sea. How on earth have you got hold of one, all this way inland?"

Orestes's face lit up in a grin. "Orrin had one of the merchants bring it up from Argos. Do you think we could keep it here? We could put it in the fountain."

"Somehow I do not think your mother would take too kindly to that. Besides, it needs salt water, if it is to survive."

Orestes was crestfallen, but this would last only until a new creature caught his eye, at which point he would repeat the process all over again.

"How do you know all this?" Clytemnestra heard him ask Aegisthus one morning. "How did you learn what they all are?"

"Like any man does, Orestes, from someone much older and wiser."

"Do you think it is possible to know the names of all the animals in the world?" he asked, his ability to question unending. Clytemnestra looked on from a distance, grinning at the pair. By this point, she would normally have tried to distract her son with something else, maybe by suggesting a snack. But, as Aegisthus continued to answer with the same level of considered care that he had the previous one hundred questions, she was loath to interrupt them.

"I think you would need a very long life," he said, "and a lot of spare time to track them all down."

Orestes's face fell. "I will get no free time when I am king. Even now, I have to sit in on long meetings, even though I am forbidden to speak."

"You do not have to talk to learn," he replied. "In fact, often it is better if you do not. Far better to listen."

"That cannot be right."

"Why not? Animals do not speak, and it gives them more time to learn about their surroundings. Think how much harder it would be for them to survive, if they had to talk too."

Tilting his head to the side, Orestes considered this idea.

"Maybe," he said. "But I still do not like all the meetings." And they laughed, filling Clytemnestra's heart with joy.

Electra remained the only fly in the ointment. Her relationship with her mother had gone from frosty to nonexistent. In Aegisthus's first year living at the palace, the princess could not have said more than ten words to him, and that number barely doubled during the second. She would not speak his name or dine with him. She ignored his offers to train with her and made every attempt to demean him in front of members of the household. It was the one blot on Clytemnestra's happiness, the one dark cloud that hovered over them. But she learned to endure it. There would be years to make amends to her daughter. Years for Electra to see that the wonderful father she had built up in her mind was a figment of her imagination. Since her arrival in Mycenae, she had felt herself shrinking into a shallower version of who she had once been. Aegisthus had brought her back to life, and around him she felt herself start to shine again. She was not prepared to give that up. Not even for Electra.

As the tenth year of the war came to pass, she considered her life and her kingdom complete. While she knew that Aphrodite would not have entirely forgiven her father for his impiety, she allowed herself a glimmer of hope that, perhaps, she had completed his punishment. That losing Tantalus, Alesandro, and Iphigenia had been enough to repay his debt. She almost came to believe that it was true. Until the beacon burned.

The summer day had been scorching and dry. Brittle earth covered the surrounding hills. It had been too hot to meet in the throne room for long, so Clytemnestra had taken her leave of the Council, removed Orestes, and left Aegisthus to continue the discussions.

Now twelve years old, Orestes was still smaller than other children his age—shorter and thinner—although he appeared not to mind. He had taken Aegisthus's advice and become a listener, and would contemplate deeply every decision he made. It was a good trait for a king, she and Aegisthus agreed. To show that degree of consideration in everything he did would serve him well.

They were sipping wine that evening and discussing the fact that Orestes needed to take a greater role in the Council, when she was suddenly distracted by a light, flickering faintly from across the horizon. At first, she wasn't sure what she was seeing. But as the night drew in, the flicker became a steady glow, which seemed to be coming from the direction of Mount Arachneus. It had been many years since they had prepared the bonfires. A beacon was only to be lit there after a signal from Messapion, and that only in response to one from Lemnos. Fires on mountainsides across the Aegean meant just one thing. Troy had fallen. The war was won. Agamemnon would be coming home.

"Do you think it could be a mistake?'" Clytemnestra heard the tremble in her own voice. "The earth has been very dry. Maybe it started as just a shepherd's fire and someone mistook it for a signal."

"The beacons are guarded day and night," Aegisthus said, holding her closely in his arms. "A soldier would not make that mistake."

"So what do we do now?"

"I do not know."

She could hear his voice contained as much fear as her own.

An hour passed and the pair did not move from the veranda. Finally, he pulled her away. "It will be days, if not weeks, before the ships arrive. You need sleep. Tomorrow, when you are rested, we will make a plan."

Her eyes remained locked on the distant flames. They looked almost alive, as if they were clawing upward, taunting her.

"Yes," she whispered. "We will make a plan."

That night, she did not sleep, nor did she lie in the bed next to Aegisthus. Instead, she took to the citadel. With a cloak over her head, she roamed the cobbled streets. Alleyways that would be full to bursting during the day now echoed with nothing more than the scuttling of rats. Stalls were empty and closed for the night. The muted glow of soft lamplight shone from the windows of homes belonging to people she did not know. People she would probably never meet. How was it possible to be so alone in a city of so many?

Finding little peace in the deserted town, she headed next to the temple. It was busier than she had anticipated, but she should not have been surprised. The war was over, but that did not guarantee the safe return of the sons of Mycenae. Seas were treacherous. Journeys always claimed lives. But were any of the women there praying as she prayed? she wondered. Pleading not for their husband's safety, but for his demise.

Smoke wove in delicate tendrils from candles. She found a space among the petitioners and knelt, but she could not find the words she needed. So instead, she waited for the gods to tell her what to do. Hours went by. A simple sign was all that she was asking for, to show her that they understood, that they would protect her and her children from whatever future awaited them. But as more time elapsed, she realized that they had nothing for her. No help would come, and she had run out of time.

Finally, as the first rays of sunlight splintered over the citadel, Clytemnestra returned to the palace, coming to rest outside the children's chamber. The three of them were sleeping, almost sound-lessly. The soft blankets rose and fell with the rhythm of their breath-ing, each so different in their slumber: Electra, lying flat on her back, Chrysothemis curled up tightly into a ball, and dear Orestes stretched right out, so that his feet and fingers peeked from under the sheets. No matter their differences, she had three beautiful children in her life. But how long would it stay that way? She had birthed five, and

Agamemnon had taken two. What new agreements had he struck while he had been away fighting, using his two remaining daughters as bargaining tools? To which tyrant princes were they to be wed, to extend his circle of power? And what alliance would he force on Orestes? Two innocent children had been stripped of their lives by his hands. What of the ones who remained?

What she needed was a plan, one that would ensure he could never hurt any of them again. Moving quietly, she returned to the chamber where Aegisthus was still asleep in their bed. Gently, she took him by the shoulders and rocked him awake.

"Clytemnestra? What is it? What is it, my love? Is he here already? Surely not."

"No," she shook her head. "I do not know where he is."

"Then what do you need?"

Her pulse was as steady as if she were plucking grapes from a vine as she looked her lover squarely in the eye and spoke with a newfound certainty.

"Agamemnon must die."

TWENTY-ONE

I T IS THE ONLY WAY TO KEEP THEM SAFE—SURELY YOU UNDER-
stand that?"

It had been five days since they had first seen the beacon
burning on Mount Arachneus, but there was still no sign of the fleet.
Word had it that a storm was raging across the Aegean Sea, one they
suspected was stopping the men from leaving Troy and returning
home. If the gods were merciful, the royal ship would capsize, or
Scylla would drag it beneath the waves and feast on Agamemnon's
bones, and she wouldn't need to slit his throat, the way he had her
loved ones.

"Perhaps he would let you go?" Aegisthus suggested. "Try asking
him."

"Let us consider how well his brother handled Helen's desire to
do the same thing," she replied. "Besides, even if he did, what about
the children? What would happen to them?"

He chewed on his lip. "He might let the girls come with us," he
said.

"And what good would that be, abandoning Orestes in the

house of a bully? No, I will not do it. When Agamemnon is left on his own with my children, they end up dead. Besides, Electra would not come with us. As long as he lives, she will follow him, the stupid girl. This is the only way. You must see that."

He rubbed the bridge of his nose. Frown lines, once so fleeting, now seemed a permanent fixture and showed no signs of fading. "We need to consider our options, that is all I am saying. I have killed rashly before, when I was certain it was the right thing to do, remember? Think of what that cost me. Cost us both." He tipped her head toward him and planted a kiss on the top. "We must not be hasty."

Days passed, each one bringing her husband's return closer. Meetings with the politicians were a thing of the past now. They were not interested in submitting to her authority when in a short while their true leader, the King of Kings, would be there. Her mind replayed the same, single thought: he must die. Agamemnon must die.

"Mother. Mother, can you hear me? Mother, are you well??"

Clytemnestra was startled to find Orestes standing beside her, a look of concern on his face.

"Sorry, my love, did you say something?"

"We are going to the tower to look for the ships. Do you wish to come with us?"

The question was not registering. Scratching her head, she fought for clarity.

"The ships? Are they here? Can you see them already?" The blood was draining from her face.

Orestes's reply stopped the rising panic. "No, not yet. But Electra thinks it will be any day now. Do you wish to come and look with us?"

The tower was outside the palace limits. Not far, but beyond them all the same.

"Who is taking you there? You cannot go alone."

"We will not. Orrin will be with us. And you, too, if you so wish."

His big brown eyes were like pools she could lose herself in. Never would she be parted from them. Not if she had her way. Shaking her head, she smoothed down his hair.

"You go. I will stay here. Let me know what you see."

He nodded, the look of concern still evident in his eyes.

"If they do not arrive today, maybe tomorrow you will come with us?"

"Maybe tomorrow."

Even sparring with Aegisthus could not distract her. She found her nerves so frayed that she would overestimate his moves, flinching or darting when she should have been holding still. The guards watching her did not help either. Their eyes seemed to be judging her every action. If she faced Electra in her current state, she would be beaten, without doubt. She shuddered at the thought.

She tried other ways to occupy her mind, to stop it wandering into dark places, but failed. It kept coming back to the only thing she could do if Agamemnon returned to Mycenae. And, inevitable as it had always been, that day soon arrived.

She had been waking before dawn each day, ready to start searching the sea for signs of the ships. So many days had gone by, that she had started to believe it would never happen. But that morning she had woken with a feeling of dread in the pit of her belly. This would be it, she somehow knew, before she had even taken her first sip of water. This would be the day he returned. And so, she had headed to the tower and waited, standing with her hands resting on the parapet, not moving, her heart beating erratically, her eyes trained on the same patch of sea beyond the port of Argos where they would dock.

What, in the early morning, had started out as a speck on the horizon was, by midday, as big as a thumbnail as the fleet finally took shape.

Later, the sound of laughter and happy voices had risen from the citadel below her, singing and cheering filling the air, as people praised the gods for the return of their menfolk. But she had not joined them. She had waited in silence as the children chattered excitedly next to her and the sun made its journey all the way to the top of the sky and back down again. She would have stayed there through the night too, had Chrysothemis not reappeared at the top of the steps.

"Mother, the palace needs instructions. What should they prepare for the feast?"

"The feast?"

"For Father's return. We will feast, will we not? Celebrate that he has come safely back to us?"

"We...we..."

Her daughter stepped forward and took her hands.

"Mother, this is a good thing. I know how hard it has been for you. And I know there are...complications to consider, but Father will be here soon. Your true husband is almost home."

She made no attempt to nod or agree. She could do nothing other than hold on to her daughter.

"They will be in port soon. It will just be a matter of hours. Electra and Orestes want to meet them, but it is up to you what we do, Mother. You must return to the palace. They need you to arrange things. You are expected."

Clytemnestra knew that she was right. She must act like a dutiful wife, start playing the part again. She had done it for so many years before. She could do it again. After all, it would not be for long.

The palace was a flurry of activity, unlike anything she had ever seen, even on feast days. Flowers were being arranged, garlands hung, and colored silks wrapped around the pillars. Candles had been placed on every surface, in preparation for nightfall, and the smell of roasting meat was so strong, it caught in her throat and almost made her gag. She had barely started to think of all the other things that needed to be done, when Laodamia appeared at her side.

"My queen, others can prepare the palace. We should get you ready. You must look your best."

Look your best and play your part just one last time, Clytemnestra thought. Silently, she led the way to her chamber and allowed the servants to get to work. By the time the women had finished with her, she looked as beautiful as a bride. Oiled to a lustrous sheen, her hair was in delicate braids, interlaced with leaves and then knotted at the base of her neck. A gown of deep green had been chosen to complement the foliage. The final touch of flowers in her hair was being completed when there was a knock on the door behind them.

"Excuse me, my queen."

"Aegisthus." She rose from her seat. "Away, all of you! Go now!"

Hurriedly, without even bothering to gather up their things, the servants scampered from the room. When the door had closed behind them, she rushed to her lover's side.

"Where have you been? I have needed you."

"I have been making arrangements, my darling. Securing myself a new place to stay."

"What? Why? You will stay here, with me. We will do the deed tonight. The moment he sets foot in the palace."

"Clytemnestra, you are smarter than that. Things have to be considered. We need to think through what we are to do."

"What do you mean?" she demanded. "You know what that is."

"My love, there has to be another way. Let us get through tonight, at least. See how he behaves toward you."

"Why? What in the gods' names could he do that would change my mind? My children deserve vengeance. You said so yourself. A mother should be able to avenge her child, just like a son can his father."

"And what of your children who still live? What of Orestes? How will he feel?"

Her previous confidence in him was fading. Trembling, she stepped away.

"You do not wish to do this with me. You do not support me."

"I do not wish you to get yourself killed," he replied. "If you must do it, then I will not stand in your way. But, please, let the king be at peace in his palace tonight. You do not know what state of mind, or body, he has returned in. From what I have heard, many men are injured. And many are afraid that the gods will punish them for the sacking of Troy. Let him dine with you and the children and make him feel as though he is safe. Think about it. You do not know for sure what rumors he has heard."

She was just about to reply when Orestes came racing into the room.

"They are nearly here! The horses are coming through the Lion Gate now!" Twelve years old, yet as excited as a small child.

Clytemnestra hesitated, her eyes once more on Aegisthus. "Go," he said, turning and speaking to Orestes. "Fix your chiton. Your mother will be close behind."

Orestes's eyes lingered on her.

"Go," Aegisthus repeated.

This time, he dashed away. When the boy was out of earshot, Aegisthus took her hand. "Think about this, my love. Let us find another way to make the children safe. I am certain if you go through with this you will be punished by the gods."

"No, I do not believe that. The gods will be merciful, Aegisthus. I feel it in my heart. I have earned it."

"I am not denying that, my love, but I worry for you."

"Why? You do not understand, do you? You will never understand."

She felt a pang of guilt. How was it possible to explain to someone who did not have children of their own? Who had never felt that burning love, so raw, so overwhelming, that everything else faded by comparison?

"Then let me do it," he said finally. "Let me kill him. Our families have generations of bad blood between us. Let it look as if that was my reason for returning to Mycenae. It is what most people believe, anyway."

She shook her head. "If you kill Agamemnon, it will only serve to maintain the endless bloodletting. My love, do you not see that if you were to do it, Orestes would be forced to seek vengeance? To kill you? The man who has raised him? You cannot do that to him. He is a good child, a pure child. Do not put that burden on his shoulders, or mine."

"So I just sit back and wait? Do nothing?"

There was such pain in his eyes, yet combined with so much trust and loyalty. She should consider herself lucky, she thought. Few women found one man who truly loved them in their lifetime, and she had found two. But she was still right. This cycle of bloodshed should end with her.

"There is a flower," she said. "I heard the women of Sparta talk about it, only never in the presence of a man. It is the color of a poppy, but with petals like those of the peony. They said the stalks of this flower, if cut up and simmered in sow's milk, make the most delicate of concoctions—a liquid with no smell or taste, yet more potent than hemlock, with the ability to stop a man's heart and make it appear like a natural passing. If I could kill Agamemnon that way, if I could make it look like it was an act of the gods and not man, then his death would be far easier for the children to accept."

"You wish me to find this flower for you?"

"If you are willing."

"Of course. But it may take some time. You say it grows in Sparta?"

"They said it grows there, wherever the sea and fresh water meet. That is what I remember."

"Then I will go. And you must greet your king. He will be here any moment. Just promise me you will do nothing rash while I am gone."

"I promise you," she said, then kissed his lips softly, tenderly. She wondered if he could taste the lie that she had just spun him.

With Aegisthus taking a back route out of the palace, Clytemnestra moved to the front, where her children were ready and waiting to greet their father. Stone steps provided an impressive entrance to the portico, where the pillars had been adorned with flowers. Several long red tapestries had been laid on the ground, providing a rich carpet for the king, and the guards, dressed in their ceremonial uniform, stood on either side awaiting the procession. The cheering was enough to set her ablaze with fury again. The whole of Mycenae had flocked to see the return of their victorious army, and she had no choice but to keep her mouth curved upward in a smile, her cheeks burning with the effort.

"What do you think he has brought us?" Chrysothemis asked excitedly as the sound of the horses' hooves grew louder. "Do you think it might be jewelry?"

"Naturally, although I would prefer to see what additions he has for the armory," Electra replied.

The only other person in Mycenae who remained silent, besides herself, was Orestes. When Agamemnon had left, he had been little more than a baby, and she was doubtful that the boy had any memories of his father at all.

"Will I please him, Mother?" he whispered at her side. "Do you think he will like who I have become?"

She thought back to the days of her husband's violent outbursts. To his lack of tolerance for anything emotional or sensitive, and wondered what he would make of this son, who loved to sleep with insects in pots beside his bed and feared the noise of a violent storm. Her heart trembled at the thought of the names she knew Agamemnon would call him, the taunts Orestes would have to endure for as long as his father lived. Tears welled in her eyes.

"He would be a fool not to be proud of you," she replied.

Their conversation was cut short by a loud fanfare that echoed all around as a bay horse, flanked by two large grays, came into view.

"He is here!" Electra exclaimed, straightening her back before changing her mind. "Bow. We should be bowing."

All around Clytemnestra everyone, including her children, dropped to their knees, but even as she bent her own, her eyes remained raised.

The war had not served Agamemnon well. Fatter than ever before, his shoulders seemed pulled down by the size of his belly. His skin was sallow and riddled with thread veins, from years of overindulgence, no doubt. The horse walked forward regally, its stride long and its head held high, as if unaware of the bulbous mass on its back.

But her attention did not remain on him for long. Her eyes were immediately drawn to the figure riding just behind him, and for a moment, her heart nearly stopped. The torchlight glinted off the saffron of her robe. Her skin was fresh and her hair fair. Was it possible? After all she had endured, had the gods granted her this? Had he brought their daughter back to her? Yet no sooner had the thought entered her mind than the whispering began.

TWENTY-TWO

I T IS THE PRINCESS CASSANDRA. HE HAS CLAIMED THE KING OF
Troy's daughter for his own."

"Princess? More like *crazy* Cassandra."

"Cassandra the witch."

Realizing her error, Clytemnestra's mind snapped back to the
present, and her heart, which only moments before had almost
stopped, now beat with a force so fierce, it almost made her ribs
rattle. Of course it could not be Iphigenia. She cursed herself for even
imagining such a thing, for allowing that hope to form. Agamemnon
was greeting his subjects with a whore at his side. What would that
mean for her and, more importantly, for her children?

Ignoring the furtive looks that she knew were coming her way,
she turned to them.

"Hurry, children," she said, quickly placing her hands on their
shoulders and turning them back toward the palace. "We must go
inside. Now!"

"Why?" Electra asked, the only one to question her mother.

"Because I said so."

"No. Father is here. He has seen us. Look."

There was no denying it. As his horse took its last few strides toward the steps, the king's eyes were on them. Bile scorched her throat. Even she would not be foolish enough to turn her back on him now, with all his Council and subjects present. Perhaps the girl was with child, she thought. She might even have already given him children, a strong young boy who had not cried throughout the night and tested his father's patience, as Orestes had. Perhaps his intention was not merely to replace her but the entire family. A new sense of urgency coursed through her. Aegisthus would be on his way out of the citadel by now. That was something at least. It would be easier to do the deed with him gone. And the sooner, the better.

Agamemnon dismounted with all the elegance that his bloated body and bulging limbs could afford him, which was very little. He dropped to the ground, creating a flurry of dust and visibly wincing in pain. Several men rushed to his aid, but he shooed them away, only accepting an ornate gold-topped cane that was handed to him. Up close, he looked even worse than he had done on horseback. His swollen legs had the telltale purple hue of gout, and his face was pitted in a way common to those who drank to excess. But, as grotesque as he was, she kept her eyes firmly on him for fear of what she might say or do if she looked instead at the girl.

Without a word, he shuffled up the carpet toward them and, with each step, she felt her breath grow shallower. He was soon barely an arm's length away, close enough for an embrace, or a slap. She did not know which she would despise the most.

"Orestes, my son." Agamemnon bypassed Clytemnestra entirely, turning his attention straight to the boy at her side. "You have grown." He placed his hand under the boy's chin and tipped it upward so roughly that she feared he might snap his neck. She saw the pain register in his eyes, and yet he held his head up as his father twisted it from side to side. "Yes, you have grown," he repeated.

"Yes, Father."

"You have been fighting?"

Orestes nodded quickly. "Yes, sir, with the sword. I have been training hard."

"As have I, Father. I have been training with Orrin every day, for nearly ten years now."

Unimpressed by the interruption, Agamemnon peered down his nose at the girl.

"Electra?" He spoke her name with a question mark at the end, as if he was not sure he recognized his own daughter. Clytemnestra tasted the tang of blood in her mouth as she physically bit her tongue. He only had two daughters left now; was it so difficult for him to recall them?

"Yes, Father. As I said, I have been training too. Since you left—"

But his attention had already moved on.

"Come, Cassandra," he said to the girl, who had also dismounted and now stood beside him. "My wife will see you to your room."

In that instant, her temper snapped. To ignore her in favor of their son was one thing. To treat her as a maid to his conquest was another entirely.

"Is that it?" she demanded, not caring how sharp her tongue sounded. "Is that the only greeting you have for your wife?"

He sniffed. "From what I hear, you are getting enough attention from my cousin. Now, show Cassandra to her chamber. She will have the one with the sea view. The one next to mine."

Clytemnestra scowled. "That is my room," she said.

"So it is. I suppose you will need to find somewhere else to sleep."

It was the end of the discussion. There was no room for further debate. With no words left, she accepted her dismissal. If she had ever been in any doubt about her position in the palace, it had now been made abundantly clear.

Soundlessly, she climbed the steps, her mind almost numb, as he began to bark orders at the men, and although she heard the faint patter of feet behind her, she did not turn to see if the girl was following.

"Take those crates into the throne room!" Agamemnon shouted. "And be careful! That one is worth more than you would see in a thousand of your peasant lifetimes!"

Soon she was too far away to hear the insults fly. As she passed Laodamia, whose expression was a mixture of confusion and horror, Clytemnestra was struck by another thought.

"The children," she said to her maid. "I left them out there, with him!"

"Do not worry, my queen. I will get them. I will bring them to you."

"Take them to their room, please, and stay with them. I will escort them to the throne room as soon as I am done here."

The slight delay, as she spoke to her maid, had given Cassandra the chance to catch up, and as she moved on again, the girl was there by her side. With one glance, Clytemnestra quickened her pace.

How old is she? she wondered. *Twenty? Twenty-one?* She was certainly no older than Chrysothemis. And it was no surprise that Agamemnon had taken a liking to her. Her delicate curves and slender neck reminded Clytemnestra of herself, many years ago.

"I am sorry," the girl said as she hurried along the corridor after her. "I did not ask for this."

"And yet I did not hear you object," she replied.

They continued in silence until they reached what was now to be Cassandra's room.

"I have only a few things," she said, her eyes on the mosaic floor. "I will not need much space."

"You will touch nothing in here! I will have my things removed, if necessary. We will see first how long this lasts. Until then, you touch nothing. Do you understand?"

"I do," she said, dipping her chin.

"I do, *my queen*," Clytemnestra snapped back.

"Of course, *my queen*. I understand, *my queen*."

She turned to leave, only to spin back to face the girl.

"When your things arrive, you are to change immediately and give that robe to one of the maids, who will have it burned."

A deep line appeared momentarily between the girl's brows. And, with that, Clytemnestra left.

The palace was teeming with people, most of them unfamiliar to her. There were more servants than she had seen in a decade, and many pretty women too, who, she suspected, were more of Agamemnon's whores. Some old advisers and friends were also present, flocking toward the throne room. Her throne room. She hurried to collect the children, to take them to whatever meeting he was about to call. When she reached their chamber, Electra was waiting, hands on hips, face like a thundercloud.

"What did you think you were doing, ordering us back to our room? You had no right. Now that Father is here, I shall see to it that we are not hidden away any more like children."

"You are my children, Electra, and you are acting like a badly behaved one right now." She did not have the capacity to think of a more diplomatic reply, with all that was going through her mind. "Orestes, when you enter the throne room, you will sit on the left-hand side of your father, as I have shown you. You remember?"

He nodded quickly, his Adam's apple bouncing as he swallowed.

"There is no need to worry. He will have plenty to talk about. It will likely be a long night. Do not interrupt him, and try not to look tired. Avoid the food, and do not touch the wine. It will be far easier to stay awake if your stomach is empty."

"Yes, Mother."

"And stay away from the breads and sweets too. They may help for a short while, but exhaustion will strike even more fiercely later."

"I understand."

"What about us, Mother?" Chrysothemis asked, having removed the braids from her hair so that it fell in curls down to her waist. "Where do we sit?"

Clytemnestra wiped her palms on the skirt of her robe, trying to stem the sweat that flowed from them.

"I will sit on the right of the king; that is the queen's place. You will sit on the steps beside my throne. You next to me, Chrysothemis, then Electra. And remember what I have just told your brother—the same applies to you, so stay alert and look your best."

While Electra checked her sheathed dagger, Chrysothemis adjusted the front of her robe so that it fell just a fraction lower. Clytemnestra swiftly pulled it back up.

"There will be time for that later," she said.

For many years, the throne room had been a peaceful place, one of discourse and the sharing of knowledge. There were plenty of other areas in the palace where people could be entertained, and merrymaking had been reserved for the courtyards or down in the citadel. Yet what she stepped into that evening resembled a bawdy tavern scene. The voices and laughter were so raucous she wondered if the war had turned half these men deaf or whether they had simply forgotten how they were supposed to behave in such surroundings. Bread and wine spilled onto the floor as men slapped each other on the back with scant regard for manners. And the way in which some of them lounged on the steps had her wondering if they were intending to turn her throne room into a sleeping chamber.

Only when they became aware of her presence did the laughter abate. Voices quietened as she wove her way down the steps between them. She assumed all eyes were on Orestes, their future king, but she soon realized their attention was on her. And it did not take long to realize why. There, sitting to Agamemnon's right, still dressed in the saffron robe of the Goddess Artemis, was Cassandra.

Clytemnestra looked straight ahead and lengthened her stride. The seat to Agamemnon's left was still empty, and Orestes took his place there. The urge to glance down at Cassandra's belly grew more overwhelming by the second. She must be with child. Why else would he offer a whore the queen's seat if it were not his plan to replace his family with another?

Wordlessly, she took a place on the cold, hard steps, a chill and a fire rising simultaneously within her—a cold fury and a burning rage. The quiet unease that had fallen on the room the moment she had entered remained, although many men were starting to clear their throats and shuffle in their seats.

"Patience. We have a very special guest about to join us for the festivities," Agamemnon announced.

With a murmur of expectation, heads turned toward the doorway; then there was silence. Clytemnestra's view of the figure who entered across the sea of heads was blocked. But as the crowds parted to make room for the new arrival, the air in her lungs turned to ice.

"Aegisthus!"

TWENTY-THREE

H ER JAW DROPPED AND A PAIN LIKE A THOUSAND NEEDLES
seared through her chest, but she could not draw her eyes
away. Aegisthus, her lover and partner, was walking toward
them, now just feet away from the king she had betrayed. He was
meant to have gone. He was meant to be far away from the palace,
searching for a mythical flower of her own creation, safe until she
had rid the world of the monster that had plagued them both.

Her reaction did not go unnoticed.

"Yes, Clytemnestra, I invited Aegisthus to join us for this little
celebration. You do not mind, do you? I assumed that given you two
are so well acquainted, it would not be an issue. You can join him
over there, if you wish, sitting with the other metics."

Just when she had thought that the height of her humiliation
had been reached, more was being heaped on. *Metic.* It was not a
term used in Mycenae. It was an Athenian word, reserved for those
who didn't come from their great city and were considered menial
by comparison. A few of the guests looked uncomfortable, but most
realized the insult was not aimed at them. The words had been meant

to degrade her alone. But she refused to accept them. Straightening her back, she turned to the king.

"There seems to be some misunderstanding about who has run this kingdom for the last ten years," she said, throwing a glance at Cassandra. The girl's eyes were half-closed, as though she were totally at ease.

"No, there has been no mistake here," Agamemnon replied. "Now tell me, Aegisthus, how did you find my wife's performance in the bedroom? I had always been told that Spartan women were supposed to have a certain fire. I think I might have seen the tiniest spark, when she was younger. But it did not last long. I guess I should thank you for doing a job I would rather not be bothered with myself. I am not saying it is a suitable punishment for your crime. I have not yet had time to think about what that will be. You are lucky that I have arrived home in such a good mood; otherwise I would be offering her your head on a spike."

This was greeted with a few coarse chuckles. They knew, as she did, that the words he spoke were entirely true. Although Clytemnestra had steeled herself in preparation for this, her children had not. The blood had drained from Orestes's face, while tears brimmed in Chrysothemis's eyes. The queen's heart bled for them, but there was nothing she could do. She could not comfort them, could not give them the warmth of her embrace. So, instead, she offered them her most defiant look and prayed to the gods that they would make it through the evening alive. There was only one person in the room who needed to die that night.

"No doubt you will have questions for me," Agamemnon said, once again addressing his audience. "I am sure you will want to hear the stories of how I rallied Greece, to create the greatest army the world has ever known. Or perhaps you would like to hear about how I made Achilles cry like a little girl." More laughter. "We will have time for all of that, I promise you. But first, I would like to offer you some gifts. Your faith in me brought me strength during those trying years. Your belief, that I alone could be the one to lead my brother and our armies to bring home his captive queen safely, was all I needed to confirm that I had been appointed to this position by Zeus himself." He lifted a golden scepter into the air, and the room erupted in cheering.

Clytemnestra turned and saw that Aegisthus's eyes were still on her, his face white with worry.

Agamemnon indicated that the adulation should stop, and continued.

"These past ten years have been difficult times for us all. Of course, it has had its perks." He cocked his head toward Cassandra, and the men stamped their feet and applauded. "But it was not all fun and games. And, as most of you are aware, even the greatest of us is not immune to injury."

Still gripping the scepter, he pulled up a sleeve of his robe to reveal the puckered skin of a scar. That explained his clumsiness when dismounting earlier. That and the obesity. By the looks of the scar, he had been lucky not to lose the arm.

"But enough about me. I said this is about you. Let us see what you greedy bastards want to take from me now." He snapped his fingers. "Bring me the first chest."

A huge wooden trunk was brought forward, placed at his feet, and opened. It contained gold, silk, and treasures, the like of which Clytemnestra had never seen before. The Spartan in her winced at the sight. Such greed and unnecessary excess. Copper, gold, garnets. Platters as long as a man's arm. Tapestries and paintings, so fine the gods themselves could have crafted them. One by one, he handed out the pieces to his subjects. It was a wise move, she considered, as they bowed low and offered unbridled appreciation to their generous king. They would remember this, how he had not hoarded the spoils of war but shared them among his people. She knew that he would have already selected the best pieces for himself on the journey home, as did they, but still their faces gleamed with delight as they showered him with praise.

The first chest was replaced with another and yet another. Throughout it all, Clytemnestra found herself drawn to the girl, Cassandra. How she remained seated there in the same trancelike position was a mystery to her. Was this luxury nothing compared to what she had been used to in Troy? Or was she simply imagining she was somewhere else? If the stories that had come across the Aegean were to be believed, she had once possessed the gift of a true seer, but now her words were no more reliable than the ramblings of a madwoman. She had no smiles for the people gathered before her, who might one day be her subjects. She paid no attention to the gems and treasures that were being displayed. In fact, she didn't look at all like a woman intent on stealing her crown. Then again, looks could be deceiving.

As the hours passed, the gifts were all handed out, and everyone's greed seemed to be satiated. The chests were dragged out of the way and conversation quickly turned to Troy. There was talk of Odysseus. Of the massive horse that he had built and how the Trojans had opened their gates to it, without even considering that there could be anything hidden within. There was talk too, of Achilles and Patroclus and topics that Clytemnestra would rather her children had not been exposed to. While others would have offered praise, adoration even, for these great heroes, Agamemnon only made crude, derisory remarks, seeking laughter at their expense. He was pathetic, she thought. Surely, they could see what a jealous old man he was.

Soon the subject turned to one on which he was extremely

knowledgeable—the women who had been captured after the final battle and what they had done to them. By this point, Chrysothemis was the only one of her children who remained awake, although she was looking increasingly unhappy. Orestes's head had lolled forward, while even Electra had succumbed and was resting her head on her sister's lap. Clytemnestra picked her moment, during a pause in the obscene observations.

"My king," she said, "I will take the children to bed."

His eyes narrowed at her. "And what about Aegisthus? Will you take him with you too?"

Laughter erupted. She bit her tongue and smiled. "I am sure that any man would much rather be in your company than mine," she said. Then, without waiting for further reply, she moved across to rouse Orestes while gesturing to Chrysothemis to wake Electra. With both girls on their feet and still no objections, she began the long journey out of the throne room.

She walked slowly, her eyes engaging with as many of the men as she could manage. They knew how well she had run Mycenae in Agamemnon's absence. They knew her true worth. She would make them all look her in the eye, if she could. They had accepted his gifts, laughed at his jokes at her expense, and they would know that she had seen them for who they truly were. She would remember their disloyalty when he was gone.

As she reached the top of the steps, she found herself standing beside one of the chests. There was still something in the bottom, she noticed. Tarnished and splintered, it had most likely not been deemed gift-worthy. The wooden handle was chipped and rough, the metal flecked with rust. Her eyes lingered for a moment longer on the small double-headed ax lying there, unwanted and forgotten. This was what she would use, she decided. This was what she was going to kill him with.

TWENTY-FOUR

THERE WAS NO NEED TO SELECT A NEW CHAMBER.
Clytemnestra had already decided that Cassandra would
not be there long enough to make that necessary. When
Agamemnon was dead, she would set the girl free. Where she
went and what she did after that would be of no concern to her,
and judging from the way so many of the men's eyes had wandered
across her body in the throne room, she would not be short of offers.
Possessing the King of Kings' whore would be quite the prize for
some Mycenaean noble. And so, she made her way to where she had
slept for all those years before Aegisthus's arrival at the palace. The
children's chamber.

"Clytemnestra."

"What are you doing here, Aegisthus? He will see you."

"He will not notice. He is too busy lapping up all the attention.
I am so sorry. The things he said to you in there. To us—"

"Will all be irrelevant when he is dead and gone."

Fear shone in his eyes, but that did not worry her.

"Did you see? Did you see how she dressed?"

He lowered his eyes. "I did. I am so sorry, my love."

"It was his doing. I know it was. Another way to taunt me. To remind me how he had taken Iphigenia and could do the same to the others. I thought it was her at first. The yellow robe. I thought that he had somehow brought her back to me."

"I cannot imagine the pain." He took her in his arms.

"I think he wants her on the throne," she said, fighting back tears she refused to let fall. "And I believe he plans to replace my children with hers. She may even already be with child."

"Surely not?"

"I will not put them at risk, Aegisthus. As long as he lives, they are in danger. I need to do this as soon as I can."

He pressed his lips together and she awaited his protests, but this time none came.

"When?" he asked instead.

"As soon as I have the chance. And then we will be safe." She freed herself from his embrace. "I will do whatever it takes."

He nodded. "I may not be able to get the flower you spoke of in time, but there is an apothecary. A man of great discretion."

"No. I have changed my mind. He is too paranoid for that to work. I will do it. I will get him on his own and spill his blood just as he has done before."

He took her hands. "Please do not put yourself at risk. I cannot lose you. The children cannot lose you either."

"Do not worry. However little he may think of me, he is too conceited to believe that his own wife could possibly do the deed in his own palace."

"But will you be able to do it? Taking a life. It is…unimaginable."

As she considered her reply, a new determination flowed through her. Maybe she wouldn't succeed. Perhaps Agamemnon had in fact already seen in her eyes what she intended. But if she did not kill him, she would die trying.

"He wants me to grovel, to fall on my knees, begging for his forgiveness," she said finally. "And that is what he will get. But it will not be me who is laid low for all eternity."

For three days, the king barely left the throne room, not even to sleep. The stream of guests who came to pay tribute to him was as unending as his desire to hear their sycophantic adulation. He ate more in a day than she could have managed in a week, which demanded the slaughter of more animals than in a month of his absence. And he drank continuously of the best wines in the cellar.

While his daughters had been dismissed, Orestes was forced to sit by his father and listen to the grizzly tales he recounted. While some boys of twelve might have reveled in stories of blood and guts, Orestes was not one of those. Instead, he sat in silence, trying to hide his revulsion. Fighting the loathing she felt being in her husband's presence, Clytemnestra would sit beside her son, offering him all the support she could with her silent presence. Sometimes Cassandra was also there, with that same faraway look in her eyes. Mostly, she was not. The double-headed ax, the spoil of war thought unworthy of gifting, remained forgotten in its chest.

When she returned to the throne room on the fourth day, she found it almost empty. Agamemnon was slumped in his throne, a line of drool caught in his beard, as he snored like the animal he was. Beside him, Orestes had also fallen asleep, but he was rigid and somehow still almost upright.

"Orestes, Orestes," she whispered as she rocked his shoulders.

"Go to bed, my darling. You will do yourself no good here now. Come on. You need your sleep."

His eyes blinked open.

"Mother?" he said, then quickly sat up straight. "Father?"

"He is asleep, see, as you should be. Come. Let me take you to your chamber, and I will fetch you some proper food, too."

Now wide awake, he shook his head. "If Father wakes—"

"Do not worry about him. Come."

After passing him over to the loving hands of Laodamia, she returned to the throne room. One by one, she roused the few remaining guests and told them to leave before instructing the servants to clear up the detritus that Agamemnon had seemed happy to ignore. They may have lived like animals in their camp in Troy, but it would not happen here, in *her* palace.

Moving to the man himself, she attempted to brush the crumbs from his robe.

"Are you still here?" He glowered at her from beneath half-closed eyelids. The stale odor of his breath caught in her throat.

"Of course, my king. You are my husband. Where else would I be?"

He snorted in response, but she pretended not to notice, instead brushing the dried food from his beard.

"Why not go to your chamber, my love? You must ache from sleeping here. And from all those years in Troy. Surely your body is yearning for a soft bed?"

Again, more snorting. "My body is of no concern to you."

Stepping back, she offered her most wounded look.

"Why are you being so cruel? Because I took a lover? Would you rather I spent ten years withering away? He was a plaything, my king, that is all. A distraction to keep my mind from the constant fear of losing you."

This time she received a grunt, only slightly less derisive than the snorting had been. "I struggle to believe that."

"Here," she said. "Let me show you how much I have missed you."

Spinning around, she crossed the room and strode up the steps, gesturing to the servants with a wave of her hand. "Out, all of you. Out now."

He shifted in his seat. "What are you doing?"

"Do not worry, my king. You can stay exactly as you are."

She had not planned this, but it would work. Just a short distance from her was the open wooden chest containing the ancient ax. All she needed was a minute alone with him. Her pulse raced as the servants scurried past her. When the last had finally gone through the door, she closed it. She steadied her breathing, took one last glance toward the weapon, and turned back toward her husband. Her heart nearly froze when she found him only inches behind her.

"So, what now?" he demanded. Any hint of the tiredness had gone from his eyes, which were staring at her with a ferocity that caused the hairs on her arms to rise. She remembered only too well how he had bested her in the temple after Iphigenia's death. But the tables had turned. He was no longer the mighty warrior king he'd once been, and she was no longer the feeble queen. She had not been strong enough to save her children before, but now her body and skills were finely honed for combat, like a true daughter of Sparta. She was more than a match for the Agamemnon who stood before her.

"On the throne," she said, her voice steady and calm. "The way it used to be. I can show you that the fire is still there."

He did not move. Instead, he continued to stare at her. Her pulse rate was edging upward. Then he clapped his hands loudly.

"Guards!" he called.

Two of his men entered the throne room.

"Yes, my king," they said in unison.

"Mind the door and see that we are not disturbed."

"We shall wait outside, my king."

"Nonsense—you will remain here."

As he spoke, his eyes remained fixed on Clytemnestra. Her mind raced to think of a way of turning this around. Hesitate now and any future opportunity might be lost. Finally, with no other choice left to her, she let a smile form on her lips.

"Show me this fire you speak of," he said.

Taking his hand, she led him back to the throne and lowered him gently onto it before kneeling down in front of him and parting his robes.

Every moment, from start to finish, she thought she might vomit, or faint, or simply cry out at the injustice of it all. The names he had called her, the insults he had thrown at her, never before had she considered any of them true. Yet, kneeling there on that stone floor, debased and humiliated in front of his men as he moaned in pleasure, she knew that she was no better than Cassandra. What it all came down to in the end was survival. Survival, at any cost.

When the deed was done, she kept her head down and pinched her cheeks to force the color back into them. Rising, she looked her husband in the eye.

"Shall I get the servants to run us a bath? I assume you recall those times as vividly as this?"

"Perhaps I need a little reminder of that too," he said with a lecherous grin that caused her whole body to shudder. "Although after food. Food first."

"Why not at the same time? I shall see to the bath now. You can bring us some wine. And see if you can find some of those dates I love. You remember which ones, do you not?"

His eyes narrowed by just a fraction, and then his face hardened.

"Tell me, of all the men that roam the world, why Aegisthus? Why him?"

"Really?" The question was as bold, her eyes as wide with confusion, as she could manage. She tilted her head to the side, trying to ignore the pounding in her chest. "I thought you had already figured that out."

"Figured what out?"

"He is in love with me. He has been since the first time he saw me. And I thought what better revenge for my husband than killing his father's murderer. And not just that. At the very end, he would know that he had been fooled—that I had helped you do it."

The king's expression changed, although it did not soften entirely. But a flicker of doubt now crossed his brow. "All this, between you and my cousin, was to help me enact my revenge?"

"Of course it was, my love. Why else would I lower myself to be with a man like that, after so many years with you? The gods require your father be avenged, Agamemnon. You told me that the very first time I met you, all those years ago in Sparta."

"You remember?"

"I remember quite clearly. And a revenge this long in the taking will likely be the sweetest of all."

TWENTY-FIVE

THE MOMENT AGAMEMNON AND HIS GUARDS LEFT, SHE FELL
to her knees again, breathless. The pain in her chest felt like
an iron brand was being pressed into her flesh. She gagged
at the taste in her throat. She would have preferred to spend the rest
of the night drinking strong wine, in an attempt to remove every
trace of him, both physical and mental. But, during the time spent
satisfying him, she had devised a plan. One that would work if she
acted quickly.

She pushed herself onto her feet, raced up the steps, and pulled
the ax from the chest. It was heavier than she had expected, and
larger in her hands than she had imagined too. Should anyone see
her with it, there would be no logical explanation. So she pulled a
small tapestry from the wall and wrapped it up. Then, cradling the
bundle in her arms, almost as she had the body of Iphigenia, she
scurried out of the throne room and headed back toward the palace
sleeping quarters.

Given that Agamemnon had failed to remember, even as a newly-
wed, any of her preferences, she had no doubt that it would take him

a little time to gather together a platter worthy of their bath-time tryst. Not to mention the fact that he would be sure to sample several of the wines before selecting which one he wanted. There would be time. She just had to keep moving. Her first stop was the bathroom. With no orders yet given to the servants, the room was still empty. Using her shoulder, she closed the door behind her and dropped her burden to the ground, the thickness of the tapestry muting the fall of the ax on the tiles.

There was a woven screen by the wall. Easing it out slightly, she created a gap, too small for anyone to step into but large enough to conceal the weapon. Then, she lifted the bundle back up and unwrapped it. This time, she set the ax down gently, draping the fabric loosely over the top so that it could be easily removed. Confident that it was sufficiently hidden, she ordered the first servant she saw to fill the bath, then returned to her chamber to fetch the final items she needed.

Cassandra was lying on the bed. Clytemnestra didn't bother with greetings.

"I have come to fetch something," she said.

"You have not taken your things yet," she remarked without malice. "You intend on moving back in here, do you not? But I know you need to accomplish something first."

"You know nothing."

"I know so much, so, so much, my queen. But it is of little consequence any more. Of little consequence at all."

Ignoring these crazy ramblings, she moved across to a large oak chest. Digging deep, she removed something suitable: a sheer gown. Over the years, he had often made her wear such items. Things that didn't leave anything to the imagination but left her fully exposed to him. *Not for long this time*, she thought. Casting it to one side, she continued to rummage until she found the other article she was looking for. Another garment, full of happy memories of Electra and Iphigenia and all the joy her children had brought her. Her heart ached at the thought of having to sully it. But it was for them that she needed to use it. All would then be put right.

"The king and I will be taking a bath," she said, finally looking her usurper in the eye. "I would appreciate it if we were not disturbed."

"Of course. I understand."

"No," she replied. "You do not."

"Yes, I do. But you need not worry."

A cold chill went down her spine. She shook it away. "Just stay in here," she barked.

When she returned to the bathroom, the servants had filled the tub. Sweet-smelling oils had been added, causing spectrums of color to float on the surface.

"That will do," she said to the woman who was scattering petals on the water. "You can leave now. And we are not to be disturbed, under any circumstances."

"Yes, my queen."

"No one shall enter here, except the king, until I say so."

Gathering up her things, the servant nodded once more and backed out. With the room now empty again, Clytemnestra checked the ax. The fabric had not been disturbed. She moved it just a fraction and tilted the handle upward slightly. Now she knew its weight, it would be easier to lift. Confident that all was as it should be, she slung both the gowns over the top of the screen, then stepped out of her robe and into the water. Even in the warmest weather, she found comfort in a bath. She loved the silky feel as her shoulders slipped beneath the surface. Aegisthus had joined her in this very tub, a hundred times or more. He would spend every moment caressing her skin, tracing every line with his fingertips. They would kiss and caress, as if every time they saw each other's bodies was the first, not leaving until they realized the water had turned cold, when their arms started to prickle with goose bumps.

"You look comfortable there."

Agamemnon stood in the doorway. Behind him, a servant carried a platter of fresh fruit, not a date of any description in sight.

"I am; you should join me."

"So soon?"

"Have the years changed you that much, my king? I can remember the days when we did not know if it was sunset or sunrise outside. Now, let me see that scar of yours. Maybe a wife's lips can help it heal a little quicker."

She certainly did remember those days. She had felt little more than a slave, trapped in her chamber, never knowing when he would return or what he would ask of her. She knew he would not recall the way she had sobbed silently as he forced himself into her, again and again. He only ever remembered what he chose to.

With only the briefest hesitation, he dropped his robe and stepped into the bath. A wave of water rushed over the sides. He was a fat oaf, round and disgusting, and the sight of his bulging belly repulsed her to the core. But she didn't show it. Instead, she threw back her head and laughed.

"We are not quite so young and lithe anymore," she said.

A smile rose on his lips as he reached for her breasts. *Good*, she thought. *The more relaxed he is, the less he will see it coming.*

"Does it still hurt?" She ran a finger over his scar, which was even longer and deeper than she had first observed. "Who did this?"

"All these questions," he said. "All this affection. I did not expect such a warm homecoming from you."

173

"No?"

His eyes bored into hers, and she was grateful for the steam, which disguised the sweat building up on her neck.

"You realize the sacrifice was for the good of us all, don't you? The good of the men. Your sister too. You do understand why the child had to die?"

The child! she wanted to scream at him. *Our child.* Did he even remember her name? He had probably slaughtered so many others during his time in Troy that they all blurred into one.

"I will not deny that it took me many years to accept it," she said, lowering her gaze to the oily sheen on the water. "But I know why you did what you did."

"Good. I am glad you do not retain any bitterness. There is little as unattractive as a disapproving woman. Particularly an older one."

She would have dearly loved to push his head under the water right then and hold it there. But even in his reduced state, she did not doubt who would win, if it came to a battle of strength.

"Let us move to your chamber," she said. "Let me show you what this older woman can do."

A cascade of water streamed down her body as she stood up. Agamemnon seemed transfixed by the sight. She was an older woman, of course—she no longer had the youthful glow of Cassandra—but the hard training she had been undertaking to ensure her children's safety had left her body toned and firm. Her exertions with Aegisthus, both in and out of the bedroom, had produced muscles across her stomach that belied the birth of five children. And whatever his criticisms and preferences, Agamemnon would have had to accept whatever whore he could get his hands on during the past years before the defeat of Troy.

In one sweeping step, she left the tub, then crossed the room to the screen and the sheer gown hanging there. She slipped it over her head and then pulled it down her glistening body. The material clung to her wet skin, and still he could not draw his eyes away.

"You are magnificent," he said.

A broad smile crossed her face.

"Come," she said. "I brought a robe for you too. Let us retire to your chamber. I have had ten long years in which to devise new ways to tease you."

Grinning so broadly that she thought she could detect drool running down his chin, he hoisted himself out of the bathtub.

"Here," she said and tossed him the second garment.

The moment his head ducked underneath the hem of the fabric, she raced around the screen and pulled out the ax. This was it. This was the moment.

"What is this?" he asked, in a muffled half chuckle. "I cannot find the neck. How strange. Clytemnestra. Clytemnestra?"

"Yes, my love?" she answered, lifting the ax high into the air.

His arms were flailing around as he sought the place for his head to escape. This gown, which had once caused his children such laughter, would now bring them security.

"What is—"

He never finished the question as, with every ounce of strength she possessed, she ploughed the ax deep into his sternum.

"Cly—"

Her name was cut short as blood filled his lungs and degenerated into a wet gurgle. The gown remained over his head, the white fabric now blooming with a red flower, which grew larger and larger with every failing heartbeat. She twisted the ax, hearing and feeling his bones crack beneath its rusty blade.

Her one regret was that she could not look him in the eye. It was such a shame that he could not see her final retribution, for all that he had done to her and her loved ones. But, as he staggered backward and toppled into the steaming water, she realized she did not care. This was enough. Leaning over his body, she watched as the pink bubbles grew fewer and fewer, until they had stopped altogether.

She had done her job. She had protected her children. The king was dead.

TWENTY-SIX

C LYTEMNESTRA HAD INTENDED TO MAKE HIS DEATH LOOK like an accident, but looking at the scene now, she knew that would be impossible. The ax was buried deep in his ribs, and even if she could manage to pull it out, she would never be able to hide the evidence of what had happened to him. What could she say had caused such an injury? Short of a raging bull in the bathroom, there was nothing.

So she would plead self-defense, she told herself. She would say that he was the one who had brought the ax, wishing to punish her for her affair with his cousin. He had lulled her into a false sense of security, then brought out the weapon. If people asked, she would say that, by some gift of the gods, she had wrestled it from him. Besides, it was not as if he hadn't raised his hand to her in the past. And everyone had seen the way he had treated her since his return. But what about the neckless robe? Her mind raced. That would look very suspicious. Maybe she could rip apart the seam where the head was meant to go through. Her sewing skills were so poor, it should be easy.

She plunged her hands into the bath. A layer of oil still floated on the top, and the water below was now red and viscous. She gripped the silky fabric between her hands, only to have it slip through her grasp as she pulled on it. She tried again and then yet again, but each time, it eluded her, the weight of his body keeping it below the surface. She could cut it, she thought, then immediately dismissed the idea with a shake of her head. A haphazard cut would stand out. And so, what? Another accident? A simple mistake in choosing a gown she had forgotten even existed? That would have to do. But then how could he have raised the ax to her, if he could not see what he was doing?

She stepped back, her knees and legs trembling. She closed her eyes and forced herself to take deep breaths. The details did not matter, she told herself. She had succeeded in what she had set out to do. He was dead. She had avenged her true husband and her murdered children, and her living ones were safe. She was queen in her own right now, and no one would be in a position to question what had happened. Her heartbeat steadied a fraction and then a little more. She would rule until Orestes was ready to take his place on the throne as rightful king, one who would be kind, fair, and just to all his subjects.

Visions of a brighter future were playing out in her mind, when a creak caused her eyes to snap open. There, in the doorway, stood Cassandra.

"What are you doing here?" Clytemnestra bolted across the room. "Leave. Leave at once."

The girl didn't move.

"The king told me I was to join him here," she replied. "He said that the three of us would bathe together."

Clytemnestra would have been repulsed at the thought, but she had little time to dwell on the matter.

"The King is preoccupied," she said, placing her hands on the girl's chest to push her back. But Cassandra was quick-footed, her dry feet more secure on the tiles than Clytemnestra's wet, blood-soaked ones. In an instant, the young girl was standing by the bathtub, looking down at the ax and the dead king that it was buried in. Clytemnestra's heart skipped a beat.

"It was an accident," she babbled. "It was just an accident."

A chuckle arose from Cassandra, soft at first, then louder and louder, until tears streamed down her cheeks. It was the first time Clytemnestra had heard her laugh, or seen even the smallest hint of emotion in her face, yet the sound brought her no comfort at all.

"No, no, it was not, but oh, there have been so many men in my short time on this earth who I wished would have an accident like this one," she said, leaning over the body. "You have done it. You have done what you were always going to do."

"You are talking nonsense!"

"Am I? Please, do not think me that naïve. Do not imagine I have not considered killing him myself. Killing any and all of them. But, for me, it would have meant an immediate death sentence, even if I had succeeded. This was not an accident, but what will happen next..." She became serious. "That saddens me. It saddens me that my journey ends now. I think, perhaps, had things been different, you and I could have even been friends. After all, I would have said whatever you wished me to, *my queen*. Whatever story you wished to spin, I would have agreed to. I could even have been a witness for you. I would have done so, for you."

Clytemnestra's skin tingled with goose bumps.

"I am sorry about what happened to your daughter," Cassandra continued, walking toward her. "I cannot imagine what that must have been like."

"You are right, you cannot, so please do not humor me with your attempts."

She nodded slowly, as if only half hearing. "Gods are strange beings, are they not? So, so powerful, it makes you wonder why they even bother with us at all. But I suppose we are like pets to them. Your children, they keep animals, do they not? I believe Iphigenia loved them."

"Do not speak of my daughter!"

"Your husband did not talk to me much," she continued, ignoring Clytemnestra. "He did not choose me for my power of conversation. No one ever did. He thought me incapable of understanding anything of importance. But I do. All of it. Everything. More than you or he ever will."

"You are mad."

"No." Cassandra glowered at the queen. "Though it would be easier for you if I were. He told me about the temple and how difficult it was for him. How pleased the child had been, once she had learned the true purpose of the visit, to be obeying the will of the goddess."

"You are choosing dangerous words now, even for a crazy woman."

"No, not crazy. I know what is coming. Just like your daughter Iphigenia knew too."

"You lie."

"Never. Agamemnon only spoke to me of her the once, after too much wine, which I suppose is not surprising. But it was with the most warmth I had ever heard him use about anyone. He was so proud of her. Of the strength she had shown, as she knelt before the altar, knowing it would be her final prayer. She made the act so much easier for him."

"No! No!" The blood rushed to Clytemnestra's head, and she felt the room spinning. "You lie. She did not know what was coming. He would not have told her. He could not have been so cruel as to let his own child know she was walking to her death."

"What is cruel about knowing your fate? She chose how to accept it. Just as I am now. Not screaming, not fearful, but in the same manner in which she lived her life. Peacefully."

Nausea churned in Clytemnestra's gut. "She did not know. She could not have known."

"Why are you so upset by this news?" Cassandra frowned. "This should be of the greatest comfort to you. Surely it was better that way. That she gave herself willingly to the Goddess for her father's cause, rather than be snatched from life with no hope of making her peace with the world? The honor was so much the greater."

"The honor? There is no honor in the death of a child."

"I am sorry that you see it that way."

The condescension in her voice brought the queen to new heights of anger. How dare she, a woman, no, a mere girl with no child of her own, speak to her of such things?

"You talk of honor," she spat. "You, who sold yourself to the highest bidder."

"You think I had a choice? You are not that naïve, dear Clytemnestra. My sisters, my mother, we were the spoils of war. Do not pretend to be ignorant of what happens when we both know that is far from the truth."

She could barely hear her now, for the blood pounding in her ears.

"You wore the saffron robe. You sat on *my* throne and gazed out at *my* subjects as if they were your own. You took *my* chamber, without a glimmer of remorse. You may not have had a choice in who took you, but you chose to act the part."

"Tell me then, how should I have behaved? I had a role to play. Surely you see that? All we ever have are the roles they force us to play."

"I do not believe that."

"Then what would you have had me do? Refuse his orders? Refuse to sit at his side?"

"Yes! Yes, you could have done that."

"And if I had, would you have stood by me? Who would have protected me? You have a family. And a lover. I, as you are so keen to point out, am just a spoil of war. We have been fighting the same battle, Clytemnestra, against gods and kings and people with power and privilege. They are so terrified of losing their control over us that they crush us at the slightest sign of our own independence or happiness. I am on your side, Clytemnestra. I always have been."

"There is only one side I stand on, and you are not there."

Cassandra stepped forward, hands reaching out, but the queen swung her arm to block her, pushing the girl to the side. It was not a strong blow, far more moderate than she would have used even playing with her children. But the girl was not built like them, and the tiled floor was slick with spilled water and blood. She began to topple, arms flying out in an attempt to regain her balance. But as her feet slipped away and she fell backward, her head smacked hard against the edge of the bath with a sickening crack, and she slumped to the floor. Dead.

PART II

TWENTY-SEVEN

O
RESTES! ORESTES!"
He felt his shoulders being shaken and heard the
voice in his ear, but there was a disconnect, caused by the
blanket of a deep sleep in which he wished to remain.

"Orestes, you must get up now! Now! Get your things. We need
to go."

"Electra?"

He opened his eyes to find his sister leaning over him, hers wide
in alarm.

"What is it? What are you doing?"

"You must get up straight away. We must leave. It is not safe here."

"I do not understand." Blinking, he shrugged away the shroud of
sleep, finally registering the horror on his sister's face. "Father? Mother?
Where are they? What has happened? Where is Chrysothemis?"

"There is no time for that now. Please, Orestes, all that matters is
you. We can get away, but we have to go immediately."

Stumbling to his feet, he looked around the bedchamber. It
seemed like it always did: spacious, yet warm and comforting. In

these four walls, nothing had changed, but then he heard the distant screams echoing from down the corridor.

"Electra, what has happened?"

"I will tell you as soon as we are safe."

With that, she grabbed him around the shoulders and forced him out of the doorway. Servants were running back and forth, many pale and weeping, while some stood in groups, comforting one another with hushed words. In the shadows, he saw a familiar figure, crouched low against the wall, beckoning them.

"Laodamia? What is going on?" he asked. "What is happening?"

Without so much as acknowledging his question, the maid spoke to Electra.

"I do not know if this is the right thing to do," she said, handing her a bundle of clothes. "Perhaps we should wait."

"It *is* the right thing to do," she assured her. "The only thing we can do. Is everything arranged?"

Pale and unsure, Laodamia nodded quickly. "Orrin is waiting by the Lion Gate. He will take you from there. Do not stop. Do not speak to anyone. Just get to the gate as quickly as you can."

"Thank you. Thank you."

Electra moved to go, but Laodamia caught her by the hand. "This is not for long, is it? She loves you all, you know that. How long will you be gone?"

"As long as needs be," she replied.

Together, with cloaks pulled up over their heads, they scurried out of the palace and through the citadel. Whatever tragedy had struck, it appeared to have been confined to the palace. The streets were empty, shutters fixed and lamps burning in an eerie stillness. Shuddering against the cold, Orestes raced onward, dragged faster than he could comfortably manage by Electra, whose hand gripped his wrist painfully. Where was Chrysothemis, he wanted to ask again. And where were his mother and father in all this? There were things he should do. Protocols to keep him safe if the citadel was under attack. Fleeing like this with Electra had never been one of them. When they reached the Lion Gate, Orrin was there on his horse, just as Laodamia had said; beside him waited a second mount.

"We must hurry," Orrin urged them. "They are waiting for you."

Without a word, Electra pushed Orestes up into the saddle, then scrambled up behind him and kicked the animal into action with her heels. They galloped away from the citadel. Away from their home.

When the lights had faded into pinpricks to the south, Orestes tried again.

"What has happened?" he demanded. "Where are we going?"

"We are heading across the sea."

"Where to?"

She did not reply but gripped him tighter and urged the horse to move even faster. Then somehow, without being told, he knew.

"Is our father dead?" The words tumbled from his lips. When again she didn't reply, he asked, "What about Mother? Was she spared? Did they kill her too? Who was it? Who did it?"

"There is not the time for this now," she said. "We will talk later. First we must board the ship." She kicked her heels again, and they sped north into the night.

The Gulf of Corinth, which nearly severed the southern part of Greece from the rest of the country, was calm, but Orestes was unaccustomed to being on the water, even for a short period. In the days before the war, when he was still a baby in his mother's arms, he had been on trips across the Aegean. He had visited the homes

of kings and cousins throughout the region, but he had no memory
of this. In more recent summer months, when the family—which
at that time had included Aegisthus—would head to the shore to
paddle in the cool shallows, they would see the local children heading
out over the waves on rafts they had built themselves, trying to catch
fish with old bread and coarsely knotted nets. He had listened to
their shrieks of delight on the rare occasions when Poseidon had
granted them a catch, and he had ached with disappointment for
them when their trophy slipped between their fingers and back into
the sea, before they'd even had a chance to gauge its size. He would
have loved to take part in their fun, but he was not a local child, and
should something have happened to him, the repercussions would
have been more than simply a mother's broken heart. Then, as now,
he had to be protected at all costs.

As soon as they had boarded, he had been ushered down below
deck and shut away in a tiny cabin, with only a small hard bed for
comfort. The air was clammy and smelled of sea salt and dried fish,
and he struggled to know whether his sweating was due to the heat
or his fear. So many times he had longed for the day when he might
stand on a ship and cast his gaze out at a great expanse of water, the
way so many princes had done before him. So many times he had
imagined setting sail and watching Mycenae disappearing over the
horizon. But never had he dreamed it would be like this.

The sound of waves against the wooden hull made him nervous:
the irregularity of the hammering, the constant crescendos and
diminuendos. It was impossible not to feel on edge and relax. He
was safe here, he told himself repeatedly. Ships set sail every day.
Hundreds of them, probably. But how often did they leave like this
one had, on a cloud-covered night with no light to guide them? he
wondered.

He positioned himself on the edge of the bed, with his feet flat on the floor, and tried to go with the swaying motion, but he soon found that didn't help and lay down again. How many hours' sleep had there been before Electra had woken him? Not many. And none at all since they had set sail. How long ago was that now?

As he debated whether he should try sitting up again, the door to his cabin creaked open and his sister stepped in.

"Mount Parnassus is in sight," she said. "We will be ashore soon and then make our way to Phocis."

"Phocis?" He frowned.

"King Strophius is there. He will protect us. He is Father's brother. We will be safe there until we are ready to act."

"What do you mean?"

His question was met once again with silence. A knot was forming in his belly. He had another question, which he had been unable to ask. One he feared he already knew the answer to.

"It was Mother, was it not?"

Electra pushed the door closed behind her.

"I am sorry, Orestes. I know you still have feelings for her."

"Feelings?" He frowned. "She is our mother. She raised us. She loves us."

"And yet she killed her own husband to give her lover the throne."

"No!" He moved to stand, but the ship lurched, and he nearly fell. Clutching a beam, he took a moment to balance himself. "You saw how Father abused her. She did what she did to protect herself. To protect us."

She sniffed dismissively. "No, she did what she did because she is weak and easily manipulated. Because she let herself be overcome with lust for a man who was not her husband. She put him above her own family. Aegisthus came to Mycenae with one intention—to take our father's crown, the same way he took our grandfather's. Believe me, he intends to destroy our family. He never cared for her. For any of us."

"That is not true." Orestes felt heat building behind his eyes. He adored his sister. She was his closest sibling and greatest confidant, but he had never understood why she had been so against Aegisthus, when all he had done was show them kindness. He refused to think ill of the man who had treated him like a son these past four years.

"You must take me back," he said, struggling to keep himself upright. "There are things you do not understand."

"Things I do not understand?" Her jaw locked and eyebrows arched. "Oh, please, little brother, pray tell: What is it that you might know that I do not? At twelve years of age, what insight do you have into the mind of our deceitful, murderous mother that has somehow escaped me, at eighteen?"

Orestes felt himself shrink at her outburst. He had been sworn to secrecy, for no other reason than to protect his siblings. But how could she understand their mother's actions, when she didn't know the truth?

"Please, let us return. I am safe with her. We are *both* safe with her."

"We are *not* going back!" Her gaze narrowed. "What is it you are not telling me, Orestes? Did you know of the plan?"

"Of course not! I would never even have dreamed of such an act."

"Then what is it? There is something you are not telling me."

There seemed no way of prevaricating. With Electra's tenacity, he knew she would get the answer from him, one way or another. Swallowing hard, he gripped the beam again to steady himself.

"I only learned of it last year, at the Festival of Thargelia. You know how Mother always found it difficult praying to the Goddess Artemis after she had taken Iphigenia."

She rolled her eyes. "It is the same excuse she uses all the time for her bad attitude. Women have lost far more than a single child yet do not choose to milk the bereavement the way she has these last ten years."

"But that is exactly it. That is what you do not understand. She has lost more than that."

"What are you talking about?"

There was no going back now. Aegisthus would understand. Orestes was only breaking his word to him so that he could return to his mother's side.

"At the last Thargelia, Mother sent the snake charmer to see us, do you remember? She said it was for all of us, but I knew it was really for me. You know how I love snakes."

"Please, get to the point."

"Well, she could barely leave her chamber that day. She knew Calchas's prophecy was close to fruition, that the war would soon end and Father would return. I was angry with her for not spending time with me, but Aegisthus stayed by my side. He ate and drank and held the snakes with me. And when I called our mother unkind names for being absent, that was when he told me about what had happened to her first husband, and her first son, our half brother. They were killed, Electra. Father murdered them, so that he could take her for his own."

He waited, expecting her to be shocked, perhaps even shedding a tear for their lost sibling. Instead, she merely shrugged.

"So?" she asked.

"So?" He searched her face for any trace of sympathy or understanding but found none. She merely stood there, her hand on the hilt of the dagger that she always kept sheathed at her hip. "Surely you can see she was terrified of him? Then he took Iphigenia from her too. Now do you understand that she only did what she did, because she thought she had no other choice? She was frightened it would not be long until he took another one of us."

Without a moment's hesitation, she dismissed this with a snort. "These were Aegisthus's words, a man who had already usurped the throne once."

"They were the truth, Electra. He swore on the gods it was the truth."

At the mention of the gods, his sister paused. Another swell lifted the ship and dropped it suddenly back down again. While Orestes struggled to keep his feet, Electra seemed to not even notice the motion.

"And was she terrified of the girl Cassandra too?" she finally asked.

A new knot formed in his gut. "What do you mean?"

"What do you think I mean? Do you think she was terrified of a girl barely older than me?"

"What...? Why?"

"It was not just Father she killed, Orestes. Not just Father who was found murdered. She killed his whore, too. Tell me, brother, do you really think that our mother, with her Spartan blood, who trained you and me and could hold her own against any guard in Mycenae, was so scared of a young captive girl that she felt she had no other choice than to crack her head open?"

"I...I..." The stifling heat had returned, and Orestes found himself sitting back on the bed once more, the swaying of the ship increasing the unsteadiness of his mind.

"Mother killed Father for one reason only, Orestes. She wanted him gone so she could take the crown for her lover. That was their plan all along."

"No, you do not know him like I do."

"You mark my words, he will be on that throne by the time we arrive at Mount Parnassus, if he is not there already."

"He would not do that."

"No doubt there is a bastard child already swimming in her belly, ready to take *your* rightful place."

Her words reverberated around his skull. He was growing more confused by the second.

"No. No, Electra," he stammered. "We must go back. You need to let me speak with her."

But she was already at the door. As she stepped outside, she turned for a parting shot.

"The next time you set foot in Mycenae, Orestes, will be when you are ready to kill them both."

TWENTY-EIGHT

WHEN CLYTEMNESTRA LATER RECALLED THAT FIRST year, with two more of her children gone, she thought it a wonder that she survived it at all. Every waking moment of her life had been filled with a grief so raw that some days she barely stirred from her bed. Orrin had taken them; she knew that much. A man she had considered loyal to her had stolen the person she held most precious in the world. Yet she could not blame him entirely. His true loyalty was to Mycenae and, by extension, to the true king, Orestes. In the chaos of Agamemnon's death, it would not have been hard for Electra to convince him to act as he had.

As her only remaining child, Chrysothemis had tried to comfort her. Battling through her own grief, she had visited her chamber daily, taking her mother bread or flowers, even the tapestry that she was working on, in the hope that something might bring even the smallest modicum of happiness. But her mother was beyond any such solace, and her appearances only served to remind her more of what she had lost.

Two months after Agamemnon's death, she ordered a ship to take her remaining daughter away, to the Temple of Athena.

"Why would you do this, Clytemnestra? She has never craved the life of a priestess," Aegisthus had asked when he learned of her plan.

"She should not have to endure the burden of my grief as well as her own."

"You know this will not make her happy. Think about it, until the next moon at least."

Any misgivings she felt were far outweighed by her certainty that this would be the best course for Chrysothemis. Better for her to be away from this family and the curse that plagued it.

"I have already made up my mind. A ship sails for Athens tomorrow. Chrysothemis will be on it."

"Clytemnestra—"

"We are done talking about this. I am queen here, remember. She leaves tomorrow."

She heard her daughter's wails from her chamber and later learned that the guards had needed to drag her out of the palace. She could not see it now, she told herself as the tears pricked her eyes, but it was for her own good. Her own safety. One day, she would understand.

And with Chrysothemis, the last of her children, gone, she no longer had to pretend or try to conceal her pain.

The running of the kingdom, something she had once taken such a pride in, now fell on Aegisthus's shoulders, a burden she knew he did not wish but which he carried for her all the same. Days merged into weeks. Women no longer came to the courtyard to gossip and enjoy music. Men scurried past her, averting their eyes, as if she might possess the power of Medusa. Tapestry was her only distraction, and she'd pass hours at the loom, slowly—and badly—weaving the threads in and out, missing the way Chrysothemis used to help and guide her. But the mindless repetition numbed the pain a little.

So unlike Agamemnon had ever been, Aegisthus was patient with her in this time of mourning, and as her strength gradually returned, she allowed him back into her life and then, eventually, her bedroom. Even so, what happened next came as a complete surprise.

At first, she thought it was grief causing the waves of nausea to strike her at all hours of the day. And the tenderness of her body, she easily attributed to her advancing age. But then, other telltale signs showed themselves. Ones she had not encountered for well over a decade, such as a sudden dislike of meat and a cramping feeling in her pelvis.

With Aegisthus busy on matters of state, Clytemnestra enjoyed all the quiet moments that she could with her unborn child. She gradually loosened her robes, knowing there was only so long she could disguise her condition.

"I will keep you safe," she said, running her hand over the taut skin of her belly. "I will protect you from everything. There is no one who can harm you now."

Some days, she would head out into the citadel at sunrise and not return until the midday sun was burning bright above her. Others times, she would sit in the courtyard, muttering quietly as she picked at olives and spiced nuts. At night, she would feign a headache or complain about the heat to discourage Aegisthus from coming too close. As such, it was not until after she had felt the first movements that he finally realized the truth.

"You have been avoiding me," he said, "turning away from me at night."

"I have had trouble sleeping these past weeks."

"That is not true, Clytemnestra. Do you think I am blind, or just a fool? We have to talk about this. You cannot hide it any longer."

"What is there to talk about? Hide what?"

He offered her a withering look. "You are carrying my child, Clytemnestra. Do you not see what this means? If Electra learns that you are pregnant, she will think that this was our plan all along. That this was *my* plan. She will think that I came to steal the throne, and she will want my head for it."

"This baby is a gift," she replied, her voice gentle as she rubbed the growing bump. "He is a gift from the gods, in repayment for all my losses, for all I have been through. Do you not see that? That is why they have given him to me. I will not fail this one. I will not let him down."

Aegisthus paled. "Why do you say 'he'? Have you been to the seer?"

She shook her head, the motion of her hand continuing in circles now.

"It is the way he is positioned. The way he sits outwards, see? The girls were never like this, but both of my boys were. My darling Alesandro. My blessed Orestes, and now my beautiful Aletes."

Aegisthus stepped forward, lowering himself to the ground and placing his hands on her knees.

"My darling, I hope that you are wrong about this. To have a boy…Electra would show him no mercy."

"Electra will not get near him."

"She will think he is going to take the throne from Orestes."

"So what if he does? Do you see Orestes here at my side, learning how to run the kingdom? Do you see him thanking me for everything I did to protect him? How many more messengers do I have to send to him? How many more times do I have to ask him to come home and listen to me, to hear my side of what happened? I have offered to travel to meet him, from Olympus to Hades, if need be, but he does not wish to know. He has abandoned his mother, his family. And now…now you wish me to do what? To give our child away? You wish me to toss aside what will probably be the last hope of something good in my life to recompense me for all the bad? This boy is a prince, Aegisthus."

"Yes, but a bastard one. I am not a king here."

"No, but I *am* the queen, and I will have this child, and I will keep him and raise him, with or without you by my side."

There was a fire burning in her, one that had been absent for too long. And now that it had returned, she was even more certain that she would do whatever it took to protect this baby.

Still on his knees, Aegisthus placed his head on her stomach. When he eventually lifted it back up, he looked her straight in the eyes.

"I have told you before and I will tell you again, the only thing that matters to me is keeping you safe. If you cannot live without this child, then I will stay by your side and raise him with all the love in my heart. But I am worried about this, Clytemnestra. I am worried what will come from this."

"What will come from this is joy," she said, and at that moment she truly believed it.

Just as Electra had predicted, their uncle, King Strophius, had been most welcoming to her and Orestes. Immediately upon their arrival at the palace, they had been taken to their new quarters, which were almost as lavishly furnished as those they had enjoyed in Mycenae.

Strophius instructed his son, Prince Pylades, to keep Orestes company while Electra discussed with him and the royal council the intricacies of the betrayal.

Although Pylades was only two years older than Orestes, he was far wiser in matters of the heart, and a far more accomplished swordsman, and yet he took Orestes under his wing like a brother. He tolerated the young boy's quirks and foibles far more than Electra ever had, showing interest when he would stop on one of their rides to point out a colorful bird, or to leave his steed altogether to inspect a lizard he had spotted in the undergrowth. While Pylades preferred to speak of poets and playwrights, he listened to Orestes's chatter, and he never pried into their arrival in Phocis. Not that Orestes was naïve enough to think he did not know what had happened. Everyone did.

While Pylades put no pressure on Orestes to relive the painful details of his flight from Mycenae, Electra refused to let him be.

"It is the law of the gods," she would keep repeating, "that fathers must be avenged."

"Then you avenge him," he'd snap back, "for I am tired of hearing this."

"This is not for me to undertake. It has to be done by you. You are the rightful heir."

When he could stand it no longer, he would move to another part of the palace, hoping she would not follow. Or else he would join Pylades, whom she dared not upset for fear of word getting back to his father, which might in turn affect his kindness toward them.

One day, about a year after their arrival, she found Orestes on the palace grounds and started up again. He had been happily sketching a frog that was perching on a lily leaf and had not moved for over an hour, save to flick out its tongue or blink.

"Have you heard?" she demanded, frightening the small creature away.

"Heard what?" he asked, although he knew only too well what was coming. Pylades had spoken to him the night before, after dinner, concerned how his friend might react if the news reached him by way of idle gossip. But he need not have worried. Orestes had no qualms about his new sibling.

"She is with child, Orestes," she snarled. "She and her murderous lover have spawned a usurper to your throne."

"Really?" he asked, turning back to the undergrowth to see if he could spot any sign of the little amphibian.

"'Really'? Is that all you have to say? Do you not understand what this means? You know she has banished Chrysothemis."

"Banished her? I heard she was sick and that Mother had her taken to the Temple of Athena, to seek help."

"Your hearing is very selective," she mocked.

"And yours is not? You would believe a rumor stating that Mother had turned into a three-headed serpent if you thought it would make me return to Mycenae and put a dagger through her heart."

Her face contorted. "How many times do I need to tell you? You cannot escape this. The Kingdom of Mycenae is slipping from your grasp. The child will claim the throne!"

Abandoning all hope of ever finding the animal again, he stood up and faced her.

"The child is not even born yet, Electra. It might never be born. It might be born a girl. It might be born sick. Even with the chance that Mother does have another healthy son, what would you have me do, kill it? Kill a newborn? I am not the monster that Father was, and I never will be."

"Defending a throne that is rightfully yours does not make you a monster."

"Five years…ten years. Let us see what the situation is then. At least let me find out if this child is a threat before you demand I go and cave its skull in."

A scowl was such a permanent fixture on his sister's face that he wondered if she could manage any other form of expression now. He certainly couldn't recall the last time he had seen her smile.

When news reached them that the child had been born and was a boy, Orestes discovered that Electra requested a ship of King Strophius for their return to Mycenae. But he refused to leave, and even Electra knew that she could do nothing without him.

She did threaten to go and do the deed herself. But he knew that it was just hot air. In her eyes, vengeance was for him to take, whether he wanted to or not.

"Electra's problem is that she refuses to believe that there are any gray areas in life," he told Pylades. "'*All sons must avenge their fathers.*' That is what she is always spouting. Well, what about mothers avenging their children? That is what my mother did, but Electra refuses to accept that, or that she might possibly be wrong."

He traced a line in the sand with his sword. The last few years had seen him become unrecognizable from the spindly child who had arrived in Phocis. The combination of puberty and time spent training with his friend had created muscles that rippled along his arms and across his back. Not that he was comparable in stature to Pylades, or even most of the other young men in the palace for that matter. But he didn't mind. Everyone knew that what he lacked in physique he made up for in quick wittedness and compassion.

"I just wish she would step back. Relax a little. She is fixated on a day that might never come."

Realizing that the sparring session was over, Pylades also lowered his sword. It was no longer his father's requirement that he spend his free time with Orestes, and yet, after so long together, he couldn't imagine anyone else he would rather be with. With each moon that passed, the pair became more and more inseparable.

"There is a way," Pylades said, "for you to know that you are right in your decision not to want vengeance."

"I *am* right."

"We know that, but Electra does not. There is a way you can get her off your back for good. A way to make her never question you again."

With the sword now hanging loose in his hand, Orestes studied his friend's face. He already had, here on Phocis, what he'd always dreamed of: a simple life, one without the constant dread of the future overshadowing him.

"How can I do that?" he asked.

"We go to Delphi. We ask the Pythia."

"The Oracle?"

"She is more than just an oracle. She is the High Priestess of the God Apollo. Her word is as good as his. If she says that no vengeance is required on behalf of your father, then there is no way Electra could ever disagree. Not without invoking the wrath of Apollo himself, which I take it she would not be keen to do."

It was such an obvious answer to his problem that he didn't know how he hadn't thought of it himself. It almost sounded too good to be true.

"Can I do that? Can I simply ask her for Apollo's word on the matter?"

"Of course you can. You are the future King of Mycenae. You would be seeking her advice on a matter of life or death. Men have gone to her for far more trivial things than that, I can assure you."

The idea was becoming more and more appealing by the second.

"And you are sure that they would show my mother compassion?"

Pylades faltered now. "These are gods, Orestes. No one can be certain of anything. But if you believe in your heart that she deserves no punishment, then so do I. Besides, what other choice have you? If you do not speak to the Pythia, then Electra will never stop hounding you. There is no way even she could dispute the words of the High Priestess."

A veritable swarm of butterflies had taken residence in his stomach. He could return home, to Mycenae, meet his brother, see his mother and Aegisthus. The idea did have one major drawback, however. But maybe if he asked him, Pylades would go with him. Shaking his head, he refocused.

"When can we leave?" he asked.

"Is tomorrow too soon?"

TWENTY-NINE

IT WAS THE FIRST TIME ORESTES HAD BEEN ON A TRIP OF ANY length without his sister. Naturally, she had demanded to make the journey with them, but Pylades had been talking to him recently about the need to stand up to Electra and make his wishes heard. And so he had.

"The journey is a day there and a day back," he told her. "Pylades and I will leave at sunrise, and we should return by dusk the following day."

"What if you are attacked?"

"By whom? I will be traveling with the Prince of Phocis. I could not be safer if the king himself accompanied me."

"There should be guards with you, though. People to protect you. No, I *am* coming." Assuming the conversation over, she turned away, but he caught her arm.

"Pylades first made this journey by himself when he was eleven, Electra. And he has done it again every year since. I am fifteen, and you are the one who has been telling me to grow up, wanting me to ready myself for the throne. Suppose the Pythia does require me to take Mother's head and reclaim Mycenae—are you going to be by my side every single day I am king? Are you going to go on every trip with me? Because, if that is the case, I might as well give you the crown now."

Her exasperated expression was so similar to that of their mother that he almost mentioned it. Thankfully, he caught himself in time.

"Fine, you do this, but if the gods tell you to avenge our father's death, then you must swear to me you will do it. Do you understand? No more excuses."

"I may be young, Electra, but I am not a fool. I have no intention of incurring the wrath of the gods."

"Good," she replied. "Then I am already awaiting your return."

It felt like he was at last becoming his own person, almost a man.

While the initial decision had been to take horses and make their journey as swift as possible, the two young men changed their minds, just a few minutes before departure. With so little to carry, and Orestes's predilection for stopping to look at every creature he came across, they decided instead to go on foot.

Spring had seen the kingdom come alive with color. Hummingbird moths, with their delicate wings and elongated features, hovered by lavender bushes, while lizards basked out in the sun, waiting for its rays to energize them. And he did take his time, observing and studying, while Pylades stayed at his side, mainly watching him.

"Do you think you will head straight back to Mycenae?" the older boy asked, when they stopped after an hour to feast on fresh peaches. "If the Pythia says your mother is blameless, will you go home immediately?"

Orestes shook his head. "I thought I might travel a little first. I know Electra hates to admit it, but from what I have heard, Aegisthus is running the kingdom well in our absence. And I am sure he would be happy to keep doing so until I am ready to return."

"Where will you go?"

He rolled over on the grass, leaning on his elbows as he spoke. "Do you know that there are some snakes so big, they can swallow a man whole? And spiders whose legs are so large, that they cannot sit on your hand?"

"They do not sound like things I would go looking for," Pylades said, laughing.

"I wish to bring those creatures back to Mycenae. I want us to have them all."

"Perhaps you would be better suited to being the King of Animals rather than the King of Kings."

"Yes, I think I would prefer that," he agreed.

When they had finished eating, they continued their trek east, on paths that were steep although well trodden. A little after midday, the heat caused them to stop again, to bathe in a stream. Orestes had already seen Pylades naked a hundred times or more, yet he found himself unable to draw his eyes away from him. One day, he would pluck up the courage to take his hand as they walked, or plant his lips against his when he spoke, or simply brush the wet hair from his eyes as they bathed. But today was not that day. Today they had a more important task at hand.

As they walked through an undulating valley, it was only when they crested the final hill that the city came into view.

"That is it?" he whispered, his eyes lost in the vista before him. "It is magnificent!"

As Pylades pointed out the distant temples and stadia that sat within Delphi's limits, it seemed more like a world of its own than just a city. Buildings were balanced on the edges of the hillsides and continued down into the basin of the valley, where the vivid green of lush grass was interspersed with the pale yellow of the rock. He could see so many of nature's treasures down there. Trees, not just those bearing fruit, but also willows and birches, oaks and poplars, flourished everywhere. So many specimens, he could have spent months simply noting them all down and sketching them. Without a word to Pylades, he found his feet moving faster and faster.

"What is that?" Orestes asked, pausing to point to a structure perched on one of the hills, where three large pillars reached up toward the cloudless sky.

"That is the Sanctuary of Athena Pronea," Pylades replied, grinning at his companion's delight.

"And that, over there, what is that? A theater?"

"No, the theater is farther away. That is the stadium."

Orestes continued to race toward the city, for once so distracted that he didn't even notice the black-winged kites that soared above them. Soon, yet not soon enough for him, they were standing amid it all.

"Why have you not brought me here before?" he asked, his mouth now watering from the aroma of the meats that sizzled and spat on open fires.

"I see that was a mistake," Pylades said, laughing. "I promise, we shall return each year, if that is what you wish."

"It is," he sighed.

People of every complexion and costume bartered and bantered as they milled around, arms laden with all manner of items from fruit and eggs to incense and silver. Some had scarves over their heads, while others wore their hair loose, down to their waist. Some had ink markings on their skin, woven in thick bands or delicate patterns. Others' bare skin was unadorned. And among them all, animals roamed. Not just asses and camels, but even a great herd of swans, which extended their necks, demanding bread from anyone they spotted carrying it. Their hisses were muted by the endless trills of musicians who, despite their number and distance apart, seemed to have no difficulty keeping time with one another.

Mesmerized, Orestes breathed it all in. Of course people would come to the Temple of Apollo and feel inspired, he thought. He was the God of Music and Dance, not just Prophecy. How could anyone fail to feel exhilarated in a place as beautiful and captivating as this?

"Are all these people here to see the Pythia?" he asked, turning to Pylades, who had been watching his reactions with ever-increasing pleasure. "Are they all seeking her counsel?"

"Not all. Many are here just to pay tribute to the god. Some hope to find work. Others to sell their goods. We can look more at that later. I sent word ahead to tell the High Priestess we were coming. We should go straight to see her. It would not do well to keep her waiting. The temple is over there."

A row of huge stone pillars marked the entrance to the Temple of Apollo, one far grander that any Orestes had seen in Mycenae. One day, he would travel to all the great temples, he told himself, as they wove their way through the crowds who lined up at the foot of the steps. Athens, Aphaia, he would visit them all and be inspired, just as he was here.

"Come, follow me," called Pylades. "I will show you where we need to go."

They made their way up into the temple. A delicate scent of citrus and cinnamon filled the cool air, giving a welcome respite from the heat of the day. Although the light was dim, Orestes had little difficulty in seeing the hundreds of offerings that had already been placed on the altar of the God, including a delicately inlaid lyre that immediately caused him to think of his sister Chrysothemis.

"Prince Pylades, it has been some time." A priestess approached them dressed in an orange robe.

"Forgive me, Priestess; you are quite right. Please, accept my offering." From out of his small bag, he produced a slim bangle of gold, which the priestess took with a nod. "I am sure you are aware that I am not here for myself," he continued. "This is my cousin Orestes, Prince of Mycenae. He seeks council with the Pythia. He requires guidance from Apollo himself."

"Of course. Please follow me." She gestured toward the back of the temple, and they headed inward, to where large swathes of fabric billowed from the ceiling, creating rippling shadows on the ground, like snakes constantly moving yet going nowhere.

Since his arrival in Phocis, Orestes's feelings toward Pylades had grown and grown. Yet he knew he would always be tied to Mycenae. But Electra's demand for the murder of their own mother would be silenced now, he was sure. Only when his friend cleared his throat did he realize that the Priestess had spoken again and was ushering him forward.

"Are you not coming with me?" he asked.

"You do not need me for this," Pylades replied. "Do not worry. You will be fine. And when you return, we will spend the entire night celebrating."

A tentative smile flickered on Orestes's lips.

THIRTY

T HERE WAS NOTHING DELICATE ABOUT THE AROMA IN THE
Pythia's chamber. Clouds of smoke rose from smoldering
incense and heated oils so thick that they clogged his lungs
and stung his eyes. The cool air too had gone, replaced by a muggy
heat that scorched his throat with every breath. There were no
windows and no way for any light to enter. The few small oil lamps
dotted around added their own odor and warmth to the mix. As
his eyes took a moment to adjust to the gloom, he saw the woman,
eyes closed, sitting on a stool beside two large bowls of shimmering
liquid. Whereas the priestesses outside had been dressed in burnt-
orange robes, that of the Pythia was a flaming red, the top drawn
over her head to form a silken hood, while the bottom pooled like
liquid on the ground.

"High Priestess," he said, stepping forward toward a cushion
placed in front of her. "Great Pythia, I come seeking the guidance
of Apollo."

He knelt, wondering for a moment if he might pass out from
the effect of all the fumes. How it was possible to think clearly in

such an atmosphere, he didn't know. He had no fear for his safety though. Pylades would not have brought him anywhere he could be harmed.

"Sweet Orestes." The Pythia's voice was almost childlike and her accent unfamiliar to him—not at all like the locals of Delphi and Mount Parnassus. "Sweet prince. So young at heart, but weighed down with a man's burden."

"I need the word of the God," he said. "I need—"

"I know why you are here, my child. Although, I must be honest, it is not my great wisdom that tells me this. I imagine half of all Greece would know your reason for coming and kneeling at this altar. Your mother included," she added.

His cheeks colored, but he stayed silent. He felt far calmer than he would have expected, no doubt the effect of the oils that burned around him. Noting the steady rhythm of his heart, he awaited the Pythia's next words.

"Your mother murdered your father. Fathers must be avenged," she said, her eyes still closed.

It was not the words of a god he heard, just the same line Electra spouted almost daily.

"I know," he replied. "But not all acts of murder require retribution, surely? My mother killed my father in revenge for the slaughter of her first husband and son. Not to mention my sister, his own daughter."

"Your sister was killed for the Goddess. Sacrifice is not the same as murder."

While Orestes had a hard time accepting that to be true, he did not wish to invoke the anger of the High Priestess and simply repeated his previous point.

"Still, her first husband and son. A king and a prince in their own right. Who should have avenged them, if not my mother?"

"I understand. What your mother did was an act I imagine would be applauded by any woman who has ever lost a child that way, at the hands of another. What could be more deserving of revenge than the spilled blood of an innocent? My heart goes out to all who have suffered such a loss."

"So you do understand," he said, feeling relieved. "The gods realize she has already endured enough—more than anyone should have to. My mother needs no punishment, and it would not be right for me to take her life."

The Priestess's eyes snapped open. Colder than ice, they bored into him. She was, as he had been told, the vessel of a god. A channel for mere mortals to hear his words, and she now conveyed them directly to him.

"Gods, not goddesses. Men, not women. Zeus, not Hera," she said. "This is the way, Orestes. Agamemnon, not Clytemnestra."

Even the heat of the room could not stop the chill that rippled through him.

"What are you saying?"

"I am saying, Orestes, that the God Apollo has spoken. It is fathers who must be avenged, whatever the circumstances. Agamemnon was killed by your mother's hand. Now your mother must die by yours."

When he finally stepped back out into the open court of the temple, he could barely stand.

"Orestes!" Pylades leaped to his side, holding a skin of water, which he placed to his friend's lips. "What did she say? Did Apollo give his pardon?"

Orestes could only drink. Drink and weep.

The Priestess had given him further instructions about the

manner in which he must end his mother's life. Although he had been listening, the only thing he could think of was his mother's face. Her eyes, so full of life. Her lips, curved upward in a smile as she ruffled his hair. How could he do this? He could barely stomach the thought of killing a rat.

After he had finished with the water, Pylades half led, half carried him outside, where they rested under a small rush canopy. His cousin did not need to inquire further of the gods' ruling.

"When?" was the only question he finally asked. "When are you to do it?"

Orestes shook his head. "Not yet. I am not ready. I have to train first. It must be…clean."

Pylades nodded slowly. "I will help you. I will prepare with you."

"I knew you would. Will you come with me to Mycenae too?" he asked. "The Pythia said that I should travel there with another man. Will you be the one?"

"Of course I will. I will always go with you, wherever you need me. Whatever you want me to do."

At any other time, his eyes would have been on Pylades's hand, which was grasping his, the other one brushing away the tears that Orestes wished he was strong enough to prevent. But he was not strong. He was weak. He was just a boy, but soon he would be a murderer too.

THIRTY-ONE

I N MYCENAE, ALETES WAS THRIVING. HE HAD AEGISTHUS'S thoughtfulness, his tentativeness. He was inquisitive, like Orestes and Iphigenia, but had the patience of Chrysothemis. In looks, he resembled Iphigenia, from the gentle curl of his hair to his long slender limbs, which seemed made more for dancing than fighting. Clytemnestra never grew tired of watching him or listening to him. She was making the most of not her second but third chance at happiness.

"How did the talks go at the Polis?" she asked Aegisthus when he returned to the palace one evening after a long day chairing discussions there. She attended now and again, but time with Aletes was too precious for her to squander on petty squabbles. He had just turned six and was already a fount of knowledge. That particular day, they had been discussing the stars. She had told him about the Hyades, who had so deeply grieved the death of their brother that Zeus had placed them together in the night sky to watch over the world. As night had fallen, they had gone outside to see for themselves.

"There was word of Orestes again," he replied, taking some bread from a basket. "Some say he is planning on setting sail before the next moon. That he will return to Mycenae to do the gods' will."

"Really? And where did this word come from? Someone in his council at Phocis? Someone who knows him? Or someone who is hoping to gain from spreading rumors of him invading Mycenae?"

"It does not matter where it came from, Clytemnestra."

"Of course it does. Until I see him standing in front of me with a dagger in his hand, I can assure you we are all perfectly safe. This is Orestes. He would sooner stay in exile for all eternity than hurt me. Or you, for that matter."

"I only hope you are right, my love," he replied, with a look of concern on his face.

Now and then he would do this. Start panicking that Orestes was about to arrive on their shores at any moment, an entirely different child from the one who had departed. But she knew her son, knew his heart, and she had never given this any serious consideration.

"How long ago did we hear about his trip to the Pythia at Delphi?" she asked.

"Two years? Three? The gods do not have endless patience. He will know that too." Aegisthus would not let it rest.

Sensing his distress would not be eased through talk alone, she walked across the room and combed her fingers through his graying hair. He was an old man now; older than Agamemnon had been when he had met his end, but anyone who looked in his eyes could see the fire still burning bright there. The fire and the love.

"Aegisthus, please, like you said, it has been years. Do you not think that if Apollo had told Orestes to murder me, I would be dead by now? Trust me, we are safe. We are all perfectly safe."

The clouds were little more than faint brushstrokes across the cerulean sky as the breeze swept them over the fields and out to sea. The sunrise had been spectacular—burned ochers blended with vivid magentas and a thousand other colors, so unique that Orestes wondered if they even had names. Would it be possible, he thought, to know the name of every color the gods had created?

"What are you thinking?" Pylades asked, intertwining his fingers with Orestes's.

The young princes lay together on a blanket, with Orestes's head resting on Pylades's chest. At this time of day, he smelled fresher than the morning dew. Crisp and new. He drew in a lungful of air and closed his eyes.

"I wish you would tell me what you are thinking," Pylades said again. "I feel I never know what is going on in that head of yours."

"There is little to tell," he replied. "Mostly my mind is filled with you."

Rolling over, he planted a kiss on the young man's lips. They had fallen in love so gently, so easily, it was as though it was always meant to be. Now, Orestes couldn't imagine a life without him.

"Well, I would like to think that I am at the forefront of your mind," Pylades said when the pair broke away, "but I suspect that is not the case today. You know I will never judge you, whatever thoughts you might have."

A familiar silence followed. One that most often arose when Orestes was being forced to discuss matters, which he had grown exceptionally adept at avoiding.

"Tell me," he said finally, sitting up and changing the subject before the tension could take hold. "What shall we do today? Go fishing? It seems like months since we last did that. We could catch our supper and cook it on the beach."

"If fishing is what you would like to do, then fishing it shall be," Pylades replied. "Although supper may have to wait. I promised

Father I would be at the palace this afternoon. He has some guests he wishes me to meet."

"Fine. We will eat the fish for lunch then, not supper. And then I will remain at the palace until you are through with your duties and have time for me again," he said with a deliberately provocative pout.

"I will always have time for you. But we live under my father's roof. We must at least pay lip service to his rules."

Orestes let out a sigh that was only half in jest.

"For now, though, I am at your disposal."

Satisfied that their time together would remain undisturbed for a few hours, Orestes dropped his head back down onto his lover's chest and closed his eyes. Would it be possible to live as simply as this forever? he wondered. Just fishing and sleeping and making love in the grass. *What more could you want from life than this?* He was still pondering the possibility of such a future, when a shrill call cut through his reverie.

"Orestes! There you are! I have been looking all over for you."

"Quick," he hissed at Pylades. "Shuffle over. Hide me. Do not let her see me."

"How? We are in an open field. She has already spotted you."

"Then send her away. You are the prince here."

Laughing, he slid out from underneath Orestes, causing his lover's head to bounce off the ground.

"This is your battle. I will not face her for you."

Simultaneously groaning and rubbing the back his head, Orestes pushed himself up to a sitting position and prepared to face his sister.

From the scowl on her face and the way her arms were swinging as she strode toward them, he could tell Electra was in her usual bad mood. King Strophius had been exceptionally accommodating, letting her train with his army. But training only used up so many hours of the day, meaning she had more than enough time left to pester him. And invariably, there was only one topic she wished to talk about.

"You have been avoiding me."

There were no pleasant greetings where she was concerned. No pleasantries, full stop.

"Sister," he said. "Why would I do such a thing? You are my favorite sibling in the whole of Phocis."

"That is not funny," she replied, although he could have sworn he heard Pylades snigger at the comment.

"You promised that we would discuss matters after the Panathenaea. That was a full moon ago."

"You are right. Maybe we should wait until the next one. It is every four years, is it not?"

Her scowl deepened. He realized that any attempt at levity would continue to be met with stony silence, and he let out a long sigh. The sooner she'd said her piece, the sooner she would go, and the sooner he could have Pylades to himself again. Sensing the softening of his resolve, Electra continued her rant.

"It has been eight years, Orestes. Eight years since we left Mycenae. I want to go back home. You have had your time. I did as I promised. I allowed you a childhood. I allowed you time to train, to prepare yourself. How much longer do you mean this to go on for?"

She hadn't even attempted to warm him to the subject. Clearly, this was not a day when she would be open to debate.

"Can we talk about this back at the palace?" he asked, plucking a blade of grass. "I was actually having quite an enjoyable morning before you showed up."

"At the palace you will avoid me as you always do."

"No, I will not. Pylades has business with his father this

afternoon. Guests he has to meet. I will be free to talk to you then. I swear."

"You promise me? You will not avoid this any longer?"

"I promise," he said, with all the sincerity he could muster. She didn't look convinced, which was probably understandable given the number of times he had previously made this pledge, only to find a last-minute excuse to be otherwise engaged.

"If you do not turn up, then I will hunt you down and drag you onto a ship for Mycenae myself. And before we leave, I might just happen to mention to King Strophius why Pylades has shown so little interest in marriage, despite all the attempts to arrange one for him."

At this, both young men flushed pink.

"I have said I will be there and I will," he snapped back at her. "Now, do you plan on ruining just part of my day or all of it?"

With a final huff, she spun on her heel and sprinted back down the hillside.

"So, about that boat?" Orestes asked, lying back down on the blanket. "How do you feel about swimming to shore when we have finished fishing? I think I might need to stay out a little longer than I originally planned."

He had expected a chuckle, or at least a smile at this quip. Instead, the remark was met with silence, and when he turned to Pylades, he saw that he was standing with a look of worry etched on his face.

"What is it?" he asked.

Slowly, Pylades kneeled back down on the blanket.

"She is right about this," he said. "About what you have to do."

Orestes stiffened. "You cannot be serious? This is Electra. All she wants is vengeance. Vengeance for a man she barely even knew and for whom no one ever had a kind word to say."

"I know that."

"And you agreed that to kill my mother would be wrong, that it was right for me to stay here."

"I agreed back then, but things have changed this last year."

"What things?"

Pylades ran his tongue across his lips as Orestes's question hung in the air between them. The two young men shared everything. Or at least Orestes had thought they did. However, the way his lover's eyes refused to meet his and the way his fingers knotted around his belt told him there was something he was not saying.

"There has been talk," he said. "About Mycenae."

"What about it?"

Pylades lifted his eyes up to the sky, as if asking the gods for strength. It was not an action Orestes was used to seeing in his cousin.

"The news of your meeting with the Pythia has spread. People know what Apollo demanded of you, and they know that you are refusing to do it."

"How could anybody know that for certain?"

"A priestess with a loose tongue, perhaps? A serpent with a keen ear? What does it matter? They know—or at least they believe—that you were told to avenge your father, and they know that it has not been done. You are regarded as a weak prince."

Orestes snorted. "And since when have I cared about rumors? You, of all people, should know they do not bother me in the slightest. Let me be a weak prince. I will be the weakest prince, if they like, for I do not care to be one at all."

"But this is not just about you, Orestes. It is about the entire kingdom. And about your mother."

"Why must she play any part in this? I have told you a thousand times, I will not harm her."

Pylades took his hands.

"You think you are doing her a favor by your refusal; I understand that. But without the true heir on the throne, people will see Mycenae as vulnerable, and they will invade. They will attack and they will seek to conquer all. Do you think invaders would be as merciful to her as you would be in ending her life?"

"We are not talking about this." He attempted to pull his hands free, but Pylades held them fast.

"You cannot avoid this any longer, Orestes," he insisted.

"Fine. So I will simply return to Mycenae and take the throne with my mother at my side."

"And openly defy Apollo? How do you think that will end? Others will still invade, and with the blessing of the gods, they will slay the weak King Orestes and his murderous mother."

Orestes looked up at Pylades imploringly. "I cannot do it."

"Yes, you can. Think of it as a mercy. You have heard the stories of Troy, the tales of what those men did to the women they captured, be they peasant, priestess, or princess. They all suffered the same fate."

"Stop this, Pylades. These are low blows."

"It is the truth, Orestes, one we have been refusing to face. I am sorry. I am truly distressed that you have been forced into this. Please, please believe me when I say if there was any other way, I would tell you to take it. I love you. You know that. And I only want what is best for you."

"You cannot believe that would be it," he replied as a stray tear ran down his cheek. Pylades brushed it away with his thumb.

"I do. With all my heart."

"She does not deserve this. She does not deserve to die."

"No, but she deserves the alternative even less. They would make a trophy of her. You know I speak the truth. And that would be even harder for you to live with."

An intense pain throbbed in his chest. If this was right, that Mycenae was viewed as weak, then the inevitable would follow.

"You swear this is a fact?" He looked Pylades in the eyes and did not need to hear the answer. He knew it from the tears now running down his face, the exact mirror of his own.

"I will be there at your side," he replied. "But it is time, my darling. It is time you obeyed Apollo's command. We must sail to Mycenae."

THIRTY-TWO

T HE SKY WAS GRAY AND THE WIND SWIRLED ABOUT THEM AS the merchant ship left port. A month had passed since Orestes and Pylades had discussed the trouble facing Mycenae if Orestes did not carry out Apollo's decree. A month of further arguments and recriminations, of tears and apologies. But, no matter how he fought both his sister and his friend, he knew in his heart of hearts that they were right. He had seen how slaves were treated, how their lives were usually valued less than that of an animal. If he did not act, the same fate could be awaiting his mother.

Orestes looked out to sea. He had brought Electra's dagger with him, given to her years ago by their mother. It felt like adding insult to injury, using her gift to do the deed, but Electra had insisted, and given his refusal to let her join them, it seemed only fair. Besides, its small size made it easy to conceal.

With nothing left to say, he continued to stare silently out at the horizon. He had no further protests to offer. He had given it his all. Now, all he could do was wait. Electra had wanted him to go back to the Pythia, to seek her further guidance, in case his memory of what she had said all those years ago had faded. It showed just how little she knew him. The words of the woman remained as freshly seared into his mind as if he had seen her only the previous day. He knew what he must do.

He had been told that they were to dress as messengers, in order to infiltrate the palace. They should conceal their weapons beneath their cloaks, and when his mother arrived to hear what they had to say, he should kill her. So simple, so straightforward. Kill her, break his own heart, and then continue with his life as though nothing had happened.

"Have you thought yet about what you will do with Aegisthus?" Pylades asked as Mount Parnassus faded in the distance.

It was a question that didn't need asking. Of course he had thought about him. He had thought about them all. His only wish was to fulfill his destiny, with as little bloodshed as possible.

"He can do as he wishes. It is his home. My brother too."

Pylades looked disturbed at the response.

"What? The Pythia did not mention Aegisthus, just my mother. She is the only one who needs to die."

"She may not have mentioned him, but that does not mean it would be wise to let him live. He has people in Mycenae who are loyal to him. They are his subjects now. Then there is the army. My father has been told that many of them think he is the greatest king ever to have ruled there."

Orestes turned away from the sea to face his lover. "Why do we even need to speak of this?"

"Because I am afraid that you do not see that it will not be as simple as just killing your mother. If you do not kill Aegisthus too, he could rise up against you."

"He would not do that. I know him."

"You *knew* him. A long time has passed, and he has become a king. He has had a taste of real power."

"He is not interested in that. He has never wanted it."

"You do not know this for sure. He is father to a son now. Perhaps he has ambitions for Aletes to be king one day. Perhaps he even thinks he is more deserving of the title, that you have abandoned your claim to the throne for so many years, that you are no longer worthy of it."

"No, that is not who he is. He is the best of us. He will understand this burden I have been carrying more than any."

"So, you will have him bend the knee and pledge loyalty to you?"

Orestes opened his mouth before shaking his head and crossing to the other side of the deck. This was too much detail. What he needed was peace and quiet. But Pylades followed him, his tenacity now rivaling that of Electra, it seemed.

"I do not mean to keep pushing you on this, but think about it. Aegisthus must bend the knee and proclaim you the true king. Or you must kill him."

"That is not an option. That has never been one."

"All right, then; pledging his loyalty to you it has to be."

A moment passed. A small flock of seabirds was circling above the ship, probably hoping it was a fishing vessel and waiting for the crew to haul up the nets so they could take their fill. He wanted to tell them that they would need to find another ship to follow, either that or be content to starve, waiting for a feast that would never arrive.

"Come, we should go below deck," Pylades said, abandoning his argument. "These clouds are growing blacker by the minute."

"You go. I will follow shortly."

With a single nod, Pylades squeezed his shoulder and disappeared, leaving the prince alone with the cry of the gulls.

Orestes stood there at the rail, staring at the almost monochromatic swirl of sea and sky. Rain spattered on his arms and clothes, but he did not notice it. Even when the wind picked up, battering the sails and whipping at the ropes, he remained, his focus on a future he did not wish to face. Only when the captain finally yelled at him to get below deck did he retreat to his cabin, where all he could do was sit and wait for the inevitable.

The storm was a violent mix of wind and rain, with waves crashing against their ship time and again, sending shudders through the timbers. The bolts of lightning were so bright, they caused the joints in the woodwork to glow a burned umber. But Orestes knew that he was safe. Zeus was watching over him. The Father of the Gods would ensure he survived to play his part.

When dawn broke, the rain had stopped and the wind had dropped, but there was now a thick fog concealing the rest of the world from those on deck. As such, it was a surprise when the lookout called that he had spotted land and Orestes realized that Mycenae was close at hand. Something deep and visceral stirred inside him, like a homing pigeon nearing journey's end.

As the merchants watched their wares being unloaded, he hung back.

"We need to head straight there," Pylades said. "The ship is not staying here. We must disembark. Someone might see us dressed as messengers from Phocis, and if news of our appearance reaches the palace before we do, they may grow suspicious and send out guards to investigate."

"Phocis has sent plenty of messengers to Mycenae since I left."

"I am aware of that, but we have not been here to see how the palace receives them, what extra precautions they put in place. We need to be smart, Orestes. And smart means fast. I will fetch us horses; then we will ride there immediately. If we hurry, we can be there before dusk."

As it was so far north of the citadel, he had never spent much time in this bustling port; it was hardly a fitting place for a prince, particularly one with a mother as anxious as his had been for his safety. Now, he wished he'd had the chance. So much must have changed in his homeland, he thought. Yet, as they began their trek to the citadel, it seemed as if he had never left: the lime trees, full to bursting with fruit, still draped over the roads; the rocky earth, almost red in places, yet as pale as moonlight in others; the olive trees, with their white-painted trunks. It was so different here from in Phocis. The sky seemed a paler blue, the grass a deeper shade of green.

As the afternoon sun was beginning to wane, the walls of the citadel came into view.

"Are you ready?" Pylades asked. "Remember, I will do the talking. It is better that you do not speak, in case someone recognizes your voice."

He nodded, silently dreading what was to come. In a last-ditch attempt to make Pylades reconsider the plan, he burst out: "Maybe I should talk to her first. If I could just explain."

"You think it would be easier for her that way? Of course it would not. No discussion. No deliberation. Just as we practiced in Phocis."

Practiced on goats, he thought to himself with a shudder. Was that really all his mother was to them now—another creature to be slaughtered?

In silence they took the curving path up between the walls toward the Lion Gate, where, upon their arrival, two guards stepped forward.

"What is your business here?" one demanded.

Orestes felt the blood rushing from his head.

"We have news for Queen Clytemnestra." Pylades spoke without a hint of hesitation. "News about her son, from King Strophius." He handed over a scroll with his father's seal, which the guard checked before handing it back.

"He will take you to the palace," he said, indicating the other. "You can wait for the queen there."

"Will she be able to see us soon?" Orestes asked, forgetting his instruction to stay silent.

"How would I know?" The soldier's eyes narrowed.

He dropped his head in response. The guard could not be any older than him, so the chance of being recognized was slim, yet a knot tightened in his gut as they were led up into the citadel and toward the palace.

In spite of the dread that filled him, there were so many familiar sights that he found his heart leaping, details he wished he could share with Pylades. The tree from which he had fallen and broken his arm when he had been trying to inspect a bird's nest. The stone seat where his mother had read to him in the evenings. But he walked silently, his heart pounding. Was this truly what the gods had destined for him?

When they reached the tall stone pillars, the guard stopped.

"I will tell the queen of your arrival. Wait here."

There was no offer of a seat, nor even a cup of water, and he wondered if his mother knew how her men treated messengers. It was not the way he had seen her act toward them in the past. But, as Pylades kept reminding him, the past was long ago. Maybe things had changed more than he had wanted to believe.

"Where will she be?" Pylades hissed in his ear, breaking his train of thought.

"Why? He told us to wait here for her."

"We are here to kill her, Orestes, not take wine and reminisce. If she comes to meet you, this will all be far bloodier than either of us wants. Now, quickly, think. Where would she be?"

It did not take much thought to figure out her probable location. He doubted anything would have changed her routine. He opened his mouth to say as much, when a flurry of footsteps drew his attention. Turning his head, he gasped.

"Laodamia."

He would have sworn that he had only said the name in his head, but the old woman's eyes instantly turned to him. He blinked, for a moment second-guessing himself, but no, he was right. His old nursemaid was standing just a few feet away from him. Had she always been so frail? he wondered. No, of course she hadn't. She had merely aged, like they all had. But the fearless woman of his memory, who had tended his every cut and bruise, who had helped them flee the palace and escape that awful night eight years ago, was a far cry from the old lady in front of him. The one who was now staring directly at him.

"Orestes," Pylades demanded. "Where will she be?"

He could not move, his eyes still fixed on Laodamia. She would scream out, he was certain, to alert the guards. But instead she pressed her hand to her heart and disappeared back into the palace.

With her apparent blessing came a strange feeling of peace. As if someone else were speaking through him, he turned to Pylades and calmly said, "She will be out on the veranda."

THIRTY-THREE

LONG SHADOWS WERE PLENTIFUL AMONG THE OPEN colonnades of the palace, and they stuck to them as best they could. Slipping past the kitchen and the stairs down to the storeroom where, so very long ago, he had hidden from Electra, they crossed the wide space of the interior, avoiding the columned porches and keeping low. Orestes's head swam. This was surreal. Surely someone would intervene; something would happen to stop them. Maybe the test was simply to come this far. Perhaps showing he was willing to obey Apollo's command would be enough. *Please*, he prayed over and over, *please let there be another way*. When he stepped out onto the veranda and saw her silhouette, he knew there was none.

She was facing away from them, staring out at the setting sun, as she liked to do. He did not need to see her face to know that this was the woman who had birthed him.

"That is her?" Pylades whispered.

He did not even have the strength to nod. He could not take his eyes from her—the familiar slant of her shoulders and the way her back arched ever so slightly as she stood in silence. There was no one else it could be. Her hair was now streaked with gray, although in the fading light it could have been strands of pure silver woven there.

Pylades pushed the knife into his hand.

"Now," he mouthed. "Do it now."

He remained rooted to the spot. How could he do this to her here? This was her peaceful place, her sanctuary. If only it could be somewhere else. Yet, perhaps this was a blessing. She would depart this life gazing out at her kingdom, at the view she loved so much.

His hand was trembling so badly, he feared he might drop the dagger. A feeling of nausea was rising fast and threatening to overwhelm him. Whatever his mother was watching, she was so focused that he knew she had no inkling he was there.

He was only a footstep away, when the sudden smell of her perfume on the night air almost unmanned him and filled his eyes with tears. Closing them, he lifted the knife and reached forward, in a movement so automatic his body needed no instruction. In one motion, his left hand clamped over her mouth and pulled her to him, exposing her neck, and his right hand dragged the dagger sharply across her throat.

It was blood, the likes of which he had never seen before. Deeper in color than the darkest poppy, it sprayed upward and outward, covering his arms. His mother's head barely turned, yet it was enough for him to glimpse the horror in her eyes.

Then the screaming began.

As her body slumped to the floor, a small figure appeared beyond her. Little higher than Orestes's waist, he had been standing right in front of her, his back to the balustrade.

That was why she had been so absorbed, so focused. She had been watching the boy.

"Oh gods!" He stepped back in horror as the child, his face splattered with his mother's blood and his eyes wide in terror, screamed again and again and again.

"Pylades! Pylades!" The shock had hijacked his entire body. "What do we do now? What do we do? They will hear. You said they were not meant to know we were in the palace until we reached the throne room."

"Give me that," Pylades yelled, racing forward and snatching the dagger from his limp hand.

"No!" he screamed, realizing what his lover intended. He lunged, but his body was too weak and shaken to reach his brother in time, and the knife struck home, deep in his heart.

The boy's screams turned to a gurgle, as his lungs filled and he toppled forward, his blood now mingling with his mother's on the tiled floor.

"No! No!" Orestes kneeled, torn between the body of the mother who had lived to protect him and the brother he should have saved. "Why? Why?"

"It was the only way, Orestes."

"What have we done? This was not meant to be! This was not supposed to happen!"

"Orestes, please." Pylades tugged at his robe, attempting to drag him away, but the prince would not be moved. "The guards will be on their way. You must stake your claim immediately. You must announce yourself the true King of Mycenae, before Aegisthus has time to discover what has happened here."

But to Orestes's ears the words seemed muffled, as though he were underwater, drowning.

"Please, Orestes, we cannot be found like this!"

His mind gradually started to clear, and he allowed himself to be pulled to his feet. He would follow their plan and head to the throne room, to declare himself king. But as the two men moved toward the doorway through which they had arrived, they saw that the route was no longer clear. A single person stood in their way.

"Aegisthus."

THIRTY-FOUR

E LOOKED EVERY BIT A KING, STATELY AND PROUD AND better dressed than Orestes had ever seen him before, in purple robes embroidered with gold stitching. His eyes widened at the sight of the prince, a smile starting to form on his lips, only for his face to twist in disbelief as his gaze took in his stepson's blood-soaked hands.

"No, you did not. You could not have."

Orestes stepped back.

"I did not have a choice, Aegisthus. The gods made me,"

"No, she promised me she would be safe. That you could never harm her."

"Please, Aegisthus. I need you to understand…"

The old man snarled as he stepped toward him.

"It was the will of the gods," Pylades said, grabbing him by the shoulders. "Orestes avenged his father as they demand. You must serve him now as your rightful king or leave. The choice is up to you."

But Orestes could see that Aegisthus was not listening. His eyes had moved beyond the two men, further even than the body of his dead wife.

"Nooo!" His scream was so terrible that it seemed to shake the very marble they stood on. "No! Not Aletes! No, no, no!"

Pushing past them, he dropped to the ground and scooped up his son. The child's small body flopped in his arms like a dead lamb.

"Aletes," Aegisthus whispered, pressing his lips against the boy's forehead. "Aletes. Aletes. My darling son." Pulling out the blade and flinging it away in disgust, he crushed the child to his chest.

"Come away," Pylades whispered in Orestes's ear. "Leave them be."

But he could not go. This was his wrongdoing, his mistake that needed to be put right.

"I…I am sorry," he stammered.

Aegisthus's head swiveled toward him, the pain in his eyes replaced by fury.

"You killed him," he said, gently lowering his son back to the ground before standing. "You killed my son."

"I did not mean to. I did not intend this. I did not want to kill anyone, Aegisthus. You know this of me."

"It was me," Pylades said, stepping between them. "I did not know who the child was. Please, it was me. This was not Orestes's doing."

But Aegisthus paid him no heed.

"My boy. My darling boy." His eyes fixed on Orestes. "This is your doing!"

"I know it is. Please, please forgive me."

Aegisthus's eyes glinted, no trace of humanity left in them. All that remained was pure hatred.

"Forgive you?" he spat.

"I did not want to come here."

"Then why did you?" he demanded.

"The gods…it was the gods…"

"You think a god's punishment is worse than this? You think that you will ever find peace now?"

"No…no…I…"

"Your mother trusted you. *I* trusted you." Aegisthus was moving toward him and he could see no way out. "He was a child, Orestes. A little boy. Your brother. I told him about you. I told him of all the time we had spent together, studying birds and animals. He knew your name and he wanted to be just like you. He wanted you to be a real brother to him."

Tears blurred his vision. "I am sorry. I am so sorry."

"Please, take vengeance on me. It is I who killed your son." Pylades touched Aegisthus's arm, but the old man flicked him away like an annoying insect. Never before had Orestes seen him raise a hand, not even to an animal, but at that moment he was reminded that this was a man who had slain a king. There was a warrior within him. One who now wanted his own retribution.

"You are no different from your father. You are no better than Agamemnon."

These words cut more deeply than any knife could have.

"I did not mean for this to happen. I only wanted peace."

"Peace? Through death? All you have brought is pain. Only pain."

"Aegisthus…"

"Stop speaking to me as if you know me. I have never seen you before in my life."

Orestes struggled to keep his body upright as the old man's breath blew hot in his face.

"I have never pretended to be king here in Mycenae, but, as the gods are my witness, I will not let a ruthless child killer take the throne I was protecting for a righteous man. A man who no longer exists."

"I am sorry. I am sorry." Orestes dropped to his knees.

"Get up! Get up so I can kill you like the murderer you are."

"Please!" He didn't really know what he was begging for—for Aegisthus to spare his life or to end it. Both and neither. Orestes only knew that he could not live like this, with a pain that felt like claws ripping out his ribs one by one.

Aegisthus hoisted him up by the neck of his robe and slammed him against the wall.

"She trusted you," he said, landing a blow square on his jaw. Blood filled the younger man's mouth. "*I* trusted you." Aegisthus hit him again, and then again, Orestes not even lifting an arm to block the attack.

Pylades was back on his feet, trying to pull the older man off his friend. Dropping Orestes to the floor, Aegisthus turned and grabbed the prince and flung him into the wall. Pylades struck it hard and crumpled to the ground, just like his cousin. Aegisthus turned his attention back to the source of his anger. The blood that had filled Orestes's mouth was now dripping from his chin.

"Orestes! Orestes!"

He glanced across to where his lover lay. Pylades was pointing to the dagger, now barely a foot from Orestes's hand. It was clear that Aegisthus had forgotten the blade. If he hadn't, he would surely have already plunged it into Orestes's heart. Aegisthus aimed a brutal kick at his ribs.

"Please, Orestes," Pylades wept. "Do this for me. Please! I cannot live without you."

This time, when Orestes turned toward his lover, it was to say goodbye. To try to tell him with a look that he was sorry for failing him. Sorry for what he had done, bringing him into this. But when he saw the tears shimmering in Pylades's eyes, his heart tore in a new way and he understood. Aegisthus was a broken old man now. He would always be crippled by the loss of his loved ones and consumed with hate. There would be no real life for him anymore. At that same moment, Orestes knew that if he let himself be killed, Pylades would spend the rest of his days hell-bent on revenge. If he even got the chance. Who was to say that once Aegisthus was done with him, he would not move on to Pylades?

And so, with every last ounce of strength he had left, he reached for the blade and drove it up into Aegisthus's stomach.

PART III

THIRTY-FIVE

H E COULD NOT RECALL WHAT HAPPENED IN THOSE FIRST FEW days after his mother's death. He had taken the crown; he knew that much from the way he was guided to the throne room and placed in what had been his father's seat. Pylades spoke for him and accepted the gifts, blessings, and good wishes, which Orestes wanted to hurl back at those who brought them. Their smiling faces made his stomach turn. They knew the truth: he deserved none of it.

Then a ship arrived, and Electra returned to the palace. She greeted him with a warmth he had not experienced from her since before they had fled Mycenae all those years ago. She wrapped her arms around him and told him he was strong and worthy, that she had known all along he would do his duty, and the gods would be so proud of him.

Would they? he wondered. Would they really be proud of a man who had slain the very people who had raised him, all for a title he could have simply asked for, had he desired it so much? If the gods were proud of a person like that, he was not sure he wanted to please them anymore.

He felt like a pariah in his own home. At the same time, he knew how his mother must have felt after Iphigenia had died, unable to even walk the corridors for the memories they held. His childhood chamber, the central courtyard, where he and his sisters had played from dawn until dusk, the kitchen, the gardens were all places he could not visit, for fear of his mother's face appearing to him. Lifeless. Murdered. Mostly, he hid away in his father's old chamber, not because he was the king now but because it was somewhere he had spent no time as a child. There were no ghosts to haunt him there.

While the rest of the inhabitants of the palace went about their duties, he often kept to his bed, although he found no peace in sleep. His dreams were filled with blood and screams as Aletes begged for his life. Whenever he woke, he'd find Pylades sitting there beside him, ready to offer him water or food, which he rarely accepted.

"I killed them" were always the first words out of his mouth. Most of the time, Pylades hushed him, gently stroking his hair, until he fell back into another fitful slumber. But occasionally, he would argue with him.

"You have done nothing wrong. You only did as the gods instructed."

"But the boy. The little boy. My own brother."

"*I* killed him, Orestes, not you. If anyone is to be punished for his murder, it is I. And Aegisthus was a matter of self-defense."

"Aegisthus. He raised me as his own."

"The same way your grandfather raised him as a son, not knowing him to be his nephew. And what did Aegisthus do to repay Atreus? He killed him and took the throne for his father without a second thought, Orestes. He killed your grandfather, and from the rumors I have heard, he persuaded your mother to kill your father, too."

He shook his head, causing a throbbing to start up behind his temples.

"I do not believe that. You know I do not."

"You have committed no crime against the gods in carrying out these acts, Orestes, which is the important thing. You do not need to let this weigh on your mind."

With sweat beading down his spine, he rolled over on the bed and left Pylades standing there in silence, watching him. It wasn't about the gods, Orestes wanted to say. What did crimes against the gods matter? They had not raised him. They were not here with him now. It was about crimes against his family. The family he had failed.

"Come outside into the citadel," Electra tried, time and time again. "This is your kingdom now. You need to show your face."

"Maybe tomorrow," he would reply, and they both knew it to be a lie. Here, confined to the four walls of his father's chamber, he could do no more harm. Let Electra run the kingdom. She had always wanted to. Or Pylades. He didn't care. He had done his part, and they had no right to ask any more of him.

Only when a month had passed was he finally spurred into action, for fear of yet another loss.

"My father has come to visit," Pylades said, whipping back the chamber curtains and flooding the room with light. Motes of dust danced in the stale air. "You will need to meet with him, to show your respects. He did house you for eight years, after all."

Groaning, Orestes shielded his eyes. "Let Electra speak to him," he replied. "He always liked her much better than me, anyway."

"Electra is occupied. Besides, she is not the King of Mycenae. You are. And I have told him you will greet him in the throne room."

"Then I abdicate all my rights to you. You talk to him."

How someone could sleep so much and yet feel so exhausted

they could barely keep their eyes open was a mystery to him. He had never felt such a heaviness in his body. It resisted any attempt to lift his head from the pillow.

"You are not abdicating to anyone," Pylades said, pulling back the sheets. "And certainly not to me."

"Then make other arrangements. Say I am sick."

He waited for the usual sound of Pylades's retreating footsteps, but instead there came a heavy sigh. "If that is the case and you will not meet with my father, then when he leaves, I shall go with him. I will return to Phocis. For good."

It took a few moments for the fog to clear and Pylades's words to hit home.

"Fine," he said at last. "If that is what you want, then go. I will not stop you."

"That is not what I want! You know it is not!" Pylades shouted at him. "What do I have to say to get through to you? I want to be by your side. To help you. But how do I do that, Orestes? How do I help you?"

Even this outburst didn't work. He simply reached down for the sheets and pulled them back around his shoulders. Maybe he was ill, he thought, for he felt as cold as if winter had arrived early.

"I do not deserve your help," he whispered.

"Yes, you do, Orestes! I love you with all my heart, but I cannot just stand by and see you like this. I do not know how to reach you, how to pull you back. And I am a coward, I know that, but I cannot spend my days watching you fade away before my very eyes. I have taken all I can."

A lump had formed in Orestes's throat at this heartfelt statement. He turned over, still unable to look at Pylades as he spoke.

"I am so—"

"No! Not another word! I won't hear any more, Orestes. If you are that sorry for the pain you have caused, then make changes. Help people. Help those in your kingdom who come to your palace each day seeking your counsel."

"I do not know how to counsel."

"Then learn!"

Pylades was raging in a way Orestes had never known his lover to do before. And it frightened him.

"I would have stayed by your side for anything, Orestes," he continued. "I would have stayed by your side if you had committed a thousand murders. But not for this. I will not watch this any longer." He stopped and dropped his head into his hands. When he looked back up, there was nothing but despair in his eyes. "I do not think it is wise that I am here anymore. In fact, I think I make matters worse. I think you do actually blame me."

"What? Why would you say that?" For the first time in days, Orestes scrambled up. "That is not true. You know it is not."

"Really? Somewhere, deep in the recesses of your mind, I think you do. The gods know I blame myself enough. If I had not killed the child. If I had just covered his mouth to stifle his cries, then you would not have been forced to kill Aegisthus."

With his eyes now filled with tears, Orestes shook his head.

"That is not true, Pylades. You were helping me, I know that. I know you have only ever tried to help me."

"But I failed. And I cannot stand it any longer."

Orestes was unsure whether he had walked into a trap or been backed into a corner; perhaps it was both, or neither. But he knew that were Pylades to leave on that ship with his father, then the darkness that threatened to consume him would quickly complete its work.

"I will come. I will come with you to see your father," he whispered.

Pylades's posture shifted. "And you will sit in the throne room and listen to your subjects? You will accept their homage as their king?"

Just the thought of this and his chest tightened. He swallowed hard and replied, "If you will stay."

"I will stay, as long as you are trying to live your life as the gods intended," he replied.

The gods. The very sound of the words caused bile to rise in his throat. But he knew he had no choice.

"Then someone had better run me a bath," he said. "For I am in no fit state to greet anyone."

From the layer of grime that floated on the surface, he dreaded to think how long it had been since he had last washed himself. His body felt angular, his ribs more prominent as he lay there. He could see that there was not a scrap of spare flesh left on him. Drawing in the heat of the water, he closed his eyes momentarily and let the aroma of the sweet oils relax him. This was helping, he thought.

"*Murderer!*"

His eyes pinged open and water rushed from his body as he sprang up.

"Who is there?" he demanded, his eyes scanning the room. This bathroom was the one he had used as a child, large and open, with nowhere for a person to hide. No screens or recesses. But the voice had been so clear, as if it had been only an arm's length away from him. His heart pounded.

"There is no one there," he said out loud, as if to reassure himself.

Picking up the soap, he sat down again and began to work at the dirt on his knees.

"*You murdered her!*"

This time he leaped from the tub, leaving a trail of water as he darted to the window. There was a sheer drop there—nowhere a person could hide, unless risking life and limb balancing on one of the ledges. Just how far would someone go to taunt him?

"Who is it? Who is there?" he yelled. "I heard you. There are guards here. Guards everywhere. Who is it?"

His questions were lost on the breeze.

"Your Highness, are you quite well?"

The naked king spun around and found himself facing his aged nursemaid. Still dripping wet, he rushed to take her hand.

"Laodamia, did you hear that?"

"Hear what, my king?"

"Someone talking. Someone accusing me."

"Come now. King Strophius is here. Do not worry; we have still got plenty of time to get you ready."

"He was here? Outside this room?"

Laodamia frowned. "No, my king, he awaits your presence in the throne room. Let me dry you." The old woman threw a towel around his shoulders and started to pat him, as if he were still a child. "Now, we need to find you something to wear," she said, leading him gently out.

As he reached the doorway, he glanced behind him to check that the room was indeed empty, then turned back to follow his servant. One step later and the voice came again, now joined by others.

"*We know who you are!*"

"*We know what you did!*"

"*And you will pay!*"

THIRTY-SIX

H E DID NOT DRINK THE WINE, MERELY GRIPPED THE CUP. That was until he saw that the liquid was splashing over onto his hand. They mustn't see him shaking, he realized and put it down at his side. Rumors of a show of weakness like that could have them plotting his downfall before the night was over. Not that there weren't already plenty.

The throne room was far busier than he had expected. The stone steps were crowded as men gathered for a view of their king. Electra had greeted Strophius upon his arrival and now moved to take the seat beside her brother's throne. Her expression was as stony as always. Orestes had expected more of her on this occasion. Most likely, she had been expecting more of him, too. Maybe they all were.

"We have come to offer you our congratulations," King Strophius announced. "You have done what many men would have struggled to achieve, and you have pleased the gods too."

He felt sick yet forced a smile. "I was guided by the words of Apollo himself," he said.

"You think too little of yourself," Strophius replied. "You always have, since you were that young boy who landed on my shores all those years ago. Be proud of who you have become. And if you do not mind, I would like to claim responsibility for teaching you a few things myself. After all, I think I can consider myself a father figure to you, can I not?"

"I like to think that too," Orestes replied diplomatically.

"*As much as Aegisthus was?*" someone called from the back of the room. "*You thought of him as a father, did you not? And yet you murdered him!*"

"*After you murdered your mother!*"

Orestes leaped to his feet, peering over the sea of heads in front of him. "Who said that?" he demanded.

Looks of concern were exchanged.

"Who said what?" Electra hissed. "Only the king has spoken."

"I...I heard."

He stared at those assembled there. Every pair of eyes that met his showed nothing but concern or confusion, he thought. But the voices. Could something so clear have only been in his head?

"I'm sorry. I must have been mistaken," he said, lowering himself back down onto the throne. He plucked the cup of wine from the table beside him, not caring now if his hands shook, as he brought the drink to his lips and downed it in one go. He did not recall the last time he'd drunk even water, let alone taken any food. Perhaps this was the cause of the hallucinations.

"We were hoping we could discuss the matter of land with you," Strophius said somewhat cautiously.

"Land?"

"Yes. After the Battle of Troy, your father made many promises to those around him—gifts that he would bestow on his allies and his subjects and their families too, in light of his historic victory.

Agamemnon was a great leader. An inspirational man. And very generous too."

Vicious and proud, Orestes thought to himself. Perhaps others found that inspiring. First the comment about him being like a son, now this. It may have been his first time seated on the throne, but he had been in this room often enough to know when a man was making a play for something he probably did not deserve.

"I know nothing of such things."

"They were made, I can assure you. Many can testify to it."

"Many who, I assume, would also gain from this supposed generosity?"

He surprised himself with the way he spoke. Strong and commanding. Pylades had been right. People had seen him as weak, and even those who had known him before, who had helped him, would be ready to test him.

"Just because they stand to benefit does not make their word unreliable."

"No, but less believable. Now, is there anything else you want, or are you simply here to waste my time and test *my* generosity?"

A hush fell on the chamber. Orestes shoved his hands down the sides of his chair to keep them from shaking. Maybe he had misjudged it. Perhaps Agamemnon truly had made such deals, and the men had waited nearly a decade for someone to fulfill the dead king's promises. As those present looked from one king to the other, a small smile appeared on Strophius's face.

"I guess I taught you well Orestes," he said, breaking the tension. A ripple of nervous laughter passed through the assembly. "And you are not the reluctant leader they said you were."

"No, he is a king!" a woman called out.

Beside him Electra smiled, and a flicker of warmth ran through him.

"*He is the King!*" came another voice. "*And he learned everything he knows from his mother. His mother, whom he murdered, to gain the throne. Is that not right, Orestes? Did you not butcher her, just so you could sit there?*"

The wine table crashed to the floor as he leaped to his feet again, his eyes trained on the doorway from where the voice seemed to have come. But, no sooner had he risen than another voice came from the other side of the room, from the top of the steps.

"*Tell me, did the color red suit her? You remember—as she lay in her own blood.*"

"What are you doing? Why are you saying these things to me?" He collapsed back down onto the throne. "Why? Why?" He could barely breathe, let alone speak.

"What is wrong?" Pylades was at his side. "Are you hurt? Is it poison?" He looked at the wine jug lying on the floor, but Electra shook her head.

"I drank it myself."

"Then what?"

Those nearest the throne were edging away while those at the back were craning their necks for a better view. In the turmoil, people were being jostled and started to shout at each other. But above it all, the voices continued.

"*You are a murderer!*"

"*A child killer!*"

"*Evil!*"

"What is it? What is wrong?" Pylades asked again as Orestes covered his ears.

"Do you not hear them? Stop them!"

"Stop who?"

"*Oh, do you mean us?*" Laughter filled the air.

As his eyes darted around the room, he suddenly saw her standing there, in the midst of all the mayhem, calm and proud, yet hideous. She was as white as the marble columns, but her eyes were darker than obsidian. It was as though every ray of light that fell on her was absorbed by her scaly skin. She was not human. Her mouth alone, with its rows of pointed teeth, was enough to tell him that, as was the glow of red flames that seemed to engulf her. It was as if the woman herself were part of an eternal fire.

"Orestes! Orestes! What is going on? You cannot behave like this, brother. What are you doing?" Electra reached for him.

But he could not respond. He could not take his eyes from the apparition as her forked tongue flickered in the firelight when she addressed him again.

"*So, you have the crown,*" she hissed. "*All you have to do now is stay alive long enough to make use of it.*"

THIRTY-SEVEN

L AODAMIA CHANGED THE COLD COMPRESS ON HIS HEAD.

"There is no fever. What you are doing is pointless," Pylades said.

"If it was poison, the cold may draw it away from his brain," Laodamia replied.

"It started the night my father arrived. It must have been administered then," Pylades suggested.

"What nonsense." Electra spoke now. "How could it have been poison, when he hadn't eaten anything and we drank the same wine? And we have given him every remedy that we know, besides. What poison causes a man to weep like this? Two weeks this has been going on. Two weeks. And he lay in the temple for three whole days. That should have remedied any ailment. This is something else. It has to be."

"Then what can be wrong with him?"

"Please, you both need to be calm. He needs quiet."

He knew they were speaking about him, fussing over him like a child, but he kept his hands over his ears to block them all out.

Rocking back and forth helped him concentrate on other things, like types of fish or species of insect. Talking out loud helped drown the voices too, if only by a fraction. Waterbirds. That would keep him focused for a while. Different water fowl. That would stop the malign spirits from making themselves heard.

"Brant, gadwall, common eider." He recited the names, louder and louder, although his was not the only voice that increased in volume, for he and his extended family were not the only ones in the room.

"*He doesn't really believe that he can silence us, does he?*" one of the demons asked. She was sitting on the end of his bed, just a few feet away. With darker skin and yellow eyes, she had that same forked tongue as the first one he had seen, the same sharp teeth, that same rabid look. Her legs were outstretched, and one foot was only inches from where Electra was wringing her hands. But his sister was oblivious to it.

"*I think he realizes by now that he cannot block us out, do you not, Orestes? You know we are not something you can ignore.*"

"*We are something you deserve.*"

"You are monsters!" he screamed at them, although his outburst only caused them to laugh even harder.

"*Us, you say? You think we are the monsters?*"

"*We did not kill our own mother. We could never do such a thing.*"

"*Tell us, Orestes, how did it feel, when the knife sliced through her flesh?*"

"Brant, eider, smew…" His words came out breathy and weak, but he kept going.

"*Was it how you dreamed it would be? To not even look her in the eyes. To not even allow her the chance to say goodbye to her beloved baby boy.*"

"Cormorant, carbo…"

"But you made sure they were reunited, did you not, Orestes? You made sure the whole happy little family would be together again. How does it feel to have so much blood on your hands?"

"Stop it!" He flung his arms out, knocking into Laodamia and causing the basin to fly from her hand. The old woman gasped in shock.

"I…I… Sorry, sorry." Orestes scrambled to the floor, attempting to mop up the water with his robe.

"Oh, he apologizes for that, does he? I did not think he apologized for hitting old women."

"We thought he killed them."

"Especially ones who raised him."

"Ones who loved him."

"Ones who kept him safe from all the demons that slept beneath his bed at night."

"Leave me alone!"

He slammed his head into the mattress, snatching up the pillow and wrapping it around his ears.

"We need to take him somewhere. He needs help." Laodamia's voice now. "I fear we cannot save him here."

"Where *can* we take him?" Electra asked. "He is raving like a lunatic. We may have been able to pass off the first episode as stress, but this has been going on for almost half a moon. If he does not recover soon, the entire kingdom will know they have a madman at the helm. Where will that leave us then?"

It was hard to deny his insanity, given that she had found him the day before cowering behind sacks of flour in the pantry beneath the kitchen. But the fiends knew this hiding place. They knew them all.

"To be fair, many kingdoms have had mad kings, but that is not the point." Pylades had taken Laodamia's position by the bedside and was stroking his hair. "If this torment is not from poison or sickness, then it cannot be of mortal origin."

The two women stiffened.

"Then what do you believe it is?" Electra asked. "And why? Why would the gods wish to hurt Orestes? He did exactly what was asked of him."

"I do not know why anyone would curse a man this way. One so good as him. He did Apollo's bidding, even though it broke his heart."

"So, what are you saying?" she asked. "I have no time for riddles, and neither, do I fear, has my brother."

Pylades nodded, lowering his hand to Orestes's back.

"I think we must go to the gods for the answer," he said. "The temple sleep did nothing to improve his condition. I think we must take him back to Delphi. Back to see the Pythia."

Pylades and Orestes had been to Delphi several times since his first meeting with the Pythia, although never to seek further counsel. They had gone for the music and the dancing, the feasts and the festivals, sometimes for the games in the stadium. But always for the chance to be alone, away from the prying eyes of the palace.

Their last visit had been so joyful, so full of passion and hope for the future. But they had been ignoring the truth that, one day, Orestes would need to return to Mycenae. They had promised each other not to mention Electra or Clytemnestra or anything unpleasant during their time there together. They had kissed in olive groves, bathed in the sea, and watched deer drinking from a lake. They had danced and sung and laughed until their sides had ached.

For good or bad, Pylades had fallen in love with Orestes the moment he saw Electra present him to his father after their escape from Mycenae. The young boy had worn his heart so openly on his sleeve, tear tracks still staining his cheeks. Pylades's contemporaries would have considered this a sign of weakness, but he knew differently. What else mattered in life if not those you love? As his father had required him to, Pylades had taken the boy under his wing. A cousin whom he should treat like a brother. But he was not his brother, and every day they had spent together, a more meaningful bond had grown.

Pylades had mused that perhaps being raised the only son in a family of women had made him so compassionate. But it did not matter. All he knew was that when something so precious comes into your life, you do everything you can to hold on to it. Even so, he had tried to suppress his feelings. Both being princes, their marriage partners would be chosen for them after years of strategic negotiations. And, as long as Orestes did not feel the same toward him, he would not risk ruining their friendship or tarnishing his reputation. But, as it turned out, he had felt exactly the same way.

Four years had passed before the day came when they had shared their first kiss. They had been far out at sea on a fishing boat. Orestes had spent most of the time gazing upward, watching the sea eagles swoop and dive, while Pylades did most of the work. They had caught their dinner and gone ashore to cook it on a small fire. They had talked about everything: the past, the future, animals—always animals with Orestes. As the stars had come out above them, Orestes had rolled over in the sand and made the comment that he couldn't imagine a day more perfect than that one.

"I could," Pylades had replied and leaned forward and pressed his lips against his cousin's. Everything about that kiss had felt so natural. When they had finally broken apart, Pylades had slipped off his robe.

"What are you doing?" Orestes had asked.

"Going for a swim. Care to join me?"

In the water, they had kissed again, their hands exploring one another's bodies as moonlight shattered on the crests of the small waves. Pylades had wanted to carry him back to the palace in his arms that night. But he had never dreamed he would need to carry him like this. Never in all his worst nightmares.

"He needs clean clothes," he said to Electra as they swayed back and forth with the rocking of the ship. "He has soiled them again."

"Then we will see to it when we reach shore. We have already changed him three times and nearly used up everything we packed. There is almost nothing left that is clean."

"Then wash something or use one of your robes or steal one for all I care, but we will not take him to Delphi like this. He is a king, Electra."

Her jaw locked, and he readied himself for more argument, but none came. Instead, she slammed out of the cabin, hopefully to fetch more clothes and some water too. Orestes would disapprove of the way he was speaking to his sister, but Pylades placed as much responsibility for his condition on her as he did on himself. It had been her desire for him to take the crown and her innate hunger for revenge that had forced this upon them. If Orestes had been just a little older, a little more worldly-wise, perhaps he would have accepted that what he had done was no worse than the deeds of many who had gone before him, and this might never have happened.

"Do not worry, my love," he said, using a sleeve to wipe his mouth like a baby. "The Pythia will tell us how to fix this. She will tell us what to do, and you will soon be back with us again. Just stay strong. I am here for you."

The door creaked open.

"One robe," Electra said, throwing it toward him. "And the color is terrible. Get him changed quickly. The shore is in sight."

THIRTY-EIGHT

THE SHIP WAS WORSE THAN HE COULD HAVE POSSIBLY DREAMED. Worse than when they had chased him through the palace corridors, their teeth dripping with blood, their constant wailing ringing in his ears as he fruitlessly sought somewhere to escape them. He had tried to hide, just as he had as a child, in nooks and crannies that he believed only he knew. But they always found him. And now, on the open sea, there was nowhere to go.

He could smell their fetid breath thickening the air of the tiny cabin. In such an enclosed space, there was barely room for the three humans and three monsters to move past one another and certainly nowhere to run. He had stopped thinking of them as women. There was nothing feminine about them. Nothing maternal or warm. Now that they had been his constant companions for so long, he knew each by their tone of voice—the guttural sounds that hitched in their throats before they began their jibes—the pattern of their scales, and the rasping of their torn robes as they dragged along the floor.

"Strong, murderous king. Look at you now."

"Did you taste her blood? Is the tang still on your tongue?"

"*Why do you not turn the dagger on yourself? That would be the easiest thing to do. Go on, Orestes. Turn the dagger on yourself.*"

Their barbs would start low, like the far-off rumble of horses' hooves. It never stayed that way, though. With each word, their venom would grow in volume and spite, until they reached a climax so vociferous he would cover his ears and scream in pain.

"*You made your mother so proud.*"

"*She was so proud of her special little prince.*"

"*Right up until you sliced through her throat.*"

The others knew nothing of this evil presence. They did not realize that demons walked among them. He could tell that much. If the others argued, the creatures were forced to shout their abuse to make their insults heard.

"*Your mother wishes you to know that she loves you still. And that she will see you very, very soon.*"

"*Your brother wishes to repay all the kindness you showed him.*"

"*And Aegisthus. Oh, Aegisthus has such a welcome waiting for you.*"

"Stop it! Stop it now! I am not listening to you!"

"*You do not have a choice.*" And in an instant, she was there, crouching by his side, the putrid stench of her breath filling his nostrils. He squeezed his eyes shut, willing her away from him, but her fingers crawling over his skin caused him to shriek out yet again.

"Get away from me!"

When he opened his eyes again, the beast had gone, and in its place, Pylades kneeled, his brow knotted and his eyes dark with worry.

"It is all right, Orestes. We have arrived at Delphi. I just need to lift you up."

"No! No!" Orestes shrank back, pulling his knees to his chest, his eyes darting back and forth. "They are here! They are hiding now! They never leave! They will never leave me alone!"

"It's just me."

Orestes turned rigid as Pylades moved to take him in his arms. They could change in appearance. Maybe it was one of them, pretending to be him! He lashed out, beating him away with his fists.

"Please, cousin, stay still."

"Why are you doing this to me?"

"The Pythia will help you. Please, my love, please, hold still."

"Get away! Leave me alone!"

"I am here to help you."

"Go! Why will you not leave me be?"

"Please, just stay still."

"Enough of this!"

The voice was so sharp and shrill it could well have been one of the creatures, but Orestes knew his sister's tone, even in the depths of his insanity. He drew his arms back, although he continued to kick out.

"Get a rope. We will tie him up. It will be safer and quicker."

"No! No!" He struggled and fought with all his might, but even in health he had been no match for his sister, let alone with his friend helping her. Within minutes, they had him bound and slung over Pylades's shoulder. No matter how much he wriggled, there was no escaping, not from the ropes, nor from the monsters that were waiting for him up on deck.

"*How appropriate,*" one of them laughed.

"*You look fit for slaughter,*" cackled another.

"*Perhaps that is their plan, although it would be too kind. You deserve to suffer. She deserves to see your agony.*"

While Electra went to find transport, Pylades lowered him gently to the ground and held a skin of water to his lips.

"The Pythia will solve this, my love," he whispered, brushing the hair from his face. "She will speak to the gods. They will put an end to this."

Orestes tucked his chin to his chest and closed his eyes, afraid of what Pylades might turn into if he looked too closely.

"Then I will take you home, wherever you wish that to be. We can stay here, or go to Phocis, or return to Mycenae. It will be your decision. Whatever you choose."

Whatever I choose? Orestes thought bitterly. When had he ever had a choice in anything?

Electra soon returned with mules. She and Pylades loosened his restraints so that he could straddle one of them. They traveled up the winding mountain paths, and somehow, with the rocking motion and Pylades's arms holding him close, he shut his eyes and faded into sleep.

Even then he wasn't free. The memory of the deaths played over and over, with no break, no pause. He forced himself to wake from the nightmare. But when he did so, they were there, waiting for him, their grotesque mouths still taunting.

"*Maybe we should push you off, so you break your neck.*"

"*I want to hear it snap.*"

"*I want him to hear it snap.*"

Squeezing his eyes shut again, he incanted the names of butterflies that Aegisthus had taught him.

"Lattice brown, scarce swallowtail…"

"I have you, my darling, not long now." Pylades held him firmly to stop him from falling.

He had no idea where they were going. Maybe they had told him, but so often now human words registered as nothing more than a distant hum. Perhaps they intended to dispose of him, miles from civilization, so no one would know the truth of his madness.

When his eyes blinked open momentarily and he saw the great yellow-stone pillars of the tholos of Delphi, he experienced a brief flicker of recognition, only to bury his head against Pylades's chest again as a violent shriek shattered the air. He prepared himself for another onslaught.

"It is fine, my love. There is nothing to be afraid of. Look. We are here."

The noise came again, although he now realized it was not the voice of one of his tormentors but the cry of a swan. A glimmer of hope sparked in his heart. They were in Delphi. For the first time in so very long, he registered his surroundings. Delphi meant the Pythia and the word of Apollo. Maybe there was the hope of redemption, after all.

"Pylades," he said, his voice cracked and hoarse from so little use. He tried to twist his neck around to look up at him, but he struggled to keep his balance.

His friend squeezed him tighter still. "We are nearly there, Orestes. We are nearly there."

"I can take him if you wish," called Electra, from her mule. "You have been managing him this whole way."

"It is fine. There is only a short distance to go. We just need to make it up the steps."

"I…I can walk."

Pylades brought their mule to a stop. "Orestes? Can you hear us? Drink some water."

"They will come back," he replied, his eyes skittering between the birds and the humans. "They are taunting me. The women. They are here for revenge."

"Who are they? Have they told you who they are?"

"Ignore him," Electra said, dismounting. "His mind is addled.

Half the time he has been talking about snakes, not women. We need to get him to the temple, now."

"Forked tongues. That was what I was talking about. Not snakes, just forked tongues."

"I know, I know." Pylades continued to speak softly to him. "Just a little while longer. Please, stay with us. The Pythia will put this right. We just have to reach the temple."

Even in his current state, he could recall every moment of his first visit to the Pythia, including the fact that he'd had to attend their meeting alone. Today, he struggled to stand on his own, even in the fresh air of the mountainside. Whether she liked it or not, she would have to agree to Pylades accompanying him, simply to keep him upright in the stifling atmosphere of burning incense.

They lowered him to the ground. Hordes of people danced, swayed, and ambled around them. Orestes had previously marveled at the chaos of it all. Now he feared it. More people meant more places for the fiends to hide. No sooner had he thought this than their tirade began again.

"*You think you will find sanctuary here? You think a god will save you? No human or god can do that.*"

"*We were here before these petty gods set foot on the earth.*"

"*We will not even let you in there. You do not deserve peace. Do you think they are at peace? Do you think your mother is?*"

"*Orestes?*"

A clawed hand reached out for him, and he leaped backward. "No!" he shouted, turning, only to find himself face-to-face with another of the beasts. "No!" He twisted again. This time one of them was waiting to grab him from the side. And then from the front. The three of them surrounded him. Covering his ears, he stumbled back into the crowd, where geese and swans swarmed. "Please, leave me alone! Leave me alone!"

Half the people edged away, while others approached, wishing to help, unaware of the figures between them, with fangs bared and tongues flicking.

"Go away! Go away!" Orestes shooed at them.

"Grab him!" Electra shouted. "Grab him and get him up the steps."

Scouring the sea of faces, Orestes searched for Pylades, but there were monsters everywhere he turned. Monsters and strangers were all he could see. The stones slipped from beneath his feet. The world was falling away, and he wanted to go with it, to plummet down into whatever awaited him. Whatever tortures and torments Hades had prepared for him, none could be worse than this.

"Yes, yes…that is right. Give in. It will be easier that way, far better."

"One good crack of the skull."

"Come with us. You do not really want this life any longer."

His eyes rolled back as his thoughts turned to water. And then, with a warmth more wonderful than summer sunlight, he was swept upward and away from it all.

THIRTY-NINE

HE DIDN'T NEED TO OPEN HIS EYES TO KNOW WHERE HE WAS.
That scent, so strong, so all consuming, wove its way
through his mind, blurring his thoughts as it cast a deep
sense of calm. His limbs were heavy, weighted, but not burdened. It
was as though he had fallen into the deepest of sleeps, one that he
had no intention of waking from. Yet, as soon as the thought struck
him, his mind awoke from its hazy state. Breathing in a lungful of
incense, he opened his eyes, just a fraction at first. Orange. The color
he had expected to see. It filled him with peace, with thoughts of
home, yet he could not figure out why. Still slow to move, he opened
his eyes a little further, and the blurred images around him became
shapes and then objects.

A familiar, soft tangerine light glimmered on the marble
floors. Several priestesses in orange robes were gathered around
them. Incense burned in hammered-copper holders, tendrils of the
fragrant smoke weaving up into the air, only to lose their form in
the shadows. The temple was quieter than the last time he had been
there. Quieter, in fact, than anywhere he had been of late. He could

hear the birds nesting at the top of the pillars and the rustle of fabric when the priestesses made even the slightest movement. Quiet. His body turned rigid at the realization. It was another trap, he was sure. Any minute the monsters would leap from the shadows to torment him again. But it was Pylades's voice that came from out of the hush.

"You do not need to worry, cousin. The Erinyes will not pester you here."

He shook his head, still trembling, as he awaited their attack. A blanket had been draped over him while he slept. It was another ploy, he was sure. He scrambled upright, his eyes darting around as he pulled his knees up to his chest.

"You think that. You think that I am safe, but they will find me. They always find me."

"Not here, my love. The Erinyes will not get you here."

Orestes shook his head and held his breath. A moment passed, and then another. Still no voices. No hissing or shrieking. Nor was there the cold chill that he had grown so used to in their presence, as if they were sucking every scrap of heat and life from their surroundings. Still not daring to believe he was safe, he cast his eyes slowly around the temple. The cushions on which he had lain had molded themselves to his body. How long had he been there? He was considering this when Pylades's words suddenly struck him.

"The Erinyes? The Furies?" He turned to his lover. "That is what they are? I am not going mad after all? They are the ones who have been torturing me?" Tears filled his eyes.

"It has been them," Pylades said, with a sad smile and matching tears. "I am so sorry we did not know. I am so sorry that we—"

"That you thought I had gone insane."

"No. Well, maybe a little." His voice hitched with the effort of fighting back the tears. "Can you forgive me?"

"Of course. Always." With his heart almost bursting, he wrapped his arms around Pylades's neck. The warmth of his skin, the stubble against his cheek, the smell of musk that enveloped him—he realized he had thought he would never experience this again. "How do you know?" he asked, breaking away. "Did the Pythia tell you?"

"Not exactly," Pylades replied nervously.

"What is wrong?" The feeling of hope was rapidly fading.

"Nothing. Nothing is wrong at all," he replied, sitting back and looking up.

Orestes pushed himself onto his knees and followed his friend's gaze.

"Are you...? No... Can you possibly be?"

A figure stood there, one that should have been lost in the shadows yet shone with a luminosity that seemed to come from within. His head was crowned with a mass of golden curls, which, in their turn, were adorned with a simple laurel wreath. Appearing no older than Orestes himself, he looked as magnificent and perfect as in any story ever told of him. More so, if that were possible.

"Apollo," he whispered.

The young man continued to smile for a fraction longer before his brow creased in a deep frown.

"I am sorry for the situation you find yourself in, Orestes. I think we will need to find a solution together. Will you have a drink with me, and we can discuss your plight?"

Had it not been for Pylades's look of awe, he would have considered his insanity confirmed. Electra reached over and squeezed his hand.

"He is here for you, brother. He has come to make all this right."

After being helped to his feet, he followed Apollo as he glided through into the next chamber, where a feast fit for the God of Light had been laid out. His sister and lover on either side of him, having had longer to adjust to the situation, exchanged a knowing smile.

"He is a god. We are in the presence of a god," Orestes whispered to neither of them in particular.

"We know, brother, we know."

The table was laid with enough food for a hundred men—meat and fish, and fruit so fresh he could smell its sweetness. Orestes felt his mouth watering at the mere sight of it. For the first time since his mother's death, he found his appetite returning, although he reached for a cup of water first.

As the others began to fill their plates, Orestes cleared his throat to speak.

"The Erinyes," he said, addressing Apollo. "Who are these women? Where have they come from?"

"The Erinyes are not women," he corrected him as one of the priestesses poured him a cup of wine. "They come from the darkest corner, in the deepest region of the Underworld, and are more evil than any they pursue. Vengeance is their only calling. They take up the cause of those they believe have been wronged. Then they torment the apparent wrongdoer, normally to the point of death."

"So they were serious about wanting to kill me?" Orestes now took a mouthful of bread.

"The Underworld, you say?" Electra had shown enough respect to remove her dagger in the God's presence; however, she still saw fit to speak over her brother's question. "And they have been sent here to inflict vengeance? By whom? By our mother? Is this her doing? Of course it would be," she answered herself.

Apollo shrugged. "I cannot give you much information. The Erinyes are ancient. Older than my father's father. How they are summoned is something even we gods do not know. It could be that they are sent, or that they are simply drawn to acts of wrongdoing here on earth."

"Such as matricide," Orestes whispered. The God lowered his eyes in what he could only assume was agreement.

"But there was no wrongdoing here." Electra's voice was rising in volume. "He was only following the instructions of the gods—your own requirement that a son must avenge his father's death."

"I am well aware of what you are saying, princess, but the truth is as I have already stated. They are older than us and they work in ways even we do not understand."

"Then you are the one who cursed him!"

Gasps echoed around the hall, and the priestesses flinched. Orestes felt Pylades stiffen beside him.

"Electra," he hissed at his sister.

"You are right," Apollo agreed. "Intentionally or otherwise, I am the one who brought this torment upon you. I, the God of Music and Light, of Art and Healing. This is not what I would have ever intended, for any human."

"When will they stop? What will make them cease? What do I have to do? Make them an offering?"

"We can give them anything they ask," Pylades added.

Apollo hung his head. "I do not think there is anything. Nothing that any of us has ever discovered, at least. Vengeance is all they seek."

A knot tightened in Orestes's gut. He could not go back to their constant torture. It would be the end of him, he was certain. He would rather die.

"But, surely, you can stop them?" he asked with hope, which was dashed as the God shook his head.

"No, I have no power over the Erinyes."

"But they have not come into your temple. You said that I am safe here, so you must have some control over them?" His heart was racing.

"I am sorry. I do not. But they are not stupid. To offend a god in his own temple would not be a wise move, even for them."

"So can I stay here?" he asked. He could hear the almost childish timbre of his voice, the desperation in it, as this new idea appeared to offer the chance of sanity once more. "Can I stay here in your temple, forever?"

The God tilted his head, and a look like that of a parent concerned about the welfare of his child crossed his face.

"This is the temple of my oracle, Orestes. Not a shelter or a refuge. I cannot have you living here among the women. It would not be proper. Besides, when I leave, they would simply resume their torment of you."

"So now what? You just cast him aside? Take the blame but not the responsibility?"

Such outbursts from his sister were commonplace, but the words came not from her but from Pylades, and a fresh fear rose in Orestes.

"Pylades, please." He reached over and took his lover's hand. Angering a god at this point would do nothing to help either of them, although it seemed, from the way the corners of Apollo's lips twitched, that he was more amused than offended. A brief silence ensued, during which a glint appeared in his eye.

"Did I say I was going to do nothing? We simply need to shed a little light on the situation," he said. "Tell me, are your belongings still packed? We have a long journey ahead of us."

FORTY

THE DAY BROUGHT A STRONG WIND THAT FILLED THE SAILS and allowed the crew to rest their oars for a while. With his gaze lost on the foaming waves, Orestes fought to block out the taunts of the Erinyes.

"*We will not leave you.*"

"*You will pay for what you have done.*"

"*I would keep my eyes open if I were you. You do not know who might come up behind you and push you overboard.*"

"*Or slit your throat. You like a good throat slitting, do you not, Orestes?*"

The king squeezed his eyes shut, wondering if he had made a mistake standing out in the open. But he barely had time to consider what other alternative he had, when another voice came from beside him.

"Surely there are other people you need to torment," sighed Apollo, waving a hand dismissively toward the hags. "You are disturbing the music. Come back in an hour, when we have eaten. He will let you torment him then, will you not, Orestes?"

"*We seek only what he deserves.*"

"Yes, yes. You are the harbingers of vengeance. We have heard it all before."

Orestes was torn between laughing and crying. Just as Apollo had said, the Erinyes had been waiting for him when they left the temple. Angered at the God for stealing away their plaything, they had, for a while, thrown their worst at him. But with Apollo by his side, he felt stronger. He had pulled his shoulders back as he had returned to the ship and managed, for the most part, to stop himself from weeping at the sight of them. Perhaps it was simply having someone else who could see them—someone who was not afraid of them.

"Do they have names?" Pylades asked, poking at the air as if he might manage to strike one with his finger.

"Creatures like this do not deserve such consideration. The way they behave is reprehensible. No wonder poor Orestes thought he had gone mad. I think I would go insane if I had to listen to that drivel all day. Why not try a song, you ghastly hags? You never know, you might have a talent for it."

"*Can you still taste the blood, Orestes? Can you still see the way the light faded from her eyes?*" They glared at him as they spoke, and the familiar churn of fear started in his stomach, but Apollo swept in again.

"Please, think of some new lines. He killed his mother. We know that. And he is devastated. Even a fool could tell. If this is the type of man you seek vengeance from, I fear you have missed the mark by quite a distance. Besides, your vernacular is unimaginative and repetitive. I am the God of Poetry, remember."

With a hiss, one of the Erinyes twisted around, only inches from his face.

"*Perhaps next time, we will seek vengeance from one of the gods, for their wrongdoings.*"

"Good luck with that," Apollo replied.

The banter helped Orestes, yet he still struggled to see what could be achieved by another god, if the mighty Apollo could not rid him of their presence.

"Do you think I am destined to have them torment me through-out all eternity?" he asked Pylades that night. The wind had grown even stronger, bringing thick clouds that had darkened the sky long before sunset. Now, as midnight approached, a storm was raging, with waves crashing over the hull and slamming the ship first one way and then the other. They had hidden themselves away below deck, in one of the smallest cabins, where they held each other beneath a thin blanket. Yet the Erinyes still taunted him, their eyes peering through the cracks in the wooden door, their fingernails poking up through the floorboards.

"Apollo will not rest until you are rid of them. He said as much."

"But if he cannot do anything…"

"Then I will march up Olympus and demand Zeus himself throw them back down where they belong."

Orestes attempted a smile, but it faltered. Another question had been playing on his mind for days now, since Electra first brought it up in Delphi. He had not wanted to share it, for fear of what the answer might be. But now he felt another opinion on the matter could not be worse than the voice in his own head, not to mention the other three.

"Do you think what Electra said is true?" he asked. "That my mother sent them? That she wishes me to be punished?" He screwed his eyes closed, awaiting Pylades's answer.

"I did not know your mother," he said at last. "But I know you and I know what has been said about her. Firstly, if the gods themselves cannot control these things, then I find it difficult to believe that your mother could, even if the women in your family—well, if

Electra is anything to go by—do consider themselves omnipotent. And we both know that is not the case."

Orestes offered Pylades the smallest of smiles.

"You have told me so much of her, the way she cared for you and your siblings. You told me of the errors she made too. She was only human, after all. I cannot imagine her pain at Aletes's death, but that was my doing, not yours. She will also know the torment you suffered. She has no reason to send these things after you. I am certain of it."

Whether it was the truth or not, Orestes did not know, but he made the decision to believe what Pylades told him about his mother and about Apollo, just as he would choose to believe that his future would be free of the Erinyes. To think otherwise was unconscionable.

The next morning, the storm had broken and the wind had lessened. Calmer than it had been the entire journey, the water was, nonetheless, flecked with endless whitecaps that stretched from the ship to the horizon. Above them, the sky had cleared to the palest of blues, and a flock of seabirds drifted in circles, trying to spot fish beneath the surface of the water. Not that Orestes was aware of this. He could see none of it.

In the hope of lessening the continuous torment of the Erinyes, Pylades had suggested he wear a scarf around his eyes and ears, to deaden his senses. The idea had not immediately appealed to him. With them vying for his death, being unable to see where they were unnerved him even more. Yet Pylades had been so keen for him to try. And in truth it did help a little, if only because it meant Pylades needed to hold him close to keep him steady.

Noises came through the fabric, muffled at first, then clearer, as his ears adjusted themselves. The squawking of the seagulls, the slapping of the oars as they hit the water with a regular beat. He controlled his breathing to match their rhythm. Soon, new sounds—the clamor of many voices and the calling of traders—made him imagine he could be standing in the center of the citadel in Mycenae. Yet he knew exactly where they must be—Athens.

"Are we there?" he asked Pylades, his heart skipping a beat with anticipation for the first time in months.

"Yes, we have just reached the port," he replied.

"You can see it from here?"

"Yes, my love. I can see it."

Even fear of the Erinyes could not persuade him to keep his blindfold on any longer. His eyes pricked with tears as he gazed out at the great city. Whether the Erinyes were there or not, he did not care, his heart was so full.

As the ship docked, the four of them prepared to disembark, the mortals' few belongings carried in satchels worn by Pylades and Electra.

"Wow, this makes Delphi look like a market town—no offense," Electra said, rejecting Pylades's hand as she stepped onto the gangplank.

"Yes, it would seem my half sister's followers have been busy building, to bolster her already large ego, no doubt. Remember she is the Goddess of Wisdom, not humility," Apollo responded with a smile. "My followers prefer to spend their time creating art or composing music. Gargantuan buildings or timeless beauty? I know which I would choose. But each to their own."

But these were no mere buildings, however easily Apollo dismissed them. There was no denying the artistry in what stood before them. Domes and archways, intricate and ornate, yet so delicate that it seemed music could have flowed through the very stonework. Pillars, carved with such detail, that Orestes struggled to believe that any stonemason could live long enough to achieve such craftsmanship. Yes, this was art. The entire city was a testament to it. This was Athens.

Rumors of the God's imminent arrival had somehow reached shore ahead of them. As they staggered onto the dockside, their legs not yet used to solid ground, people rushed toward them. Orestes had been used to seeing such displays of tribute, people flocking to his mother or King Strophius when they had walked through their kingdoms. They would barely acknowledge the homage, as rich and poor, male and female would all come to seek the favor of their ruler. Their gifts might be simple—fruits, breads, occasionally trinkets from the richer citizens—or more valuable, from those who hoped for something in return. Really large gifts would be reserved for ceremonies in public halls, where their display could be admired by all.

How different it was with Apollo. Showing the same level of courtesy to every person who came to him, whether dressed in rags or silks, he accepted the gifts that they brought with grace. With endless thanks, he took their offerings, which, along with more modest items, included pieces of art and small instruments, fine vases, and barrels of wine. He ordered everything taken back to the ship to return with him to Olympus. Whether his gratitude was genuine or not, Orestes found he did not care. His admiration had grown immensely for a god who would act this way, who seemed to really care for mere mortals.

When the crowds gradually started dispersing, he replaced the scarf around his eyes and ears.

"Do not leave my side," he begged, taking Pylades's hand and squeezing it tightly as they started their journey up to the temple. This would be an ideal time for the Erinyes to make another play for him. And with such narrow paths and sheer drops to the boulders below, it would be the perfect place for them to achieve their mission.

"You know I will never leave you," his lover replied, guiding him upward.

"*Yes he will, and when he is gone, we will have you all to ourselves,*" one of the Erinyes piped up.

"*One quick push is all it would take. We can do that, you know.*" His steps faltered.

"It is still a long way to the temple," Pylades said with concern. "Would you like me to carry you? Or shall I fetch a mule?"

"No, I can do this," he replied, trying to block out the jeers.

"Good," Apollo said. "My sister respects brave men."

Finding an even footing on the rocky surface while ignoring the jibes of creatures of the Underworld would not have been an easy task even with sight, yet he trusted Pylades and his sister not to let him fall. Step by careful step, they made the ascent. The air was crisp and clean, and he wished he could stop and admire the view that must be stretching out below them now. But there would be time enough for that later, he hoped, when they would be free to enjoy it all.

Finally, breathless but not defeated, they stopped.

"We are here," Electra said. "We have reached the temple."

The excitement that he had first felt on arrival in Athens returned, although with new trepidation. Hands trembling, he pulled down his blindfold. Even the presence of the Erinyes could not detract from the magnificence of the building in front of him.

The sand-colored stone gleamed, as though imbued with the ichor of the gods. Light reflected from every angle. A warmth rose up from the earth, causing his skin to tingle. He felt that something more powerful than he had ever encountered was housed in these walls. However much humankind might fail, whatever might fall, this place, this magnificent acropolis, would outlast everything.

"It is…all I ever dreamed it would be."

He recalled, with an ache in his chest, his first visit to Delphi, when he had vowed to himself that he would travel the world to see all her treasures. This was the first step toward fulfilling that promise. He just hoped it would not be the last.

"I guess we should go in then," Pylades said, moving to climb the steps.

Apollo caught him by the shoulder.

"Better you let us deal with this," he said, nodding toward Electra. "Things tend to end badly when men enter my sister's temples. Do not worry, though. We will keep him safe."

Orestes had seen his life unfolding with increasing disbelief. What would have once seemed inconceivable—hiding to avoid terrifying beasts, which were invisible to all but him—now seemed prosaic, compared to his current situation. Even with all he had recently experienced, he was having a hard time comprehending this turn of events.

No longer was he in the presence of a god but two—two immortals—who were discussing *his* welfare. Standing there together, their combined luminosity was almost unbearable. An Erinye, the tallest and palest of the Furies, stood in deep conversation with them, while the other two remained with him and continued to hound him, whispering in his ears and causing a cold sweat to break out along his spine. As they ran their fingernails up and down his skin and across his throat, they muttered their promises of vengeance. The familiar chill had returned, causing his breath to fog the air around him. Screwing his eyes closed, he forced down the scream that was building.

It had been like this for hours; the gods lost in conversation, leaving him on his own. Electra had somehow managed to fall asleep and Pylades remained outside, unwelcome in the sanctuary of the Goddess. Occasionally, one of the gods would glance his way, and the Erinyes would lessen their torment, by just a fraction. Only when Apollo finally raised his voice to them, loud enough to startle the birds from the roof of the temple, were the monsters distracted long enough for Orestes to catch his breath.

"This has gone on long enough! There was no wrongdoing here; he was obeying the command of a god!"

"*Those two things are not mutually exclusive. Do not insult me by implying the gods are just. Do not pretend to stand on the side of the wronged. Surely, some of the acts that have taken place in this very temple are enough of a testament to that.*" The tallest Erinye glared at the Goddess Athena, but whatever it was referring to, Orestes remained in the dark, and Athena seemed nonplussed.

The gray-eyed Goddess sighed as she stepped away from the pair. Unlike the effigies he had seen of her, she wore no helmet. Nor did she have a spear in her hand. But her long gray chiton shimmered as she walked, as if her divinity extended to everything she came into contact with.

"We have been over this point before," she said. "At least a dozen times. And it seems neither of you has anything new to add to the argument. Apollo, we know that Orestes acted on your command and that a father's vengeance is paramount to our way of thinking. So, you do not believe that he should be punished."

The Erinye opened her hideous mouth to speak again, but Athena cut her off.

"I am aware of what you are about to say, yet again. It is strange how you both feel that the Goddess of Wisdom requires so much repetition in order to understand something.

"The act of matricide cannot be taken lightly. Orestes killed the mother who had nursed him and raised him and loved him in a way that far too many mortals fail to do. There is no denying that, in normal circumstances, this should not go unpunished. But these are not normal circumstances."

She paused, steepling her fingers and pressing them gently against her top lip.

"So where do you stand?" Apollo asked, breaking her moment's contemplation. "That is what we have come here to establish."

Silence hung like a shroud over them as Orestes awaited her response. Content to listen to the other two, she had seldom engaged in their arguments and had answered only a few questions during their time together. All seemed insignificant, compared to what she had now been asked. He could sense her mind whirring behind those gray eyes as she considered the question. Then, she slowly turned to face him, her head tilting to the side, like the little owl that so frequently accompanied her.

Does a god have the power to hear a man's thoughts? he wondered as she regarded him. If she did, then she was welcome to them. She was welcome to share the nightmares he had faced every night since hearing the Pythia's decree, the guilt that roiled through him like curdled milk. She was welcome to it all.

"This matter perplexes me. And for one of my abilities, that is not something I admit lightly. What is evident from this is that we alone cannot come to a decision. With one person on each side, and each of you so sure of your argument that you would never cede to the other, we could go back and forth until Mount Olympus crumbles."

"So you must decide," said Apollo. "That is why we came. Give us your ruling. Look at this man; he is as near to death as any mortal I have ever seen. What they have not stripped from him he has already taken from himself. Surely you can see that?"

"*It is no less than he deserves. The lives he has taken are worth more than his,*" countered the Erinye.

"As I have said, we are going around in circles," Athena cut in, before the debate could spiral any further out of control. "I know what you want of me. However, I do not think I am able to judge this fairly. I cannot see this with the same eyes as the mortals who have suffered through it. I have no child of my own. I cannot imagine the feeling of violation, of being so truly betrayed by one whom you have loved even more than your own life. But, at the same time, I cannot conceive of the agonies that one must suffer when tasked with a vengeance one does not wish to see through. I feel only a mortal could rule on this. Your lives may be short, but they are full of the dramatic experiences it requires to have a definite viewpoint."

"What are you saying?" Orestes asked, standing up. "Do you mean that they will be with me forever? That I will never be rid of them?"

The Goddess turned to face him, and in that moment, he saw a thousand emotions pass across her face as she paused before answering.

"I am saying that I am not qualified to pass judgment. In fact, this problem is weightier than can be decided by just one opinion. In short, Orestes, we must put you on trial. We shall see what democracy can bring to this."

FORTY-ONE

I T HAD NEVER BEEN DONE BEFORE, AND IT TOOK MORE TIME TO arrange than Orestes would have hoped. For two days, Athena had scoured the city to assemble a jury she considered just and fair.

Apollo told him of the final arrangements, on the eve of the trial. "Six men and six women," he said. "She has shown us no partiality in whom she has chosen, but she has done us no disfavor, either. That, I suppose, is all we could hope for."

"So how does it work?" he asked. A trial by jury had never taken place before. As a boy, he had watched in the throne room as his mother had resolved endless minor squabbles in the citadel and several major ones too. He had seen farmers pay fines in sheep and gold, and countless other sentences handed down. There had been no debate, no discussion. His mother's word was law. But he did not stand to lose livestock or savings here. It was his sanity at stake, his life, in fact. If the jury found against him, as the Erinyes hoped, then that would be the end of him.

"Athena has given every person on the jury equal standing. They will vote as individuals, but their collective decision will be what counts."

"And I will have the chance to speak? To put my side of things?"

"You will. You will speak for yourself, and the Erinyes will speak on behalf of your mother."

"And Aegisthus and Aletes? They will talk about them too, will they not?"

Apollo shook his head. "No, I think not. Of course they could, but it is only the matricide for which they wish to punish you."

Orestes was silent.

"Just a little while longer, my love," Pylades said, "and you will be rid of them."

Yes, Orestes thought, *one way or another.*

In the hours preceding the trial, the Erinyes took their persecution to a whole new level. Not a moment passed when they were not present, hurling insults or clawing at him.

"*You could save your family this further humiliation if you just ended it all now,*" they taunted. "*Do you not think your sister has already suffered enough because of you?*"

"*I saw a well back there. Maybe I should just push you down it?*"

"*No, you do not need to go to the trouble of doing that. He is perfectly capable of doing the job himself, are you not, Orestes? Or there is a good thick rope in that cupboard.*"

"*And a sturdy sycamore tree outside.*"

"*But that would be too clean. You know how he likes blood.*"

"*That is true. He should use a blade.*"

He pulled the scarf tighter around his head.

"We must speak to Athena," Pylades said, massaging Orestes's temples. "You must be allowed to rest and prepare, if you are to represent yourself tomorrow."

"I think that is their point," he replied, pressing his fingers to his ears for a moment, before sighing and loosening the knot in the blindfold enough to pull it down.

"What are you doing?" Pylades asked. "You said the blindfold helps."

"It does, but I need to see you. I need to see your face to speak to you."

He turned to focus his whole attention on his lover. One of the Erinyes continued to hiss in his ear, but he pushed the sound to the back of his mind. It took all his concentration to achieve this feat, and he found he was struggling for words.

"It is hopeless."

"You cannot think negatively. You have Apollo on your side."

"That is true, but I fear it means less than you imagine. These demons are older than the gods, remember."

"Still, you must stay positive."

"Pylades," he struggled on, "I have something I must say to you."

Pressing his lips together, he gave a sober nod. "Go on."

"If they decide that I am guilty, and that the Erinyes are justified in what they are doing, then I cannot continue."

"Orestes, you do not mean that."

"I do, Pylades, for so many reasons. I can barely live with my guilt as it is. But with them, with these creatures…"

Their cackles resonated around him as they sensed him weakening.

"I cannot endure another day in their presence."

Pylades had paled and tears gleamed in his eyes, although he stayed silent and allowed Orestes to continue.

"When… If…" There was no way of saying it that did not cause tears to stream down his cheeks. "If I am gone, you must marry Electra."

"What?" Pylades shot up. "You cannot be serious."

"Of course I am. Mycenae will be weak and will need a king. Some might ask for her hand. Others will just try to claim the throne by any means they can."

"No! You are delirious!"

"No, I am not, and you know it makes sense."

"It may have escaped your notice, Orestes, but I am not the marrying kind. And your sister would most definitely not be my type, even if I were."

"And it has obviously escaped yours that a prince has no choice, wherever he is."

Pylades fell silent.

"You will have to continue your line. You will need to father children," Orestes continued, his voice growing stronger with the certainty of his words. "And they will be perfect. Because they will be a part of you, and almost a part of me, and there could be nothing more wonderful than that."

"Orestes—"

"Please, say you will. Your father would be more than happy with the union. You know that. No one would dispute it. Promise me. Promise, if I fail tomorrow, you will do this."

"You will not fail."

"Promise me!"

Closing his eyes, Pylades dipped his chin before taking Orestes's head in his hands and pulling it toward his chest.

"I will," he said.

And, even with the Erinyes present, Orestes kissed Pylades as if they were alone, for he feared this might be their last night together.

When dawn broke, he awoke in confusion, although it only took a moment for it to clear. They were sleeping on a thin mattress, and Pylades's arm was draped across his chest. He gently lifted it off before getting up. Outside, he could hear the first birds of the dawn chorus, and only when he turned around and saw the golden-haired god hovering by the door did he realize—the demons had gone.

Apollo smiled.

"Athena required their presence at her temple," he said, as if reading Orestes's thoughts. "I will be honest, I asked her to keep them there as long as she could, to drag the meeting out as much as possible, to give you the chance to prepare. I wondered if there was anything I could help you with?"

He shook his head. "I will tell the truth and hope that is enough."

"It will be."

"I pray you are right."

"I am. Now, let us eat breakfast. I have the feeling we have a long day ahead of us."

The hearing took place on the Areopagus, a rocky outcrop a short distance from the temple. The bare natural marble was rough and craggy, a far cry from the sleek and polished pillars of the Acropolis, but Orestes was not concerned with aesthetics. Nor was there time to admire the vista that stretched out to an almost infinite skyline of distant jutting mountain peaks.

Stools had been placed on the southwest side, with views overlooking the city of Athens. Twelve of them, placed centrally, were already occupied. Standing in front, dressed in her full regalia, was Athena. With helmet and spear, she appeared twice her previous height and every bit the Goddess of War and Wisdom. Orestes felt himself shrink at the sight of her. He could not feel confident that she would remain truly impartial as she claimed she was.

Despite the crowds that had flocked to the hearing, there was silence when he entered. As he moved to take his seat, there was a sudden gasp of fear from the people.

"Orestes! No!" Electra grabbed his arm, gripping it to the point of pain and causing him to stop in his tracks. "H...how?"

He turned, seeing at once the reason for her discomfort. What had once been reserved just for him now stood, fully exposed and corporal on the stones of Athens. The Erinyes were visible to all. Men and women shrieked in fear, although for once he remained calm.

"Those...those *things* are what you have had to endure?"

"Day and night," he replied, avoiding their gaze as they leered at him.

"How are you still standing?" she asked.

His sister was not the only one in disbelief at the sight. The crowds edged away from the monsters. People who had clambered up on rocks to get a better view of the proceedings now scrambled down again. Others covered their eyes. Surprisingly, he found all this a comfort.

"Come," he said, removing his sister's hand from his arm and taking a seat on the stool next to Apollo. "We will see plenty more of them, I expect."

Having regained her composure, Electra took her place beside him. "You must look the jurors in the eye," she advised, adjusting his robe, unable to control the trembling of her hands. "You are human. They are monsters. There is no way they can side with them. See, they are already repulsed by the creatures."

"Terrified of them," Pylades countered.

It certainly seemed that way. Those who were not looking toward Orestes were conversing with each other. All eyes avoided the Erinyes. He was about to comment on the fact when the crowd fell silent again.

"We are to begin," Pylades whispered. "Look."

The hairs stood up on Orestes's skin as the two gods walked to the center. Apollo stood momentarily by his sister. His laurel wreath seemed larger than usual and his presence even more imposing. He nodded to her before striding back toward Orestes. If he survived this, he thought, he would build a temple to Apollo.

"It will all be over soon." Apollo grinned as he took the seat beside him again. "It will all be over soon."

Athena stepped forward. The hem of her robe hovered just a fraction above the ground, her spear and helm glinting in the sunlight. Her gaze went first to the jury, then to the Erinyes, and, lastly to Orestes. She then turned to face the crowd.

"We have gathered here today to decide the fate of Orestes, son of Agamemnon and King of Mycenae. We will listen and learn of his matricide. Orestes, you wish to address us, I believe."

His throat felt as though he had swallowed a thousand daggers, and the air seemed to thicken around him. Was that it? Was that all she had to say? He knew the Goddess to be economical with words, but he had hoped for a little more than that, and a little more time to ready himself.

"Just speak the truth," Pylades whispered to him.

Not able to reply, or even nod, he stood and stepped forward, sweating so profusely that his feet slipped in his sandals.

The jury was, as Apollo had already told him it would be, a mix of men and women, adults of every age. *Look at them,* that was what Electra had told him. Yet it was harder to do than he would have imagined. Hard to look these twelve humans in the eye, hoping they would recognize the truth in his words. Blinking back the tears, he began.

"I did not want to kill her," he said, his voice catching in his throat. "I truly did not. I knew that a son must avenge his father, but I could not do it. I wanted her to live. I stayed away for eight years, but the Pythia speaks the word of the gods, and she said my mother must die, that my father must be avenged. But I am... I was ..."

He was struggling to keep his mind focused. Somehow, even silent, the Erinyes' accusations were inside his head. Clytemnestra had trusted him, and yet he had murdered her. Slit her throat.

"She did not see me coming. I did it as quickly as I could. I did not want her to know, to suffer." He replayed it in his mind, as he had done so many times. That dreadful gurgling sound as blood filled her lungs. "I did not want to do it. I loved her, but I was ordered... She should not have died. She should not have had to die at my hands. I am sorry. I am so very, very sorry."

There was nothing more he could say. His legs buckled and he fell.

FORTY-TWO

THE HARD ROCK STUNG HIS KNEES AS HE LANDED IN THE dust. The crowd murmured and whispered. What a pathetic display, he thought. What a king he must look to them, unable to defend even himself. He hung his head, weeping. Then a hand gently slipped into the crook of his arm and pulled him to his feet.

"I have you, brother," Electra said, wrapping the arm around her shoulder. "I have you."

"I...I am sorry. I am sorry."

"We have you." Pylades took his other arm.

What a memory to leave his loved ones, he thought, as they helped him away from the jury. And he would be leaving them, for, if he could not justify his actions, how could anyone excuse them?

As they lowered him onto his stool, he prepared for the Erinyes to inflict their final damning words, this time to an audience. But it was Apollo who now stood in front of the jury again.

With his head tilted to the side, and the smallest of smiles on his lips, the God looked just as at ease as one might expect him to be at a play or musical performance. He looked around before settling his gaze on the twelve men and women.

"Ladies and gentlemen of the jury, forgive me. As you can see, Orestes is suffering greatly and has done so for some time now. I hope you will permit me to speak for him?"

Whispers passed through the crowd. Worried glances and hurried words were exchanged among the jurors, but not one of them, whether through fear or confusion, responded. In the end, it was Athena who addressed her brother.

"You may," she said. "But remember—only the facts."

"Of course," he grinned. "Those are all that I have at my disposal."

He paused a moment and then, after a final smile, took on a far more sober countenance. Closing his eyes, he lifted his chin, before stalling further with a deep breath and then sigh. Only then, with his eyes once again open, did he begin.

"A father—a king, no less—was murdered." He paused.

The crowd was silent. Every person was enthralled by the God in front of them. If nothing else, attention had been diverted from himself, Orestes thought.

"A father was murdered, and that requires vengeance. This is the way it is. This is the way it has always been. Such a task may not be an easy one to carry out, as Orestes—King Orestes—has demonstrated. But he did what had to be done, what he was commanded to do by me, a god. This boy should not be tormented but celebrated for his ability to act beyond such mortal deficiencies as maternal devotion and sentimentality. He should be rewarded for the strength he has shown. That we are even here today, discussing this at all, is absurd. And anyone who agrees with the vile lies these...these *things* put forward, violates the sacred word of Zeus, just as much as the monsters do themselves."

The speech came to such an abrupt end, it was only when Apollo sat back next to him that Orestes realized it was over.

"See, you will be fine," he said, brimming with a confidence Orestes found hard to share. Surely, if it was purely a matter of the gods' will, they would be past all this by now. But they were not, and the Erinyes still had their turn before the jury.

"There, you have had a god speak for you," Electra said, squeezing his hand. "This will be over soon. The worst is already behind you."

And yet, in the pit of his stomach, he could only feel that the worst was yet to come.

"Tisiphone," Athena remained seated as she spoke. "You are to speak for the Erinyes?"

Tisiphone. So they did have names, he thought, as the tallest of the creatures stood up. Her mouth was closed, fangs and forked tongue hidden, yet it did little to improve her appearance. She stepped slowly to the center, the ripped fabric of her robe trailing in the dust behind her.

"*No, my goddess,*" she hissed. "*I am not here to speak for us. I speak for the murdered. I speak for those who cannot speak for themselves. I speak for Queen Clytemnestra.*"

Orestes shuddered. Several of the jurors had averted their gaze, but unlike before, this offered him little solace. They only needed to consider the words she spoke, not the way she looked. In long strides that would have put a horse to shame, she moved across the Areopagus and came to a stop in front of them. Whether they wanted to or not, they couldn't avoid looking at her now, and her eyes were on them. They shrank back in their seats.

"*I see my current embodiment makes you ill at ease,*" she said. "*I would hate for it to be a distraction from what I have to say to you. Here, let me rectify that.*"

In an instant the revolting creature was gone, and in its place stood an elderly woman. She wore the same robes, but they were now worn rather than ragged, and that was where the similarity ended. There were no fangs. No talons. Nothing fearful at all. Rather than scales, her olive skin showed liver spots and was creased in laughter lines around her eyes, while her silver hair, oiled and braided, flowed down below her waist. She was now shorter than Orestes, and her shoulders were slightly hunched, and her stomach was prominent, as if she had in her lifetime birthed many children, and her fingers were curled, as though they'd seen decades of hard work.

"Hopefully this is better," she said with a voice now as fluid as milk. "Where were we? Ah, yes. We were hearing how a father's murder must be avenged. I must admit, I see how convenient it must be, to look on life from such an uncomplicated viewpoint as dear Apollo. Never to have to worry yourself with details. To assume that, because of the position you were born to, you need do no more than make a sweeping statement, and people will assume you are right. Because he has that advantage over me, does he not? His smooth skin. The boyish glint in his eyes. His effortless articulation. That smile. But a smile can be deceptive. It can be used as a mask, as each person here today is well aware. It can hide one's true nature and intentions.

"So, let us get back to the great God's words. What did he actually tell you? There was the trite line about vengeance and sons that has been spewed for centuries without question. Without refutation. His words were vague as he brushed over the pain Orestes caused by his actions. But I will tell you the truth of the matter. Because the truth, as the Goddess said, is what we are here to establish today. Truth and then justice."

Now that she looked no more alarming than an old nursemaid,

the jurors stared at her with rapt attention. Even Orestes, who knew what lay beneath, could not help but feel himself drawn in by her words.

"When these gods tell us a father should be avenged, what do they mean exactly? Every father? Every murder? What about the father who beats his child constantly for the slightest mistakes? Should that father be avenged when he finally gets the knife to the throat he so rightly deserves? What about the one who drinks and gambles away all the family's money and then forces himself on his wife when he comes home angry and drunk? Should his murder, too, be avenged? Or those who have slain other men or who lie and cheat? Those who send their young children to work in the fields until their feet bleed and their hands are raw?" She tutted as she turned to Apollo. "All fathers? Have you even considered what that means?"

With a sweep of her robe, she continued.

"So, let us get to the truth of the matter here. High-ranking gentlemen, that is who he is talking about. Kings. Noblemen. Those whose wealth puts them above us mere minions. Should money be able to do that—absolve you of even the blackest deeds? I would like to think that is not the case. That there is something left that even gold cannot buy.

"Some fathers do deserve to die. That is the simple truth of the matter. And if they should be avenged ought not to be determined by whether they are kings or slaves. It should be by their living deeds that their right to retribution in death is judged.

"Agamemnon was a man who had murdered his wife's first husband and child so he could take her for himself. He bludgeoned a tiny baby to death, and why? Because he stood in the way of what he wanted. But this was not the end of his barbarity.

"Clytemnestra. Remember that name when you think about why we are here today. She is not some shadowy, distant figure. She was a real woman. A mother. And Agamemnon abused her, year after year. It was not just the beatings and cruel words, although there were plenty of those. He stole yet another child from her, murdered his own daughter, and tore Clytemnestra's heart from her chest once more, in a way that only a mother would understand. And yet, she remained strong and determined. She did not give in, take her own life perhaps, the way many would have. How did she manage this? Why, because she had to, to protect her remaining children: the warrior princess, Electra; the compassionate, maternal Chrysothemis; and Orestes, her beloved son. The future king. Her murderer.

"I am here for Clytemnestra. A mother who gave everything for her children. Who wept and bled for them. Yes, and killed for them too. She killed to save them. If you had lost two children at the hands of the same man, would you not fear for those who remained? Would you not do everything you could to keep them safe? When she was betrayed and most in need, who came to her aid? No one. And the gallant Orestes showed his gratitude by slitting her throat from behind, too cowardly to even look her in the eye as he cut her life short. And yet, by the gods' rules, *she* is not deserving of vengeance. She *deserved* her death. After all she had done, all she had been through, that is what the gods think of her."

Orestes sensed a mood shift. Every word the old woman had said was true. Apollo had assumed that the people would listen to him, that they would pay no heed to the Erinyes' side of the story, because of who he was and what they were. But he had been wrong. They were listening to a truth he could not deny, and he was afraid.

"We are standing outside the temple of a goddess," Tisiphone continued, still in human form. "It was not to a god that mighty Apollo came for a solution to this problem, just as it would not have been to his father that Orestes would have gone with his troubles as a child. The goddesses, the mothers, they are the ones we turn to. And yet it is a god's word that we have to obey, one that tells us that a man must be avenged, but not a woman."

She took a step back and lifted her arms to the crowd.

"One is not worth more than the other. Men are not more worthy. Fathers are not more worthy. Do you think a god would be here defending a girl who had killed her father? Of course not. She would be hanged or worse. Do not be swayed by his golden curls and easy manner. Be guided by your own moral compass. Your own mortal moral compass. That is why you are here today, to see right from wrong. To repudiate this repugnant, patriarchal society. You can dress it up with fine words and talk of prophecy if you want, but the fact remains: Orestes murdered his mother. He murdered Clytemnestra, who raised him and loved him and would have willingly given her own life for him if needed. If she were here, she would tell you this herself just as she told me. Instead, he took hers. And that woman deserves her justice. She deserves so much more than she was given in her lifetime. Do not make her suffer in the afterlife, too."

Silent tears streamed down Orestes's cheeks. Beside him, even Electra had now lost all hope. He could feel the energy draining from her. Was it true, what Tisiphone had said? Had she conversed with his mother in the Underworld? Had she herself brought this upon him? With every fiber of his being, he wished it to be a lie, and yet, in the depth of his soul, he knew she spoke the truth. Clytemnestra had sent them. She wanted Orestes to pay.

"I will leave you now to make your decision." Tisiphone, still in human form, stepped back. "This is not a matter of the narrow-minded rules of the gods. This is a matter of justice for the deserving. There is nothing more that I can say to you."

FORTY-THREE

T HE SPECTATORS BEGAN TO WHISPER, THEIR VOICES QUICKLY rising in volume until they were soon so loud, they could have drowned out even the Erinyes' wails. The people were on her side. Orestes could feel it. They wanted his blood as much as his mother did, possibly more, for the sport it would offer them.

Athena rose from her seat and silenced them.

"The jury must now decide," she said, turning to face the twelve chosen men and women. "This will not be a debate, and you are not to be swayed by emotion. Your decision must be driven by the facts and the evidence that you have heard here today. You will each rise and tell me whether you find Orestes, son of Agamemnon, King of Mycenae, guilty or not guilty of the murder of his mother, Clytemnestra. If found guilty, he will be left in the hands of the Erinyes, to do with as they see fit. If not guilty, they will leave him and cease their torment immediately."

She stepped toward Orestes, her robe billowing out behind her, then turned to the assembly.

"In the case of an even vote, I will cast mine to decide the matter.

And let it be known that this will be final. My decision has already been made. So now it is in your hands, my jurors, to bring us the justice that is deserved. This is a case like no other. You are the first of your kind. Do not take this responsibility lightly."

With sweat streaming down his back, Orestes stood to face his fate. The Goddess was partially blocking his view of the jurors, and it was only when he heard her speak that he realized the first had stood to give her verdict.

"Guilty." The woman's clear voice was like a blade in his gut. Behind him, Pylades gasped.

"It is only one," Apollo whispered. "There are eleven more to go."

The second juror got to his feet, this time in Orestes's line of sight. He looked at the king.

"Guilty."

It was as if all the air had been sucked from his lungs. He couldn't breathe. He couldn't even hear anymore. Across the stone slabs, the Erinyes rubbed their hands together as the third juror stood.

"Not guilty."

A whisper of air, but enough. The fourth rose, and then the fifth.

"Guilty."

"Not guilty."

By the time they were halfway through and the sixth juror had offered a "not guilty" response, the clouds had covered the sun, cooling them all. Yet Orestes felt as if he were burning up.

"Not guilty."

"Not guilty."

"Guilty."

"Guilty."

"Guilty."

"Not guilty."

All the jurors were standing now.

"What does that mean? What did they say? Which way did it go?" He couldn't think straight. Was he guilty? Or was he innocent? Which had the last one said? He had not heard clearly.

"It is an even vote," Electra whispered, her voice quivering. "The Goddess will now decide."

"She has already decided," he reminded her.

Now he would learn how much longer he would have in this body of his, which had already been through so much. If the Erinyes got their way, this would be his last day in the mortal realm. And surely Athena would side with the women. Then again, would she wish to go against her brother Apollo?

He caught sight of a small creature in a nearby tree. A little owl with eyes so big, they seemed to leave no room for other features. It ruffled its feathers and stared back at him.

"I told you that I had already made my decision, but I feel I should explain it to you. Our choices are shaped by our experiences, and our experiences by those who surround us from our birth. I was not birthed. I sprang from the head of Zeus, fully formed, clothed, and with a spear in my hand. I had no maternal guidance. I was raised among gods. Trained to fight with them. I cannot imagine the pain of Clytemnestra. It is not possible to say we truly understand someone if we have never walked that person's path. While I cannot truly empathize, I can at least sympathize.

"We have come here today for justice. Murder, matricide—these are bleak words and true ones. But there are other truths, too, such as the loyalty that a man would show to a god. The suffering he would endure for him. For eight years, Orestes ignored the will of the gods to try to protect his mother from a fate that *he* had not decided, that *he* did not want.

"In our darkest moments, we should recognize not just what has been lost but who continues to stand beside us. Orestes arrived here in the company of a god, a sister, and a friend, and their devotion is unquestionable. Love like that does not come from fear or coercion. He is not an evil man. His deeds were not entirely of his own volition. And, despite everything, I believe his love for his mother remained true to the end. Which is why, in my final ruling on the matter, I find him...*not* guilty."

The words echoed around them, and yet he could not believe what he had heard.

"Did she...did she?"

"Not guilty," Apollo confirmed. "You see, I said you had nothing to fear."

Not guilty. Freed from torment, at last. Could it really be? he wondered as arms were flung around his neck.

"We can go home now," Electra said, tears in her eyes. "We can go home to Mycenae, and you can rule."

"Is it really true?" He looked to Pylades for confirmation, as if the word of the God Apollo was not enough.

"It is. Just look."

On the other side of the Areopagus, the Erinyes, all in their true form with talons out and teeth bared, were squabbling among themselves. The Goddess approached them, and Orestes could not help but strain to listen to what was said.

"*You chose wrongly!*" one spat at her.

"On this occasion, I do not think so. Although there have been times in my life when I have acted irrationally. When the fire of anger has seen me lose my patience too quickly, and I have acted or reacted in a manner that I later came to regret. But this was not one of them."

"*So, you have come to gloat!*" another sneered.

"No. I have not. I realize that I could make use of your perception, your sense of morality and code of ethics."

They seemed to flinch.

"*What are you saying?*"

"I am asking whether you would consider a slight realignment of your vocation?"

"*Realignment? What does that mean?*"

Orestes found himself moving nearer the women. The crowds were already dispersing, some notably relieved by the outcome, others disappointed. But he ignored them as he inched toward the Goddess and the Erinyes, the weight already lifting from his shoulders.

"When I listened to you here today," Athena continued, "your argument seemed considered, well reasoned. You may have come here to seek vengeance, but I believe that what you truly wanted was justice for his mother. Justice, not vengeance."

"*I believe they are too close to be distinguishable.*"

"They are not. There are often two sides to these problems. Take one, the world gets better and becomes a brighter place. Take the other, there is only darkness and torment. Work with me. Make the change. You have been too long in the Underworld. What do you say?"

They turned to one another, although no words were spoken that he could detect.

"*What would you want from us?*"

"I would give you a place in my court. A place of light, where your actions can bring relief to those who have been wronged, but without the torment."

A hand appeared on Orestes's shoulder, and he turned to see Pylades's smiling face.

"Come, my love. We should go. Surely you have seen enough of those vile creatures to last you a lifetime?"

"I…" He turned back, but both the Goddess and the Erinyes had gone.

"I should be leaving too." Apollo appeared at their side, ringlets gleaming.

"Thank you," Orestes said, falling to his knees. "Thank you for what you said and did today."

"There is nothing to thank me for. However, if you would like to hold a feast or two in my name when you return to Mycenae, you know I would not object."

"I will. I will hold a thousand feasts."

"One or two would be plenty." And with a final smile, he turned and wandered off into the crowd, which swarmed around him as people sought his blessing.

And then, only the three of them remained. He assumed Electra would have something to say. Some cutting comment to mark the occasion the way she always tended to, but instead what she said was, "Come, let us go home now. We have been away far too long."

EPILOGUE

ORESTES SAT QUIETLY IN THE CENTER OF THE GRAVE circle. Sometimes, he would weave between the monuments, reading the various epitaphs, but it was always the same three that he came back to. To those of a mother, her son, and her lover.

For five years, he had ruled as King of Mycenae, always trying to show kindness and fairness in preference to power and might, and so far he was succeeding. His subjects no longer saw him as weak but compassionate. They had come to realize that he would not just spout fine words but put them into action, and they admired him for it.

Other things had changed at the palace. Laodamia had passed on the previous year, and Pylades had left him too, not taken by death but by a marriage he could no longer put off. At some point, he would have to consider doing the same. He knew that a king must have an heir, and an heir meant a wife, but for now he would mourn the loss of the man he loved, and he would live each day as simply as he could.

The hours ahead would be filled with meetings and then a state dinner, and he knew this quiet moment on his own would not last long. He stood up, thinking about the list of duties that awaited him. He should head straight back to his quarters, he thought. Maybe tomorrow he could find a little more time to himself. Yes, tomorrow he would build a new altar to Apollo, for the old one was looking tired.

As he started back, a flash of red in the grass caught his eye. A bird perhaps? He had not seen anything of that shade around here before. And yet, when it moved again, he noticed that it kept low to the ground. It was a shame he didn't have his notebook with him, to sketch the creature, he thought, as he crept forward as silently as he could. Maybe if he got a good look at it, he could later recall it well enough to draw it from memory. Better still, he could grab the little animal and carry it back up to the palace.

Another step forward and he saw it, in all its beauty. A viper with a blood-red crown and vivid yellow scales on its belly was now coiled up on a rock in the sun. Aegisthus had taught him to read the movements of snakes from a young age, and this one did not look as though it was readying itself to strike. He could catch it, he thought, taking another half step forward. Yes, he would pick it up and take it back with him.

APPENDIX

The House of Pelops, like many of the lineages in Greek mythology, is complex to say the least, but few are quite so besmirched with betrayal and bloodshed as that of King Pelops of Pisa.

Grandson to Zeus, Pelops was murdered and fed to the gods by his own father, King Tantalus, in an attempt to trick the immortal beings. However, they were outraged at the act and sentenced his father to a lifetime of eternal hunger and thirst. Pelops himself was returned to life.

Eager to make his mark on the world, he headed to Pisa, where King Oenomaüs had sent out a challenge: if any could beat him in a chariot race, then they would win the hand of his daughter Hippodamia. But attempting this did not come without risk: if the challenger did not beat Oenomaüs, they would be sentenced to death. Deciding he needed an advantage, Pelops bribed the king's charioteer, Myrtilus, to sabotage his master's chariot. True to his word, the charioteer did as he had promised, and during the race, the axle on the king's chariot broke. In front of cheering crowds, he was dragged by his horses through the dust and dirt, screaming and wailing, until his neck snapped. Needless to say, Pelops won the race and married Hippodamia. He also promptly threw Myrtilus off a cliff. As the betrayed Myrtilus sank beneath the waves he cursed Pelops and his heirs.

In his new position as husband and king, Pelops fathered two legitimate sons with Hippodamia, Atreus and Thyestes, along with an illegitimate child, Chrysippus. This boy was conceived during an illicit union with a naiad—a water nymph—and Pelops showered great affection on him, affection that did not go unnoticed. Jealous of this favoritism and fearful that Chrysippus might make a play for the throne, Atreus and Thyestes murdered their half brother, casting him into a well.

While having eliminated their competition for the throne, the two brothers had failed to consider that their father might seek vengeance on them, and the pair subsequently fled to Mycenae, where King Eurystheus offered them sanctuary. Eurystheus was still bitter about the humiliation he'd suffered when Hercules had successfully completed the famous Twelve Labors, which he had challenged King Eurystheus to undertake. When he heard of Hercules's death, Eurystheus decided to set about eliminating his many children. As he headed to Athens, he left Mycenae in the care of Atreus and Thyestes. Unfortunately, he and his sons were all killed in the battle with the Heracleidae, and Atreus took the crown for himself and became the King of Mycenae.

Thyestes, now jealous of his brother's crown, began sleeping with Atreus's wife, Aerope, although infidelity was only the start of his plan. With her help, he stole Atreus's golden fleece—a symbol of authority and kingship—and tricked him into relinquishing the throne. Thyestes's reign as king, however, was short-lived as, with the help of Zeus, Atreus wrested back control of Mycenae through trickery of his own.

However, the restoration of his kingship was not enough for Atreus. During what was supposed to be a reconciliatory feast, he took the ultimate and most despicable revenge on his brother.

Unbeknown to Thyestes, Atreus had earlier that day murdered his sons. But their death was just the beginning. With the feast in full swing, he brought out their heads and revealed to Thyestes that he was dining on his own children's flesh.

The crime, so horrific that it is said that even Helios the Sun God turned away, set upon the family a curse that saw bloodshed and betrayal continue until the conclusion of Orestes's trial.

Keep reading for a look at Hannah Lynn's next retelling,

QUEENS OF THEMISCYRA

ONE

HER BLADE WHISTLED THROUGH THE AIR, SURE AND UNWAVering, first through the warrior's leather armor, then through the soft flesh of his belly. A spray of blood arced upward as he toppled from his horse. Already racing away, Hippolyte paid him no mind. Her mare's hooves churned the dry earth beneath them, sending up clouds of dust as the queen locked her aim on her next victim. Within moments, he too lay face down in the dirt.

From all around came the clang of metal—swords against shields, arrowheads against breastplates—and the stench of blood, bitter and cloying, hung densely in the arid air. The aroma was one she knew well. One of battle. Of sweat and pain. Burning skin under the glare of Helios's sun, of horses slick with perspiration. But above all else, it was the scent of victory.

Their adversaries, who only an hour ago had been screaming in rage and fervor, were now crying in fear, begging for mercy, choking as they drowned in their own blood. If they were fortunate, her women would offer them a swift death. Flies had already arrived in droves, settling on open wounds, buzzing around the corpses already graying in the dirt.

By the time the last scream had faded, and the sun had reached its zenith, the earth was crimson with the blood of the fallen.

Hippolyte cast her gaze across the scene. These were young men. Some barely in their teens. It was a weak king who thought to send such boys to face them.

"Back home to Pontus and Themiscyra, my queen?"

Hippolyte turned to face Penthesilea. Her sister sat upright upon her horse, her embroidered tunic, leather trousers, and boots—the traditional warriors' garb—possibly even more stained with the colors of battle than Hippolyte's own. The princess's bow was stowed in a sling on her back, the elegant weapon with its double curve, smaller than those their enemies favored. Smaller than those that littered the ground around them.

The bow had been carved, planed, and strung by Penthesilea's own hand. Wood and bone, shaved off in the finest of slivers, imperceptible to some, yet enough to shift the weapon's balance and ensure the truest of flights. Hippolyte could not imagine how many arrows had been loosed from it that day, how many bronze tips had met their target, piercing hearts or skulls. Penthesilea's arrows did not miss.

"Back home to Themiscyra, sister," the queen replied. "Although first we must collect our payment."

It was a handsome settlement; the best they had received in months. The bulk was in metals—gold, iron, bronze—that would be hammered out or melted down, but there were other items, too. There were jewels, both raw stones and those already cut and polished. There was pottery. There was even a lyre, and although she did not play herself, Hippolyte knew many of the women would strike a fine tune from it.

Within the city walls, the king had thanked them profusely,

bowing low to the ground in the awkward, angular movements of one unaccustomed to such humility, even less so toward women. Hippolyte was almost as uncomfortable with the display as he was. Afterward, settled into a more reposeful posture, he asked if they wished to stay the night. Most kings prayed she would refuse and offered only out of courtesy, and this was the case today. She could not help but note the flash of relief dart across his face when she declined his offer and found herself feeling a pang of sympathy for the man. This was unlikely to be the last battle they fought for him.

Their saddlebags full and their horses rested, they began the ride east, back to the region of Pontus and their citadel home, Themiscyra.

The journey to the edge of the Black Sea would take two days at a leisurely pace. If needed, they could ride at a gallop and without stopping unless unavoidable—that was the way they had ridden to reach here—but the women and the horses had earned a little respite.

Blue skies, scattered with feather-like clouds that hovered motionless in the still air, stretched above them as they rode. On a clear day like today, from its southernmost point, they could see all of Anatolia. To the north, beyond the Sea of Marmara, was Thrace, and west, across the Aegean, lay Thessaly and Athens. They had traveled to these places, and further still. They had traveled to Thebes and the Peloponnese, called to fight for kings who might otherwise have lost their lands. Called to rain their arrows on armies with whom they had no quarrel. And paid handsomely for it. Sometimes the battles would come one after another, and they would race from one belea-guered land to the next, always ready, always victorious. But for now, they were headed home to rest, basking in the scent of the ferns that littered the hillsides around them.

Women chattered as they rode. There was always a rush that came after battle. The adrenaline that had lent them such force and ferocity now drew words from their lips as quickly as the blood had spilled from their enemies. Such exuberant conversation between her women might endure for miles, over plains and through valleys, across rivers and around grand lakes. Yet inevitably, at some point before the sun set on that first day after a battle, the quiet would descend. The quiet in which they recalled those they had lost. Those that had been granted the most honorable of deaths. A warrior's death. An Amazon's death.

"Four women made their first kill today."

It was Antiope who spoke to the queen through the quiet. "Four who can ride with us to the Gargareans next spring."

"That is good news. I will meet with them personally upon our arrival home."

Shortly after midday, they halted at a shallow lake that had survived the droughts of summer. Shingle stones shimmered beneath the surface as the women knelt to wash the blood and grime from their skin and watched as swirls of red eddied from their palms.

While Hippolyte and her sisters considered Themiscyra their home, this was not the case for all Amazons. Certainly, many dwelled within the citadel walls, with the protection and luxuries provided by so many warriors living in close proximity, but there were those who found such a life constrictive and claustrophobic. These nomads spent their time away from the battles wandering the steppes and camping out beneath the stars. They hunted with bow or spear, preferring to make small fires and pick the meat from the bones of the birds and beasts they had caught alone, rather than with the company of the other women. They craved solidarity, returning to join the rest of the warriors only on those occasions that required them to do so. At festivals, or to fight, or to embark upon the annual springtime trek south to the Gargareans. There was no enmity between the two groups of women. The queen had no preference in how the women lived and did not judge one way of life more favorably than another. Each woman could choose to spend her days in the manner in which she found the greatest delight, and each woman would therefore fight for it with the strongest fire.

By the time they had pitched their bivouacs, the sun had long since sunk below the horizon, and streams of stars glimmered above them. A chorus of cicadas hummed and buzzed, a complement to the chatter of the women. Lying with her back on the grass, her sword by her side, Hippolyte listened. This was her favorite time to learn—the night after a battle had been fought and won. The women would regale their comrades with stories of their opponents: how they fought, how close they came to striking them down. The maneuvers they had mastered and those that had nearly lost them their life. The queen would seal it all away in the back of her mind, ensuring they would not make the same mistakes again.

They had lost a dozen women that day. Nothing when set against the hundreds their opponents had suffered, but more than was acceptable. They had brought the bodies with them, wrapped tightly in linen to be returned to their homes in Pontus. They would perform a proper burial there, committing the women to the land with their weapons and horses and all the honor they deserved.

Next time, Hippolyte told herself as the fire sizzled and spat, she would not lose any. And she would offer a greater sacrifice to her father. Her father. Her immortal father. Ares, the God of War.

READING GROUP GUIDE

1. In the Foreword, the author states that when contemplating the stories of Ancient Greece, one must "clutch at that fiber, hold it close, and have faith that the path you are taking is one that will lead you all the way through the heart of the web and out the other side." What does she mean by this, and how might that affect one's experience when reading retellings?

2. The story begins with Agamemnon, King of Mycenae. Why is he visiting Calchas's, and what does the old man tell him to do? Does he go through with it?

3. What is Clytemnestra's reaction to the death of her daughter, and what kind of mother does she become to her other children after? How did this make you feel?

4. What kind of ruler is Clytemnestra? How does her power in Mycenae change over the course of the novel?

5. Explain why Agamemnon is in Troy. What is so important about his journey that allows him to justify sacrificing his own child?

6. Electra and Clytemnestra have a tumultuous relationship, one that ends in tragedy. What is the cause of this? Did you have sympathy for Electra after the things she does?

7. Vengeance is a theme that courses through the story. How does vengeance play a role in all the characters' motivations, especially Clytemnestra's and Electra's?

8. This novel is filled with morally gray characters. Were there any decisions made by the characters that made you think differently of them? Were there some you found unforgivable?

9. Why does Electra take Orestes to Phocis? Is she ultimately successful in her plans to convince him to avenge their father and take revenge on Clytemnestra and Aegisthus? What are the consequences of her and Orestes's actions?

10. Were you familiar with the story of Clytemnestra and Electra? If so, how did you feel about this version of the story? Have you heard it told differently?

A CONVERSATION
WITH THE AUTHOR

Why Clytemnestra? What drew you to her story?

So many aspects of Clytemnestra's story drew me to her, but most of all, I think it is how she behaved as a mother. How all her actions were to keep her children safe but how in doing what she thought was the best for them often resulted in yet more heartache.

What was it like to write about such morally gray characters? What did you feel was most important when developing them?

People don't normally think of themselves as being morally gray. They just need to do whatever is necessary to reach their goal, and that is how I feel writing all my characters. I try to think as they would, using their belief system to justify their actions. Clytemnestra makes mistakes, because she is a flawed human who thinks about immediate threats without considering the consequences of her actions. Agamemnon is full of hubris, and while to someone on the outside, he is clearly not a great person, he simply views himself above the people around him.

What was the research process like? Were there any unexpected difficulties while writing this book?

Research for Greek mythology is always a bit of a minefield.

There are so many stories to consider and so many tales that inter-twine. Quite often, while researching, I find myself being drawn to other characters. For example, I would have loved to have written more about Cassandra, and there are other versions where Iphigenia is saved. Picking the tale I want to tell is one of the hardest parts.

You retell a popular Greek myth from a feminist perspective. Why do you think retellings are important nowadays?

Every story has more than one perspective, and I think what people commonly refer to as feminist perspectives are simply stories told from the female point of view. The world is often a polarized place, but such distinct opinions often come from not seeing anoth-er's point of view. Anything we can do to bridge those differences and open people's minds to seeing different perspectives is, in my opinion, a good thing.

What is your writing process like? Are there any ways you like to get inspired?

Research is so important to my plotting process, but thankfully, the Greek myths provide a whole wealth of inspiration. Research and plotting with these books often takes me as long as writing the actual books. When I've finished plotting, I try to write a rough first draft done as quickly as I can, so I know the full extent of what the charac-ters have to go through and all the ways and places I wish to see them develop. After that, it's revising and re-drafting until I'm happy.

What do you hope readers take away from this story?

I would like people to see that they can sympathize with more than one side of a situation. They can sympathize for Clytemnestra but also Orestes. And I believe, had I written in such a manner, then there may have been an opportunity to even sympathize with Agamemnon, (but perhaps not as much!).

What are you reading these days?

I love reading a variety of different genres, but in mythology retellings, I'm loving *Horses of Fire* by A. D. Rhine and *House of Odysseus* by Claire North.

ACKNOWLEDGMENTS

Massive thanks must go to Jenna, Charmaine, and Carol for their amazing skill in helping me get this book edited, and to Sourcebooks for their belief in the story.

Thank you to all of my beta readers, who take the time to read early drafts and offer valuable feedback, especially the eagle-eyed Lucy, Niove, and Kath, as well as their support and encouragement.

Thank you to my husband, who helps me find the time to write and tirelessly checks and double-checks and keeps me on track.

Lastly, thank you to every reader who has taken the time to read my work and listen to my stories, and to the amazing bloggers who have done so much to help me along this journey. This book was such a passion project for me, so please know that every recommendation to a friend, share on social media, or kind message means the world to me.

ABOUT THE AUTHOR

Hannah Lynn is a multiaward-winning novelist. She published her first book, *Amendments*, a dark, dystopian speculative fiction novel, in 2015. Her second book, *The Afterlife of Walter Augustus*, a contemporary fiction novel with a supernatural twist, went on to win the 2018 Kindle Storyteller Award and the Independent Publishers Gold Medal for Best Adult Ebook. Having lived and traveled extensively, Hannah is now settled back in the UK with her husband, daughter, and horde of cats, and spends her days writing romantic comedies and historical fiction. *Athena's Child*, which was her first historical fiction novel, was a 2020 Gold Medalist at the Independent Publishers Awards and is the first in a series of novels centered around mythological women. You can learn more at hannahlynnauthor.com.